WHO KILLED EMERALD ISACSON?

Book One in the series
The Misbourne Murder Mysteries

Denise Beddows

Misbourne Press

Published in 2025 by Misbourne Press

Copyright © The author as named on the book cover.

First Edition

The author has asserted their moral right under the Copyright, Designs and Patents Act, 1988, to be identified as the author of this work.

All Rights reserved. No part of this publication may be reproduced, copied, stored in a retrieval system, or transmitted, in any form or by any means, without the prior written consent of the copyright holder, nor be otherwise circulated in any form of binding or cover other than that in which it is published and without a similar condition being imposed on the subsequent purchaser.

Any resemblance between the characters, places or institutions in this book and persons living or dead, or existing organisations is entirely coincidental.

A CIP catalogue record for this title is available from the British Library.

Chapter 1

Parking in the Buckinghamshire market town of Briarfield was murder on Fridays, because Friday was market day. And it was a murder which had brought Carole Murray to the town's *Elsinore Tearooms* on the previous Friday. She had fully intended to ask the owner of the tearooms about the murder of her sister. At least, that had been her intention, but somehow, during that first meeting with seventy-odd-year-old Euphemia Isacson, Carole hadn't felt the moment was right. It had seemed too early in their acquaintance to raise such a sensitive and potentially upsetting issue. She felt it was important to gain the lady's trust before posing direct questions about the awful incident, twenty-five years earlier, which had seen Euphemia's only sibling bludgeoned to death by an unknown assailant.

The murder of Emerald Isacson had never been solved. Perhaps, given the passage of time, it never would be. Nevertheless, ever since first hearing about the case, Carole had been eager to learn more about it. She was glad Euphemia had suggested she visit again today, on this quieter Monday morning. Today, she was able to park right outside the tearooms which, like several of the town's shops and restaurants, was closed on Mondays, and today, she was determined to broach the subject. Switching off her engine, she reached for the carrier bag containing the large box of chocolates she had brought for Euphemia and she climbed out of the car.

She knocked resolutely on the blue-painted front door which led to Euphemia's apartment above the tearooms. As on her previous visit, she got no answer to her first few knocks. She knocked a little louder. Unlike on her previous visit, however, she got no answer after knocking several times more, and as loudly as she dared without disturbing the rest of the street's residents. She told herself she would be surprised and disappointed if, having invited her over, Euphemia had gone out. Might she have forgotten their appointment? She knew the lady was a little hard of hearing, but she hadn't seemed particularly forgetful at their previous meeting.

Stepping away from the front door, Carole glanced up at the front windows of the flat. The curtains were closed, which seemed odd for ten o'clock in the morning, and she wondered whether Euphemia had overslept. She could see, at the point where the top of the curtains did not quite meet, that the main light in the living room was on. It seemed odd that the curtains should be closed and the light on when there was plenty of daylight. She suddenly had a bad feeling. Past experience, as well as her well-developed intuition, told her something might be wrong.

Walking down the little alleyway at the side of the building, she glanced up at the bathroom window and saw the light was on in that room, too. She continued around to the back of the property, opened the back gate and stepped into the little garden. Everything looked tidy and well-tended and nothing seemed to be amiss. Then, however, she noticed that the back door to the property was standing ajar. Stepping forward and pushing it open, she peered in through the doorway. She wondered briefly whether Euphemia was one of those ladies who held to the tradition that laundry should be done on Mondays. Perhaps the back door was ajar because she was intending to hang out her washing on the garden's little clothes line. But Carole could not hear the whirr of a washing machine. And anyway, didn't the world and his wife use tumble dryers these days?

'Miss Isacson. Euphemia,' she called out. 'Are you there? Hello.'

There was no reply, so she stepped in to the lobby and glanced up the stairwell. She could see a trapdoor into the loft space was open and a loft ladder was suspended from it down onto the upstairs landing. This wasn't surprising, since Euphemia had promised to retrieve from the loft some stored family photographs and documents to show her, but Carole now felt concerned in case the pensioner had fallen from the ladder and hurt herself. In her worst imaginings, the lady might have been lying there injured all night.

She raced up the stairs but saw, to her relief, there was no injured lady lying on the landing. Thankfully, all that lay on the floor at the bottom of the ladder was an open suitcase with photograph albums and letters both within it and scattered on the floor around it. Carole guessed Euphemia must have dragged it down the ladder from the loft and had begun sorting through its contents right there on the landing.

'Hello, Miss Isacson. Are you home? It's Carole Murray,' she called out.

There was still no reply, however, and Carole couldn't hear anyone moving around. Glancing into the small kitchen, she saw it was empty. Peering into the sitting room via the open door, she was surprised to see papers strewn everywhere there too, on the coffee table, on the sofa and on the carpet. A couple of the drawers of Euphemia's bureau had been pulled out and the contents tipped out too. Carole couldn't believe Euphemia would have generated this amount of disarray when sorting through documents. It looked more as though the flat had been ransacked. Her trepidation immediately increased as she stepped further into the room and saw all the chaos, but what she saw next stopped her in her tracks. The frail and motionless figure of Euphemia lay on her side on the hearthrug.

'Oh no, Euphemia!' Carole gasped.

Bending down, she grasped the lady's hand and felt her wrist for a pulse. There was none. Euphemia's skin was dry and cold to the touch. Her eyes were open but unfocused. Carole then noticed a large, mainly dried bloodstain on the rug beneath the woman's head. She saw Euphemia's silver locks were matted with dried blood. On closer inspection, she could see the back of Euphemia's head had been the source of the bleeding. It seemed clear the old lady had suffered headwounds, and yet it wasn't obvious how she could have sustained such an injury accidentally. There was no blood on the coffee table, on the hearth or on any other nearby hard surface. Given the disturbed state of the room, Carole strongly suspected this was no accident.

The irony of Euphemia seemingly having been murdered by blows to the back of the head, in exactly the same way her sister Emerald had been murdered a quarter of a century earlier, was not lost on Carole. A sense of self-preservation now kicked in, however, as she realised Euphemia's attacker might still be in the flat. Rising, she reached across the hearth and grabbed the poker from the companion set. She called out the first thing that came into her head.

'Police! Come out and show yourself!'

There was no response and so, still brandishing the poker, she crept silently around the flat, checking out the bedroom and bathroom. To her relief, there was no-one there. She decided against climbing the rickety loft ladder to see if the killer was hiding in the loft. She thought it extremely unlikely the killer would have chosen to hide up there rather than fleeing, but in the very unlikely event he had, she had no wish to poke her head up through the trapdoor and make herself an easy target. Returning to the sitting room, she knelt and placed two fingers on the woman's throat, still hoping there might be a faint pulse to be felt. However, she now reasoned that Euphemia was so very cold she had likely been dead for quite some hours, probably since the previous evening, if the living room curtains and light were anything to go by. Carole told herself the killer must surely be long gone.

She took out her mobile phone to call the police, but then paused. Old habits die hard, she told herself, as she gave way to an urge to assess the crime scene. Judging by the position of the wounds, she guessed the attacker must have pounced from behind after Euphemia had turned her back on him. Why had she turned her back on him? Neither the front door nor the back door looked as if they'd been forced, so she supposed Euphemia must have admitted her killer. She wondered whether that meant he was someone known to the deceased woman, or at least was someone she had no cause to fear. Or maybe he had simply pushed his way in and the victim had turned away from him in an attempt to flee to another room.

Carole could see no obvious weapon anywhere in the room. The heaviest and most dangerous implement she could see was the poker she was holding in her hand. There were no traces of blood on it, however, and it had been hanging in its proper place, from a hook on the fireside companion set. She doubted the killer would have either cleaned it or replaced it so carefully if he had used it to kill, so she decided the poker was unlikely to be the weapon which had been used on Euphemia.

Wiping the handle of the poker with her sleeve to erase her own fingerprints, she placed it back on its hook on the companion set. She told herself she hadn't interfered with the crime scene, at least not to any great degree – not so far. Given the fact that both sisters were clearly killed in the same way, the thought crossed her mind that they might both have been murdered by the same killer. But why? And why now? Why would the killer wait a quarter of a century after killing the first sister before killing the second one? It made no sense. The police had not solved Emerald's murder all those years ago, so perhaps they would be equally unsuccessful now in solving Euphemia's.

She wondered whether the clue to both murders might lie right here in the flat. She knew she should report the incident right away, and yet her curiosity – the instinctive curiosity of a retired intelligence analyst – was gnawing at her. She had an overwhelming urge to search the flat and to examine all the paperwork strewn about the floor. After all, Euphemia had invited her over specifically to see these papers, and the septuagenarian had clearly gone to so much trouble to drag the case full of albums and documents down from the loft, it would be remiss of Carole not to at least glance at them.

As shocking as this was, it wasn't the first crime scene she had experienced, of course. Nor was it the first dead body she had ever seen. Numerous times during her three decades with the Security Service, she had attended the scenes of murders involving someone of interest to her department. On those occasions, once the scenes of crime officers had done their bit, it would be Carole's role to survey the scene and, in consultation with the forensic experts, police and pathologist, to come up with a preliminary hypothesis as to what might have happened, why it had happened, and what sort of individual might have done it. Then, the intelligence gathering and analysis process would begin in earnest, with a view to supporting or rejecting that hypothesis. She suddenly realised how much she missed those days.

Of course, one didn't need to be a former intelligence officer like Carole to know what to do and whom to call on finding a dead body. She knew she should do the responsible thing and call the police immediately. Accordingly, she tapped nine-nine-nine on her phone. In the few short moments it took to be connected to the emergency operator, however, she took an impulsive decision. Instead of asking to be connected with the police, she asked for the ambulance service.

'My name is Carole Murray,' she told them. 'I just arrived at the *Elsinore Tearooms* in Briarfield to visit the seventy-something lady who owns the premises and I found her collapsed in her upstairs flat. She looks to be in a bad way. She's not conscious and I'm having difficulty finding a pulse.'

Carole was promised an ambulance would be despatched as soon as one was available. Naturally, she knew there was absolutely no treatment an ambulance crew could administer which would bring Euphemia back to life, but she reasoned that it might take a lot longer for an ambulance to be despatched to the scene than it would for the police to respond. She knew it was dishonest to withhold the information that Euphemia was dead, and that she had clearly died many hours earlier and in suspicious circumstances, but she wanted to buy some time in order to look around the flat. She told herself that any delay between the ambulance staff arriving and their subsequently summoning the police would make no difference whatsoever to the deceased.

She quickly dismissed any thought that this might be the work of a thief who had been disturbed in the act by Euphemia. The silver photograph frames she had admired on her previous visit were still in place on the book case. The antique mantle clock was still in place, too, as was the little collection of porcelain trinket boxes arranged on the small pie-crust table. The fact that this was the second Isacson sister to be murdered by being beaten to the back of the head also suggested this was no common burglary. But who would have had it in for these respectable, middle-class, spinster sisters?

Without touching any of the discarded papers lying around the room, she tip-toed around and squinted down at them. She suspected the killer must have been looking for something, in which case either he had found it and had taken it away with him, or he couldn't find it, and that might be the reason he killed the occupant of the flat. Maybe Euphemia couldn't or wouldn't give him whatever it was he sought. Perhaps she didn't actually have whatever item or information he wanted. Or, if she did, perhaps she thought that, whatever it was, it was worth dying to protect. However, most of the items tossed aside seemed to be old family correspondence, birth and marriage certificates and photographs.

Carole decided to search the other rooms in the flat, starting with the bedroom. Pulling the sleeves of her sweater down over her hands in order to avoid leaving fingerprints, she began opening the drawers in the bedside cabinet and examining the contents. She could find nothing of any great significance. The wardrobe, too, was devoid of any relevant paperwork. She checked all the kitchen cupboards, the refrigerator and even the freezer compartment. The bathroom cabinet yielded no surprises, and, having run out of places to look, she even lifted the cistern lid in case Euphemia had been as imaginative in hiding things as had the subjects of previous searches Carole had conducted. She could find nothing of interest, albeit that she didn't actually know what she was looking for.

On returning to the sitting room, she found her attention drawn back to the bookcase. Using her phone's camera, she took some close-up shots of the photographs on the top of the bookcase – the photographs of the people she believed to be Per and Brigid Isacson, the long-deceased parents of sisters Euphemia and Emerald. Next, she glanced along the rows of books. She saw a dozen or more books on ornithology. She had noticed them on her previous visit and their presence was unsurprising, since Euphemia had said she and Emerald had both been keen birdwatchers. What she now noticed which was surprising, however, was that the books on birdwatching seemed to include a dozen copies of the same book. She wondered why anyone would acquire multiple copies of the same book.

Carole took out her handkerchief and used it to avoid leaving fingerprints as she slid one of the books out and had a closer look at it. The identical books were all entitled 'A Bird Watcher's Guide to the Chilterns', and the author was F.E. Cassoni. Carole took out each copy in turn, held each book spine uppermost and flipped through the pages in case there might be any relevant letter or note hidden inside. Nothing fell out. In one of Cassoni's books, however, as she flicked through the pages, she spotted a handwritten dedication on the fly leaf – *'To EM with love from FE'*.

'EM' she guessed would be Emerald, and the 'FE' would probably be F.E. Cassoni. The fact that the author had added 'with love' was intriguing. Did Emerald and the author share more than a love of birds, she wondered? Was F.E. Cassoni male or female? Might this writer and ornithologist have been Emerald's lover? She decided this definitely warranted further research. Yielding to another sudden impulse, she thrust that particular copy of the book into her carrier bag alongside the box of chocolates she had brought for the now deceased Euphemia.

Checking out more of the books in the bookcase, she came across several hardback desk diaries. Removing them from the shelf, she saw these were arranged in date order but only ran up to the year 2000. Glancing inside the most recent one, she saw Emerald's name. She realised these were Emerald's diaries. The thought occurred to her immediately that the diaries could hold a clue as to her murder which had occurred in March of 2000. She began to browse the handwritten entries in the diary but, suddenly, she heard a vehicle pulling up outside. Crossing to the window she pulled the curtains open slightly and looked out. It was the ambulance. Damn! It had arrived a lot sooner than she had expected.

Her heart raced as she heard the ambulance crew knocking at the front door. She thrust the three most recent diaries into her carrier bag then went downstairs to admit the green-uniformed paramedics.

'Upstairs,' she said. 'The poor lady's lying on the floor.'

Without a word, the paramedics raced upstairs to the flat. Carole followed and remained on the landing, watching them from the living room doorway. After only a brief examination, one of the paramedics shook his head.

'I'm sorry,' he said. 'We can do nothing for her. She's deceased and it looks as though she has been for quite some hours.'

Drawing his colleague's attention to the deceased woman's head wound, he took out his mobile phone and called the police.

'Oh dear,' Carole said, feigning shock and innocence. 'Do you think someone hurt her?'

'Looks like it,' the paramedic nodded. 'This is now a crime scene. Perhaps we'd better wait outside until the police arrive.'

'Of course,' Carole agreed. 'I think I need to sit down. This has been a terrible shock. I'll sit in my car until they get here.'

As soon as she reached her car, she stowed the bag containing the chocolates, the book and the diaries in the boot, then she climbed into the driver's seat and began to work out what she was going to tell the police. She took out her mobile phone and began to tap in her home number as she felt she should call home and tell her husband what had happened. Immediately, however, she had second thoughts. She knew Dave would scold her for entering premises under what she knew were suspicious circumstances, thereby putting herself in danger. He would react as any former murder detective would do and tell her she should have called for assistance the moment she saw the open back door, rather than going in alone. She decided she would wait until she got home before invoking his inevitable reproval.

It wasn't long before the police arrived, in the form of two detectives, a man in his forties and a younger woman. They walked past her car and, after a brief exchange with the paramedics, went straight into the building. Little more than ten minutes later they emerged again and the female detective took out her phone and made a call. Carole anticipated this would be a call to summon the SOCOs. She opened her side window as the male detective approached and flashed his warrant card in her direction.

'Good morning,' he said. 'I'm Detective Inspector Bernard Hogget. I understand you found the deceased.'

'Yes, Inspector. I did. It was a bit of a shock, to say the least. I felt a bit faint and I had to sit down. I'm sure you'll have lots of questions to ask me. Would you like to sit in?' she said, pointing to the front passenger seat.

The detective walked around the car and climbed into the passenger seat.

'And your name is?' he asked, taking out his notebook.

'Carole Murray. I live at Rowan Tree Cottage, Hawthorn Lane, Chalfont St George.'

'And your date of birth, Mrs Murray?'

Carole realised he needed this in order to conduct a CRO check with a view to either confirming or eliminating her as a suspect.

'It's Miss Murray, actually. I'm married, but I still use my maiden name,' she explained. 'Fourteenth of March, nineteen-seventy.'

'So, you're …'

'Fifty-five.'

'And how do you know the deceased lady? Are you a friend or a relative?'

'No, neither really. In fact, I only met her for the first time on Friday. Her name is Euphemia Isacson, and I came to visit her then as I wanted to ask her about her late parents, Per and Brigid Isacson.'

'Why?'

'Well, you see, I'm a member of the U3A's local history group and, for our group project, we're researching some of the famous and infamous people who've lived in the area. Euphemia's parents were people of note.'

'U3A?' he queried.

'University of the Third Age.'

'Ah yes, I've heard of it. Isacson, you say,' the DI continued taking notes.

'Yes. That's Isacson with one 'a', by the way, not two. It's the Scandinavian spelling. Per Isacson was a Danish-born medical scientist of some repute, and his wife, Euphemia's mother, was Brigid Dornan, a famous opera singer in her day. I wanted to get Euphemia's recollections of them for the project. When I visited her on Friday, she kindly invited me to come back again this morning, when she'd have rooted out some family papers to show me.'

She paused to allow the detective to write down the names.

'I got here at ten o'clock as arranged,' Carole continued, 'but couldn't get a reply when I knocked, which I thought was odd, since she was expecting me. I went around the back and saw the back door was ajar, which also struck me as odd, so I went inside and upstairs to the flat, and I found her on the floor. I thought perhaps she'd fainted or had fallen over something, but the paramedic tells me she's dead, and that somebody must have hurt her. Who would do such a thing?'

'Indeed. Did you switch on the lights in the flat?'

'No. They were on when I got here. And the curtains were fully closed.'

'So, what can you tell me about the deceased. Do you know who her next of kin would be? Is there a husband or partner?'

'No, I don't believe she was ever married. But, Inspector, there's something you should know about Euphemia Isacson.'

'Yes?'

'Well, I don't know a great deal about it, but … and this could be relevant to your enquiries … she had a sister, Emerald Isacson, who was murdered. Twenty-five years ago, it happened. She was attacked up in Percival's Wood. Someone bashed her over the back of the head, numerous times, apparently.'

The detective stopped writing for a second and looked at her in amazement.

'Do you think that could be just an awful coincidence?' Carole asked.

'No, I don't,' he shook his head. 'I don't think that for a minute.'

Carole gave the detective her contact details and explained that, having taken the civil service's early retirement package, she was at home most days if he needed to speak to her again. Hogget thanked her and stepped out of the car. Carole started the engine, pulled out into the lane and headed home. If she had felt bad seeing Euphemia Isacson lying there, obviously beaten to death, she now began to feel even worse. On the six-mile drive back to Chalfont St George, Carol found her hands shaking slightly. Euphemia's wasn't the first dead body she had ever come across, far from it. But, somehow, this was different.

When she arrived back at their cottage, she found Dave exactly where she had left him – seated in his armchair, his broken ankle propped up on a footstool, as he wrestled with a particularly challenging crossword puzzle.

'You're back early,' he said. 'I expected you'd be gone much longer. Wouldn't she discuss the murder with you, then?'

'She couldn't.'

'Don't tell me she'd forgotten your appointment. Was she out?'

'In a manner of speaking. She was dead.'

'What?'

'I found her lying dead in her little flat. I called the emergency services but she'd been dead for quite a while. And, Dave, it looks like she was murdered.'

'Murdered?' Dave was as shocked as Carole had been.

'Yes. And, what's more, I can't shake off the horrible feeling that it might just have been my fault.'

Chapter 2

'Murder' was the last word Carole Murray had expected to hear at her local history group meeting two months earlier. Group member Mohamed Durrani was delivering a lengthy and rather dry account of his research into the history of the local churches and their successive vicars. Carole thought it bizarre that the task of researching the Christin places of worship and their ministers had been assigned to the one group member who was a Muslim, but that didn't seem to have diminished Mo's enthusiasm for the topic. Carole wasn't a church goer either and she suspected that, like herself, Mo regarded the local churches mainly as atmospheric repositories of local history.

At first, Carole thought she must have misheard. After all, the meeting room was rather warm and airless, and she had found her mind wandering a couple of times whilst Mo was speaking. Surely though, he wouldn't really have mentioned murder, not in the context of church history? Looking around at the faces of her fellow group members, nobody seemed quite as surprised as she, so she told herself she probably had imagined it.

It was a full turnout that morning, which was why the room was stuffy. She reflected that the local history group had proved very popular with the U3A members and its numbers had quickly grown to fill their allocated meeting room in the village's community centre. Carole knew she had been lucky to secure a place in the group at all. Initially, she hadn't been too sure about joining something called the University of the Third Age, especially since, at fifty-five, she didn't actually consider herself to be in the third and potentially final phase of her life, far from it. Soon, however, she had come to realise the group was just what she needed to satisfy her need for a project to research.

Mo was now mentioning the fact that few of the vicars had been locals, but most had re-located out to the villages of the Misbourne Valley from London. *'Just like us,'* Carole thought, recalling how thrilled she and husband Dave had been when offered voluntary early release from government service just a few months earlier. Dave had been pleasantly surprised at the price they had received for their London flat. Moving out of the city had been a long-held dream, although she felt that finding a pretty cottage in a leafy Buckinghamshire village, and embracing the charm of English village life, had been Dave's dream more than hers. Ideally, Carole would have preferred to settle back in her native Northern Ireland, but the connections with County Down were hers and not Dave's. In any case, her one remaining relative in the province, her much-loved aunt Eleanor, had passed away just the previous year.

Gazing out of the meeting room window at the pollarded willow trees which lined the River Misbourne, she remembered how the big skies and birdsong had enchanted them – at first. The Misbourne Valley had indeed offered her and Dave a verdant location for the next stage of their life together. Gradually, however, the unaccustomed slow pace of village life had begun to lose a little of its appeal. She would never say as much to Dave, but she had begun to wonder if their move might have been a mistake.

Carole had decided fairly early on that what they needed was some sort of hobby or interest to fill the void their busy working lives had left. Picking up a leaflet in the community library, she had been pleased to learn that the only requirement for joining the U3A was to be neither engaged in, nor seeking full time employment. Seemingly, one didn't have to be ancient to become a *Third Ager*, merely free and eager to learn new things. As she glanced around again at her fellow local history buffs, she guessed most of them had also decided to quit the world of work whilst still young enough to enjoy the pleasures and opportunities of retirement.

Of the seventy-plus interest groups available to members, Carole had chosen local history since it seemed the topic most likely to satisfy her obsession with research. She preferred to call it a healthy interest, of course. It was Dave who deemed it an obsession. She had also hoped joining the group would be a good way of making new friends, as well as learning more about Chalfont St George, the village in which she and Dave had chosen to commence their early retirement adventure.

Glancing around again at her fellow group members, she remembered how they had warmly welcomed this newcomer into their ranks from the start. They were indeed a friendly bunch. She hadn't known what to expect upon first joining the group and had wondered whether there would simply be history talks given by paid speakers, which would have been interesting enough, but in fact the group's activities were much more participative. She liked the fact that Mary Keswick, the group's enthusiastic convenor, had set the group members individual tasks. They had each been assigned specific aspects of local history to research with a view to reporting their findings back to the group. The tasks were all part of a group project. They were researching the more famous and infamous people who, over time, had lived in and around the Misbourne Valley.

Of course, Carole accepted that this kind of research was in no way a substitute for the sort of intelligence analysis she had spent the past twenty-seven years conducting with MI5's Counter-espionage section. Researching local history was not at all as exciting as investigating and thwarting hostile plots against the nation. It was nowhere near as satisfying as seeing her complex analysis charts support her fellow intelligence officers' hypotheses and persuade a court to convict bombers and hostile nations' assassins. For now, though, she told herself it would do. It would at least slake her thirst for discovery.

Gazing out of the window once more, she recalled how excited they had been to arrive in the village, and how busy. In the first few weeks following their move, she and Dave had been fully occupied re-arranging their cottage. Rooms had to be re-decorated, furniture placed, boxes emptied and pictures hung. The tranquillity of the village had attracted them to Buckinghamshire as much as the gentle beech woodlands which cloaked the valley. It was Dave who had first begun to express a few misgivings about their move. Carole had put that down to his accident. His insistence on climbing a ladder to lop off a crossover branch on the apple tree in their cottage's rather overgrown garden had led to a fall, resulting in the broken ankle.

She felt quite sorry for him, but not as sorry as she knew he felt for himself. That ankle was now clad in a large medical boot affair, and so Dave had been confined to the house whilst his injury healed. Carole knew that being housebound had left him frustrated at not being able to do more jobs around the house and garden, or to get out and explore his new surroundings. His horizons being thus narrowed, it was only natural that, like Carole, he would find the peace and tranquillity beginning to pall. She had to agree that things were certainly quiet in this part of the Chilterns, a little *too* quiet perhaps, but she had assured him she felt they had made the right move. They just needed time to settle in and find their feet. So then, here she was, doing what many retired people do in the country, pursuing a new pastime in order to … well, pass the time.

The group's laughter which suddenly drew her out of her reverie seemed to be caused by some story Mo was telling. Seemingly, it involved a grumpy and vengeful long-ago vicar further down the valley at Chalfont St Michael. That vicar had refused to conduct the marriage ceremony for the son of the Lord of the Manor, citing that son's non-attendance at church on Sundays as the reason. Milord had responded by exercising his right to bring in a vicar from another parish to conduct the ceremony at St Michael's, so the grumpy cleric had extracted his revenge by exercising his own right to toll the funeral bell all during the marriage service. Carole didn't think that was very funny at all. In fact, she thought it most unkind. The vindictive vicar's next posting had been as a missionary to China, Mo informed them. *'Karma'*, Carole thought.

Carole was grateful Mary hadn't allocated *her* the stuffy topic of the vicars as her contribution to the group's project on famous and infamous locals. Instead, Carole had been assigned the scientists, medics and local administrators to research. Three groups might have seemed excessive, but Mary had said she didn't expect there'd have been that many scientists and medics whom one might consider famous, so she had tacked on the administrators, potentially an even less interesting group, as an extra. As group member Mo continued to drone on. Carole felt he had really drawn the short straw with the clerics. It was surely unlikely he would find any truly interesting characters amongst their ranks. It occurred to her that investigating the more *infamous* historic inhabitants of the villages along the River Misbourne would be the most interesting part of the project, but perhaps there wouldn't have been very many of these either, not in this serene backwater, and in any case, another group member had drawn that golden straw.

Stifling a yawn, she felt guilty that the warmth in the room had caused her mind to wander a little. She had been wondering what to cook for Dave's supper, and what nice little treat she might be able to pick up at the village supermarket to cheer him up. She felt bad that he was temporarily confined to barracks, but it was his own fault. She had warned him that placing his ladder on uneven ground might be a bad idea, though, of course, she hadn't compounded his pain by saying 'I told you so'. She felt a slight twinge of guilt that she had left him at home with the Sudoku to complete in the morning paper, a book of crossword puzzles and a large mug of coffee, whilst she was enjoying the company of her fellow *Third Agers*.

But then, there it was again. Mo had just said it again – 'murder'. Carole realised she had not misheard, at all. Mo really had mentioned a murder.

'Excuse me,' she butted in, raising her hand tentatively like a hesitant schoolchild, 'but did you just say there'd been a murder?'

'Yes,' Mo nodded. 'This month sees the twenty-fifth anniversary of the village murder, and they never solved it.'

'So, if I may ask, who was murdered, and where? Not a local vicar, surely?'

It was Tom Sharples who replied. Retired fireman Tom was not only a veritable goldmine of local information but he also baked the best brownies and ginger biscuits Carole had ever eaten, and, moreover, he often brought in a batch to share with the group. As well as daydreaming, Carole had been eyeing the biscuit tin Tom had placed on the coffee trolley at the back of the room and wondering what delights he might have brought along to today's meeting.

'She was a scientist, so that should interest you, Carole,' Tom announced. 'Doctor Emerald Isacson. She was in her early fifties, I guess, and she was a keen birdwatcher. She was birdwatching up in Percival's Wood one afternoon when someone bashed her brains in. They never got anyone for it.'

'Good heavens!' Carole spluttered. 'Percival's Wood? Where's that?'

'It's …, well, where do you live, Carole?' Tom asked.

'Hawthorn Lane.'

'Right, well Percival's Wood extends almost from the top of Gallows Hill and all the way down the valley, skirting behind the houses on the east side of Hawthorn Lane and right down to the valley bottom. At the time, the police searched the woods and they even dragged the river looking for the murder weapon. Never found nothing.'

'So, what was it? Robbery? Sexual assault?' Carole asked, her curiosity radar now fully charged.

'No evidence of either,' Tom shook his head. 'They reckoned she'd been hit on the head from behind, then she fell to the ground and her killer continued to bludgeon her to death. A dog walker found the body. Cops made the usual house-to-house enquiries, and they combed every inch of the woods, but they turned up nothing.'

'Did they interview the husband?' Carole asked. 'The husband or partner is usually the first suspect the police consider. In fact, in eighty percent of cases, he's usually the killer – so I've read.'

'I don't think she was married, was she?' Tom asked, turning to Mo, who seemed pleased to be back in the conversation, the topic of which he had raised but which Tom seemed to have hi-jacked.

'No, she was single,' Mo confirmed. 'A career woman. She worked at that big scientific centre that used to be up on Gallows Hill. Like I was saying, her memorial service was held at Briarfield parish church. According to press reports, the vicar at the time went on quite a bit about the wickedness in men's souls. But they didn't know who the man was who'd killed her, or even if it was a man. Could equally have been a woman.'

'I recall the press reports about the murder,' Mary Keswick interjected. 'She was wearing her binoculars when they found her. As Mo says, they decided she'd gone up there for a quiet afternoon's birdwatching. But why would anyone murder a birdwatcher?'

'I think they decided it was probably down to some random nutter who just happened to be in the woods that day,' Mo continued. 'Like I said, it was a quarter of a century ago and they never solved the case.'

'They had DNA back then though, didn't they?' Carole pondered aloud.

'Yes,' Tom cut in again, 'and they say every contact leaves a trace, but it looked like there wasn't any contact between the killer and his victim, apart from the weapon he'd used which certainly made contact with her head – numerous times.'

'Locard's Principle,' Carole said.

'Beg pudding?' Tom looked baffled.

'Locard's Principle,' Carole repeated. 'Every contact leaves a trace. It isn't always the case, though. Not if a killer knows what he's doing.'

'There wasn't any physical evidence,' Tom confirmed. 'It was a sunny spring day and the weather had been dry for a while, so the killer wouldn't have left any footprints in the hard earth either. Killer didn't leave anything behind like they do in detective dramas. It was a weekday afternoon, too, so there wouldn't have been many people in the woods. No witnesses.'

'Well, that's enough about murder,' Mary intervened, 'and I'm not sure how you got from your vicars onto that historic homicide, Mo, but now, I think it's time for our tea break.'

'I could certainly murder a cuppa,' Tom joked.

Once they had finished their hot drinks and most of Tom's homemade biscuits, Mary Keswick called the group back to order.

'Now, before we finish, does anyone have anything else to report? Malcolm, how are you getting on with the military heroes?'

'Oh yes,' Malcolm Rawlinson shuffled his notes. 'You'll all be pleased to know that I've found out exactly where our First World War Victoria Cross holder lived. Following his discharge from the Royal Navy, Ernest Blount acquired *Ferndown House* in Gaunt's Cross.'

'For a retired naval man, he certainly settled a long way from the sea,' Mary commented. 'Wasn't *Ferndown House* that big Edwardian place which is now a hotel?'

'That's right,' Malcolm agreed. 'It's now the *Austen Arms* hotel and restaurant. Ernest's son, Anthony Blount, was also a naval commander who was decorated in World War Two. I found out there are photos of both war heroes on the wall in the bar at the *Austen Arms*. It's my wife's birthday soon, so I thought I'd take her there for dinner. Since I'll be paying their fancy prices, they might let me copy the photos.'

'So, the Blount family no longer live there?' Mo asked.

'No, and it was just Ernest and his son Anthony who were naval men. Anthony's son Michael, and his grandson Robert, both joined the Civil Service. The family had moved away by then, though. They moved out to Wiltshire.'

'That's good work, Malcolm,' Mary, congratulated him. 'A VC recipient *and* his decorated son will be great additions to our project. So, come on everybody. Get researching and we'll meet again next month.'

***

It was a quarter past twelve when Carole arrived back at Rowan Tree Cottage. Their two greyhounds came rushing into the hall to greet her. As was usual since his accident, Dave was still sitting exactly where she had left him, in his armchair. He hadn't much choice, given his present lack of mobility. Moving around the house was possible, but painful. Carole went straight into the kitchen and filled the kettle.

'Coffee, Love?' she called out, knowing Dave wouldn't have ventured into the kitchen during her absence.

'Please,' he called back. 'I'm gasping. What's for lunch, by the way?'

'I'll do us an omelette for about one,' she said, returning from the kitchen and sitting down on the sofa. 'Here, you'll never guess what I found out this morning. There's only been a murder in the village.'

'Well, at least I'm not in the frame,' Dave grinned, pointing at his injured foot which was propped up on the footstool.

'No, not a recent murder. Twenty-five years ago, it happened. A woman was clobbered over the head in those woods just at the back of us.'

'Good grief!' Dave spluttered. 'Who was she?'

'A government scientist. Doctor Emerald Isacson. They never solved the crime.'

'After that length of time, they never will. It'll be languishing in some cold case file somewhere and any suspects may be dead. Anyway, what happened to that coffee? I'm spitting feathers here, Love.'

'Do you know anyone in Thames Valley Police? This area comes under their CID, doesn't it? Where d'you think their cold case files would be kept?'

'Oh no, Carole! You're not getting involved. I absolutely forbid it.'

'Well, it wouldn't hurt just to do a little bit of research on it, would it?' she said, as she grabbed and logged on to her laptop. 'After all, I've agreed to research local scientists and medics for my group's local history project, and the murdered woman *was* a scientist.'

Dave shook his head, took up his crutches, raised himself gingerly from his armchair and hobbled painfully into the kitchen to make his own coffee. Meanwhile, Carole typed the words 'scientist' and 'Chalfont St George' into the search engine. At first, there were no results, so she tried again entering 'Isaacson' and 'scientist'. This combination was more successful, albeit that the information which came popping up onto her screen showed she had misspelt 'Isaacson'. It seemed the Isacsons – with one 'a' – were a well-known family who had lived some six miles down the road in the town of Briarfield. Carole began to take notes. Soon, she was totally engrossed in the research.

According to an online encyclopaedia, Professor Per Isacson, the head of the family, was a Danish-born medical scientist. She read how he had come to England in the nineteen thirties as a teenaged refugee from Nazi-occupied Denmark. The article suggested he had arrived on something called the *Kindertransport*. Carole had an idea she had heard of this and that it was an initiative to bring Jewish children to the UK just prior to the outbreak of World War Two, but she decided she would research that aspect properly later. According to the online article, Per Isacson had pursued his education at London's Imperial College and had, during an illustrious career, invented numerous items of life-saving medical apparatus. It pleased Carole that she had already found her first worthy individual to research for the project, and he was both a scientist *and* a medic. She felt Mary Keswick would be impressed.

Reading further, Carole saw that, just after the war, Per Isacson had married the celebrated Irish-born opera singer, Brigid Dornan, and that the marriage had produced two daughters, Euphemia and Emerald. Carole guessed that the second-born infant would be the Emerald Isacson who would be murdered half a century later. Scrolling down through the article, she found a brief reference to the murder, but there was annoyingly little detail. Still, she felt she had a starting point. She rubbed her hands together. Two scientists to research for the project, and an unsolved murder to boot. This was shaping up to be an even more interesting assignment than she had hoped.

Chapter 3

The Thursday after Carole's group meeting saw her seated at a desk in the offices of Thames Valley Police's Unsolved Cases Unit, with a stack of files in front of her.

'This is very kind of you,' she smiled at Geoff Jackson as he handed her a freshly brewed mug of tea.

'Not at all,' he beamed. 'Nothing's too much trouble for Dave Lloyd's missus. I worked with Dave when I was a sprog over in Gloucester, you know. He was a good governor.'

'What brought you into the Thames Valley force, then?' Carole asked. 'I didn't think one could transfer between forces.'

'I got shot pursuing robbers during that big bank raid in Cheltenham fifteen years back. I was in hospital for quite a while. Then I got medical retirement. Later on, the wife and I moved out this way to be near her elderly mum, and I saw a civilian desk job being advertised here at TVP.'

'It must be a bit less exciting than your previous career?'

'True, but at least I'm still involved in investigations and I get to crack cases occasionally. Some of the historic case files make really interesting reading. Plus, the wife says she sleeps better at night knowing I'm behind a desk and not out chasing villains. Speaking of which, when Dave called, he said I was to remind you you're not to go chasing any murder suspects. If you find anything the CID missed back then, you're to tell us. You're not to go off investigating it yourself.'

'Oh, don't worry, Geoff. I'm just looking into the case by way of an exercise. I'll report back to my U3A local history group about it. It happened in our village, you see.'

'Okay, well, I'll leave you to it. Let me know if you need anything else.'

'I will. Thanks,' Carole smiled. 'Oh, there is just one thing. Would you know whether any of the original detectives involved in the case might still be around and where I might be able to find them?'

'I'll check that out for you,' Geoff promised and he left her to her research.

Carole began to peruse the stack of case files. Her attention was first drawn to a photograph of the victim. It was an old photograph, clearly taken when Doctor Emerald Isacson was young and still alive. It showed a smiling, slightly-built, dark-haired young woman. The photo, showing Emerald clad in graduation gown and mortar-board and holding a scroll, was undated but Carole estimated it would have been taken around three decades before the murder, since the details on the file cover stated Emerald was aged fifty-one at the time she was killed in March 2000. Carole flipped through the file documents but there were no further photographs of the victim taken in later life, just those taken at the crime scene.

She now steeled herself and turned her attention to those crime scene photographs. The victim lay face down in a clearing in woodland. Her dark hair was matted with blood and the binoculars were lying next to her head, with the strap still around her neck. *'Why would anyone murder a birdwatcher?'* Carole wondered aloud. She avoided looking at the close-up shots which captured the extent of the victim's injuries and she turned instead to the typed case summary. Taking out her notebook, she made a list of the various individuals the police had interviewed. Using her phone's camera, she took some shots of the file notes and statements and of the map showing the location of the crime scene within Percival's Wood. Before she knew it, an hour had passed, her tea was finished, and she decided she had gleaned all she could from the police files. Soon Geoff was back. He handed her a scrap of paper with a name, address and telephone number written on it.

'Here you are. DCI Walter Gerrard. He was lead detective on the case. He's retired now. Last we heard of him he was still living in the area. But you'd best give him a call rather than turning up at his home on spec. You never know, he might have passed away, or he might be a bit senile these days. Best check he'll be willing to see you.'

'I will, and thank you so much, Geoff,' Carole shook his hand and took her leave of him.

Climbing into her car in the police station car park, before starting the engine she decided to take Geoff's advice and call the retired Detective Inspector to see if he would be willing for her to visit him. She dialled the number and eventually her call was answered. The voice was that of an older man.

'Hello, may I speak with Mr Walter Gerrard?' she asked.

'Depends why you're calling,' the man answered, rather abruptly Carole thought.

She introduced herself as the wife of a retired Gloucestershire Constabulary detective, as she thought that might make Gerrard more amenable. She explained she was herself a retired civil servant and was looking into one of Gerrard's old murder cases in connection with a research exercise for her U3A local history group.

'Which case you interested in?' he asked.

'The murder of Doctor Emerald Isacson in March two thousand,' she told him. 'Do you recall the case? It happened in Percival's wood in Chalfont St George. I understand it was never solved.'

There was a protracted silence and, for a moment, Carole wondered whether in fact Gerrard might be so elderly now and so long-retired that his memories would have faded. Or perhaps he had no wish to be reminded of a case he had failed to crack. She wondered whether calling him might have been a mistake.

'Yes,' he said at last. 'I do remember that one. Who did you say you were again?'

Carole repeated what she had said about who she was and she expanded on the reasons for her interest in the case, mentioning the fact that Per Isacson was the main focus of her research, but that his daughter's scientific career, and, of course, her fate, would also, by association, be of interest to Carole and her fellow local history buffs.

'It's all local history, whether worthy or tragic, isn't it?' she said.

'You're not a journalist, then?' he asked.

'No, just a retired civil servant. I'm looking at the case mainly out of curiosity. If you don't wish to be bothered about your past cases, though, I'll absolutely understand. I've no desire to intrude into your peaceful retirement, but if you would agree to see me, I'd be very grateful.'

She hoped the continuing silence meant Gerrard was considering her request.

'Yes, okay,' he said eventually. 'Do you know where I live?'

'I do,' she confirmed and she read the address over to him just to confirm he hadn't moved.

'I'll be home on Monday morning,' he said. 'If you call around about ten-ish, I'll have the kettle on.'

'Very many thanks indeed, Mr Gerrard. I look forward to seeing you then.'

Rather than heading home immediately, Carole next called at the offices of the local newspaper, *The Bucks Sentinel* which occupied a shop premises on the high street over in Briarfield. The young woman manning the office was on the phone when Carole entered and she seemed to be the only person on duty.

'How may I help you?' the young woman asked on ending her call.

'I was wondering whether you keep back issues of the *Sentinel* as there's something I'd like to look up.'

'How far back?'

'March two thousand,' Carole said, hopefully.

'I'm afraid we only keep issues here going back ten years, but you should be able to find the older editions online, at the British Newspaper Archive. You might have to take out a paid subscription, though.'

'Okay. Many thanks,' Carole smiled. 'Is it just you running the show here, then?'

'No, there's two of us. Justin Buchanan is office manager. He's out at the moment. I'm Trudy, the general dogsbody.'

'Ah, so where do the reporters hang out?'

'They're free-lancers. They mostly work from home and send in their copy.'

'How fascinating. I've always wondered how local press works. Do you accept stories from members of the public as well?'

'Oh yes. If you have a story to tell you can e-mail it to us and Justin will look it over. Here's our contact details.'

Carole pocketed the business card, thanked Trudy and headed back to her car. As she drove home along the A40, she began to feel a mild rush of adrenalin. She was experiencing once again that lifting of her spirits which always came with new tasking. Of course, this wasn't a counter-espionage job requiring the specialist skills of MI5's former senior analyst, but she definitely felt that same sense of eager anticipation, just as she had always felt when allocated a new intelligence operation to get stuck into.

As her adopted village came into view, the slight disappointment she had felt with her new life in the country began to dissipate. Seemingly, all was not as calm and dull in Buckinghamshire as she had begun to think it might be. There could actually be a darker side to life here in the Chilterns. It seemed there might, after all, be murders and mysteries crying out for the attention of a former intelligence analyst like Carole, and perhaps also for a retired detective turned MI5 agent handler like Dave. She couldn't wait to get home and tell Dave all about the unsolved murder of Emerald Isacson.

Chapter 4

The following morning, Carole checked the cost of subscribing to the British Newspaper Archive. It wasn't exactly cheap, but she told herself it would surely be an essential tool, not just for researching the Isacson murder, but also for any other aspects of local history she might wish to research. She took the plunge and purchased a year's subscription. If Dave didn't ask how much it had cost, she wouldn't volunteer that information. If nothing else, her three decades of experience with the Security Service had taught her how to keep secrets.

She set the parameters for her search to Buckinghamshire and the period from the year two thousand to two thousand and ten, then typed in the keywords 'Emerald' and 'Isacson'. Pleasingly, a great many results to her query popped up immediately. As she opened them up, however, she realised that these were mostly the same account of the murder which had been written by the same reporter for the *Bucks Sentinel.* Clearly, the report had been syndicated and re-printed in the nationals as well as in many other local newspapers, from the *Aberdeen Argos* to the *Wycombe Courier*. She scrolled through each report hoping to find some new aspect of the case, but there was little variation in the accounts.

The facts were pretty much as her fellow local history buffs had said and reflected what was in the police file. At the time of her death, Doctor Emerald Isacson, aged fifty-one and unmarried, had been a research scientist at the Chiltern Bio-sciences Institute, a mainly government-funded scientific centre in Chalfont St George. A keen amateur ornithologist, she had indeed spent much of her leisure time birdwatching in the various woods around the Misbourne Valley but, for reasons which were never established, on one such outing in Percival's Wood, one Wednesday afternoon in the spring of two thousand, she was brutally beaten to death. The articles all said the same thing – that the killing was senseless and the police clueless as to the identity of her killer.

Carole also found a death notice for the deceased scientist. She pulled this up, too, hoping to see what family members might have been alive at that time and whether the murder victim, although unmarried, might have had a partner or fiancé. She told herself she wasn't going to overlook the statistics which showed that, in most cases of femicide, the victim's husband or partner was the culprit. However, the brief announcement suggested Doctor Emerald Isacson was survived only by a sister, Euphemia Isacson of Briarfield. From the name, Carole deduced that Emerald's sister would also have been unmarried at the time.

Carole decided it probably wasn't worth opening every single article on the case, since most of them confirmed the fact that the killer was never identified, and that the police investigation had been wound down some six months after the incident. However, another headline stood out, and made her decide that this article might just be worth checking out, too. 'Another Death in Percival's Wood', was the full headline. The subheading announced the fact that, just eighteen months after the unsolved murder of Emerald Isacson, another fatality had occurred in Percival's Wood. This struck Carole as potentially interesting so she opened up the whole article.

It seemed that another Briarfield resident, one Charles Herron, had been found deceased and hanging by his neck from a tree within the wood. As with Emerald, the body was spotted by a dog walker. Carole hoped it was not the same dog walker in both cases. That would have been too much of a coincidence, she thought, not to mention an incredibly traumatic experience for the dog walker concerned. In the Herron case, the article confirmed, there were no suspicious circumstances and no other persons were believed to have been present at the time of the death. Accordingly, the local coroner had determined that the death of forty-five-year-old journalist Charles Herron was a suicide. Though she searched using a variety of key words, Carole could find no further reports of deaths in the two-hundred-and-fifty-acre Percival's Wood.

There wasn't a great deal of information in the article about the death of Herron, certainly nothing like the amount of detail to be found in the reporting on Emerald's murder. Carole supposed there wasn't a lot to say about a suicide. In any case, Herron's death hadn't made the nationals, only the local press, whose reporters probably wouldn't have wished to add to the Herron family's grief by speculating on the reasons for his having taken his own life. On impulse, however, she searched for Charles Herron's name on the newspaper database.

To her surprise, dozens upon dozens of articles came up, chiefly featuring him as Charlie Herron, rather than as Charles, and all were on different topics. It suddenly occurred to her why this should be. Charlie Herron was in fact a freelance journalist who had provided a great many articles for *The Sentinel* and for other newspapers. More significantly perhaps, he was *the* journalist who had provided the original, widely syndicated account of the Isacson murder. She thought it oddly ironic that the journalist who had first covered Isacson's death had ended up dead himself the following year and in the same woods.

'Where are you off to now?' Dave asked, as he saw Carole putting her coat on again.

'Going to take the dogs out for a walk.'

'Why are you taking the car keys?' he asked, his former detective's innate sense of suspicion kicking in.

'Going by car. Thought I'd pick up some food down in the village. Don't want to hump potatoes back up the hill.'

'You won't be going anywhere near those woods where the murder was, though, will you?' he asked.

'Of course not,' she replied. 'I'll give the dogs a run in the meadow next to the community centre car park.'

Securing the dogs in the back of her car, Carole headed back up the road to Briarfield. Leaving the dogs in the vehicle, she nipped in again to the offices of *The Sentinel*.

'Hello Trudy,' she greeted the receptionist. 'Me again. I just wondered if you knew anything about Charlie Herron. Apparently, he wrote a lot of articles for *The Sentinel*. It would have been before two thousand and two.'

'Oh, that's long before my time. I could ask Justin, though. He's been here longer than me.'

Trudy disappeared into the back office then re-appeared just moments later accompanied by a man in a smart suit. Guessing him to be in his early thirties, Carole realised that, owing to his comparative youth, she was likely to be disappointed.

'Hi, I'm Justin Buchanan,' he smiled pleasantly. 'You're asking about someone named Hearne, I believe?'

'Herron,' Carole corrected him. 'Charlie Herron. He wrote a lot of articles for your paper over the years, but I understand he died in September of two thousand and two. I just wondered if you knew anything about him or the circumstances of his death.'

'Well, I'd love to help you, but since I would have been around, what, nine or ten years old back then, I wouldn't even have heard of him.

We've always used freelance reporters, too, so he wouldn't have been directly employed by us.'

'Is there any former *Sentinel* employee still around locally who would have worked here longer than you,' Carole asked. 'Someone who might remember him?'

Buchanan thought for a moment, then shook his head.

'I wouldn't really know, to be honest. The chap I took over from passed away a couple of years back, and we had a series of temps before Trudy joined us. We've always been a fairly small operation, you see.'

'I see, well thanks, anyway,' Carole smiled and turned to leave.

'Don't forget,' Trudy called out, 'if you turn up anything interesting and would like to submit it as an article for *The Sentinel*, just send it to me.'

'I may well do that,' Carole promised, and she headed back out to her car.

'Did you get the potatoes?' Dave asked, as she walked into the hall, leading the dogs but otherwise empty-handed.

'The ones in the greengrocer's didn't look brilliant, to be honest,' she fibbed. 'I decided we'll have pasta instead. Fancy a nice carbonara?'

'Yes, lovely,' Dave nodded. 'So, how's the online research going?'

'Well, now, what would you think if I told you that the journalist who was the first reporter on the scene of that lady scientist's murder, and whose account of the case appeared in all the papers, was found dead himself, just a year and a half later, hanging from a tree in the very same wood where the scientist was killed. Quite a coincidence, wouldn't you say?'

'Nope. I wouldn't. You know exactly what I'd say, Love. There's …'

'…no such thing as coincidence. Yes, you always say that, Love. And you're always right.'

'So, what's your next line of enquiry, then?'

'My next move will be to interview one of the detectives who was investigating the murder. Former DCI Walter Gerrard. You don't know him, do you?'

'No. Never heard the name. But promise me something, will you, Love?'

'What?'

'Promise me you won't go upsetting him. I mean, he didn't solve the case, did he? He might not take kindly to you suggesting there were any shortcomings in his methods. It might be better not to give him the impression you think you'll succeed where he and his team failed. We ex-coppers have fragile egos, you know.'

'I can be diplomatic when I need to, Dave. I promise you I'll tread very gently with Mister Gerrard.'

Chapter 5

Walter Gerrard's home was a neat bungalow in Chalfont St Michael, or, as Dave had christened the next village along the river from theirs, 'bungalow land'. There was indeed a proliferation of almost identical single-storey houses in the village, which Dave had said probably reflected the local demographic. The population of the village did seem to Carole to be slanted towards retirees, and they also made up a large portion of the local U3A's membership.

Gerrard's house was named 'Dunsleuthin', the humour of which Carole got right away. It made her smile. The pocket hankie sized lawn in front was neat but there weren't a great many shrubs or plants in the borders. She rang the bell and waited, hoping the retired detective wouldn't have had second thoughts about speaking to her. The door was soon answered by a fairly non-descript looking man in his late seventies.

'Hi, I'm Carole,' she smiled at him warmly.

'Right, come in, then. You take a seat in the lounge and I'll pop the kettle on. Do you prefer tea or coffee? Life's full of big decisions for us retired folks, isn't it?'

'Tea would be great, thanks, Walter. May I call you Walter? And I brought some biscuits,' she said as she handed him a packet of chocolate digestives.

To her relief, he seemed a little friendlier in person than he had sounded on the telephone. Glancing around the little sitting room, which seemed as spartan as the front garden, she took in the few framed photographs. Some were of the younger Walter Gerrard in uniform and there was a nineteen seventies wedding group photo and snaps of a couple of children at various stages in their lives. There wasn't any of the usual police paraphernalia which retired policemen seemed to collect, such as caps and plaques from other nations' visiting police officers, or Interpol paperweights and the like, but she supposed Gerrard might have converted his spare bedroom into a study and might have them displayed there instead.

Carole gained the impression that Walter Gerrard might be living alone; a widower, perhaps. She didn't detect the presence of any female touches. The coats which hung in the hall were men's coats. There was a pair of men's muddy boots in the porch, but no women's coats or shoes to be seen, and the sitting room was devoid of any ornaments. A small, drop-leaf dining table stood folded back against one wall but had stacks of magazines upon it and so didn't look as though it was used for dining very often.

She was gazing at a photo of a sun-tanned Walter Gerrard, clad in sleeveless shirt and shorts, seated at a seaside café table, a grin on his face and a bottle of beer in his hand, when he returned with a tea tray.

'That's me in Fuengirola,' he said.

'Do you visit Spain often?' Carole asked.

'Got a house out there. Me and the missus bought it years ago. I don't get out there quite so often since she passed away, though.'

'Oh, I'm so sorry,' Carole said.

Walter had decanted the biscuits onto a plate. He poured out two cups of tea and offered Carole the milk jug. She declined the sugar but accepted a biscuit, took a nibble and placed it in her saucer.

'Thank you for agreeing to see me' she said. 'As I explained on the phone, I'm participating in a project with my fellow members of the U3A, researching some of the area's more famous and infamous residents. My particular assignment includes researching the scientists and medics. I found details of a prominent medical scientist, Per Isacson, who'll be a worthy inclusion. Then I saw that his daughter, also a scientist, had lived in the area, so I decided to research both of them. I was surprised to see she'd been murdered, though, so I thought I'd look into the circumstances.'

'I see,' Gerrard nodded. 'Playing the armchair detective, eh?'

'No. Nothing like that. I do think some detail about what happened to Emerald would add a great deal of interest to the project, though, especially since it was an unsolved case.'

'Okay. So, what do you want to know?'

'I understand there was nothing in the way of forensic evidence at the scene.'

'That's right. The killer left no fingerprints, no footprints, no DNA. We never found the murder weapon, either.'

'Press reports say she was bludgeoned to death. Did the post mortem suggest what kind of weapon it might have been?'

'Something solid, they thought. Metal. A car tyre iron or something similar. We had squads of police and civilian volunteers with metal detectors scour that wood, and we dragged the river, too. No potential weapon was found.'

'So, was there anyone in her life who might have had a motive? A jealous work colleague, perhaps, or a spurned lover?'

'No, no-one like that. She was a well-educated woman, good at her job, and she led a very quiet life. Lived with her sister, Euphemia, a school teacher. They didn't get up to anything more exciting than bird-watching. No boyfriends on the scene.'

'I understand they were Jewish,' Carole speculated. 'Might there have been an antisemitism angle to this?'

'We did consider the possibility, especially as there had been some vandalism at the Jewish cemetery over in Briarfield Meadows three months or so earlier. New Year's Eve, it was – you know, the turn of the century, the millennium. At the time, the administration at the synagogue put it down to drunken revellers. No CCTV there, of course.'

'Was it the Isacson family's grave that was targeted?' Carole asked.

'No. Just a few random headstones smashed.'

'It looks like Emerald's only living relative was her sister, Euphemia. Did you consider her as a suspect?'

'No. She had no motive, and she was really distressed about the murder. Distraught, in fact. I think it really frightened her.'

'Does she still live in Briarfield?'

'Don't think so. I heard a rumour she'd moved away. Some said she'd applied for a teaching post on a kibbutz in Israel.'

'Did she not keep in touch with you, then? If a sister of mine were murdered, I'm sure I'd be making a nuisance of myself ringing CID at least every few months to ask how the investigation was going.'

'No. Never heard from her again. I suppose she was frightened in case the killer was someone with a grudge against the family and they might come back and take a pop at her, too.'

'And did you establish whether anyone did bear a grudge against the family?'

'No. No evidence of that. Now, mind if I ask you a question?' Gerrard looked her in the eye.

'Not at all.'

'What's the Security Service's interest in the case?'

'The Security Service?' Carole was taken aback. 'What makes you think they …'

'Well, that's who you worked for, isn't it?' Gerrard said, giving her a steely glance.

'How did you know that?'

'Whilst you were checking up on me, I was checking up on you?'

'I no longer work for the Firm. And, although I'm retired, I'm not yet dead. I was an intel analyst and I was involved in some pretty big operations. It's hard no longer having anything to analyse or to investigate. *You* must know how that feels, Walter. Joining the U3A's local history group has given me a purpose. It's given me a project to get my teeth into. I was just hoping to get enough background on the Isacsons to make my contribution on local scientists a bit more interesting.'

'Really?'

'Yes, really. And I'm not trying to make you or your investigation look bad. I mean, it's extremely doubtful that any enquiries I could make now would solve a case that you and your crack team couldn't solve a quarter of a century ago. And it's not my intention to even try.'

Carole couldn't fathom Gerrard's expression. He looked doubtful, suspicious even, but he seemed to accept her motives. He shrugged.

'We *were* a crack team, but a small one. There were just four of us in local CID back then, and this wasn't the only case of suspicious death we had to deal with at the time.'

'No?'

'No. There was a road rage incident. Then a man who killed his wife in west London came out here to dump her body. But don't think we didn't go all out to try and catch doctor Isacson's killer. We shed blood, sweat and tears over that one, and we called in all the uniforms and local volunteers we could muster. There just wasn't any evidence.'

'I understand. Not all cases can be solved.'

'Okay. Well, is there anything else you'd like to ask me?'

'Were you aware of another death in Percival's Wood? A year and a half later, Charlie Herron, the reporter who'd been the first one to report on the Isacson murder, was found hanged there? Did you consider there might have been a connection?'

'Of course we did, but we found nothing to link the two deaths. Herron was a hack, always desperate for a juicy story. He was also an alcoholic, and his wife had left him. History of depression, that sort of thing.'

'Ah, I see.'

'I suppose, having reported on the murder and been at the crime scene, once things went wrong in his own life, he might have decided those woods would be a good place for him to end it all. Just as with

Emerald Isacson, his body wasn't found immediately. If you want to do away with yourself and you don't want to be found and revived, a wood's the best place.'

'So, were there no suspects at all in the Isacson case?'

'We tickled the collars of a few local sex offenders, but there was no evidence of that kind of interference. It just seemed a random and senseless killing. The wood is easily accessible from the A40, so the killer could have been some psycho on an away day from the Big Smoke. He could easily have headed back to London afterwards, as well. And, anyway, if a woman's daft enough to go into the woods on her own, well, she's just asking for trouble.'

Carole immediately bristled at Gerrard's odious resorting to victim blaming. She suddenly decided she didn't like him very much, and nor did she see much point in remaining in his company any longer.

'Okay, Walter, well, I think I've picked your brains enough. I'll leave you my e-mail address and phone number. If you think of anything else relevant, you can always call me.'

Carole scribbled down her contact details on a scrap of paper she pulled from her bag, then, placing it on his coffee table, she picked up the remains of the biscuit from her saucer, popped it in her mouth and rose to leave.

'No need to show me out,' she smiled with cold politeness. 'Thank you for the information and for the tea.'

As he heard the front door close, Walter Gerrard also rose and, picking up the piece of paper she had left, he went to the window to watch Carole drive away. Walking over to the bureau in the corner of the room, he took out a pen and added her car number to her details on the slip of paper. Then he picked up his mobile phone, scrolled through the contact numbers and hit the 'call' button. Moments later, he was connected.

'It's Walter Gerrard,' he said. 'You asked me to let you know if anyone ever came asking about Emerald Isacson ...'

Chapter 6

Carole decided her subscription to the newspaper archive was money well spent. Over the next couple of weeks, she found herself trawling through lots of different and fascinating press articles. The only problem was that there was a temptation to drift off at a tangent, following up other accounts of local incidents and events not related to the Isacson murder. The initial impression she had formed of the villages along the Misbourne, that they were tranquil, respectable and perhaps a little dull, continued to be dispelled.

It seemed that, whenever there was an unexpected occurrence of sufficient seriousness to create ripples on the village pond – an unexplained death, a road rage incident, a fight outside a village pub – the press reporting always emphasised the fact that such things rarely happened in these quiet little villages. Clearly, however, that wasn't the case. Carole felt that such a claim flew in the face of the indisputable fact that human nature was human nature, regardless of the location. Motives for murder and other violent crime were pretty much the same whether in town or country. That said however, there still seemed to be absolutely no obvious motive for the murder of Emerald Isacson.

One thing Carole was unable to find in trawling through the press articles was any report of the attacks on the Jewish burial ground. She searched the reports from three months either side of the millennium but could not find a single report of any damage caused at the cemetery, either malicious or accidental. Surely, she thought, that sort of incident would have been met with outrage? It would have been exactly the kind of thing local reporting would have described as 'out of character' in a quiet rural town or village. Yet there was no mention of any such attack having occurred.

Could Walter Gerrard have been mistaken, she wondered? Might he have misremembered the facts of the case? Might he have confused the Isacson case with another case in another time? That was possible, especially since it had happened a quarter of a century ago. And yet his comments about the millennium attack on the burial ground were so specific. Might he even be lying? But why would he lie about that? Why would he suggest a false motive for the murder? Did that mean he really *did* know why Emerald had been killed, and was trying to cover it up?

But why would he do that? Surely, no detective would be content to leave a murder case unsolved? She felt she had so many questions but so few answers.

***

By the time the next meeting of her local history group came around, Carole had already put together a good deal of information, not only on the Isacsons, but on several other notable scientists who had made their homes in the villages around the Misbourne. She had concluded that a major draw factor to the area, for people who followed the scientific professions in particular, was the Great Western Railways. In the railway's early years, a service which, sadly, was no longer in existence, once ran from the station at Gaunt's Cross up to Paddington. From there, London's Imperial College at South Kensington, Per Isacson's place of employment and study, was easily reached. From Paddington, it was just a gentle stroll across Kensington Gardens to that centre of excellence in sciences, medicine and engineering. These days, Carole noted, trains from Gaunt's Cross and Briarfield only ran to Marylebone, which was not quite so convenient for access to South Kensington, since further journeys by underground were now necessary.

She discovered that, back in Per Isacson's working years, there had actually been quite a scientific community in the area. Following the arrival of the railway at Gaunt's Cross in 1906, and the lyrical representation of the leafy Buckinghamshire villages along the Metropolitan Line as part of the poet Betjeman's 'Metro-Land', Great Western Railways and local developers had sold Gaunt's Cross to commuters as 'The Brighton of the Chilterns'. Carole supposed word of mouth had encouraged a significant number of Imperial's scientists to follow their colleagues' example and settle in the area. Indeed, perhaps the concentration of scientific mindsets in the area was also the reason for the establishment of the Chilterns Biosciences Institute on Gallows Hill.

Carole turned up for the local history group's next meeting eager to share her findings. She was able to tell them that, amongst his many achievements, Per Isacson had worked with other medics to develop an item it was likely most of the group members used on a regular basis – the sphygmomanometer or blood pressure gauge. Prior to the invention of that device, she informed them, testing blood pressure had been a much more intrusive process. The number of nodding heads around the room told her she wasn't the only group member who had cause to regularly check her blood pressure.

'That's a good bit of research, Carole,' convener Mary Keswick congratulated her. 'Weren't you also going to be researching local administrators as well, though?'

'Oh yes, I was. I mean, I am, but I got so tied up with the scientists, I haven't had time to look at administrators. I have to admit that I also got a bit side-tracked with the murder of Per Isacson's daughter.'

'I'll bet that's a darn sight more interesting than the local administrators,' Tom Sharples said.

'Yes, have you solved it yet?' Daisy Cooper asked.

'Well, I did meet up with the lead detective on the case. He's retired now, but it's still a mystery crying out to be solved,' Carole agreed.

'Maybe we could help you with that?' Kitty Walker offered.

'Indeed, we'd love to,' Daisy agreed, her brown eyes flashing with enthusiasm. My background is in maths and science, so if there's anything scientific you need explaining, then I'm your girl.'

'Yes, we'd love to help,' Betty Brown enthused. 'We're all keen researchers. Between us, we could help research your murder, Carole.'

'Yes, it does sound like an interesting challenge,' Mary agreed, 'but let's not lose sight of the project, which is to research *all* categories of significant locals. I know the administrators probably sound like a dull lot, but I could introduce you to Kulwinder Kaur, Carole. She's one of our parish councillors. She could show you where to find council records and details of past chairmen.'

'Yes, that would be helpful,' Carole agreed. 'If you have her contact details, I'll give her a call.'

'Oh, but don't give up on the murder,' Betty urged. 'If you find out who the murderer was, we could include him with the infamous characters in our project, couldn't we?'

'Who's the lucky person researching the infamous?' Carole asked.

'That's me,' Tom said. 'So, listen, why don't a few of us get together for coffee next week, Carole. We could form a sub-group to look into the murder. If it turns out the killer was a local then I'll have my first infamous person for the project.'

'That's a great idea,' Carole enthused. 'My husband, Dave, is a retired murder detective and I'm sure he'd like to get involved, too. But he's laid up at home with a broken ankle at the moment. So, why not come over to our house, Rowan Tree Cottage. We're halfway up

Hawthorn Lane, on the left as you drive up from the village. How about Wednesday morning at ten o'clock? I'm sure Dave would love to meet you all.'

***

'What have you got yourself into now?' Dave asked when she told him about the following week's plans. 'And why do I have to be involved?'

'But, Dave, you have the kind of skills and connections we need if we're to solve this murder. And anyway, I'm sure Tom doesn't want to be the only man in the group. You and he should get along well.'

'I'm in pain, Love. Not sure I'd be good company.'

'Well, why not just meet the group members and hear what they've got to add to the research? I'm sure it'll pique your interest. Then, if you don't fancy being involved, you won't have to be.'

'Okay. So, who are these people you've invited over?'

'Well, Mary Keswick is our group's convenor. She's quite a sporty type, a member of the local tennis club. When your ankle's healed, you might want to join. You used to enjoy tennis. Daisy Cooper, she's a brunette and she's a retired maths teacher, though she still does some tutoring, and she also convenes the family history group as well. There's nothing she doesn't know about centimorgans.'

'Senti Morgans? What's that, Welsh family history?'

'And then there's Kitty Walker,' Carole continued, ignoring Dave's frivolity. 'She's a petite ash blonde and she's just the loveliest person. She volunteers in the library and she's in something called the river watch group. I guess it's also a case of Walker by name, walker by nature, because she's also involved with the U3A's walking cricket group.'

'Walking cricket? What's that?'

'It's cricket in which you walk but don't run. That might be something else you could try once your ankle's mended a bit.'

'So, instead of scoring runs, what do they score – strolls?'

'Then there's Betty Brown. She's lived around here longer than anyone else, so she's got a lot of local knowledge. She's a red-head with a sexy voice and a wicked sense of humour.'

'Well, I'm certainly looking forward to meeting *her*,' Dave brightened, 'and who's the chap in this sub-group of yours?'

'Tom Sharples. He's a retired fireman. And he's into cooking and baking, just like you. You've got that in common, at least.'

'So, when did you say they're coming over?'

'Wednesday at ten. It's just for a chat and to pool our ideas. You haven't been out of the house since your fall. It'll be good for you to meet some new people. And these are good people.'

'If you say, so. But remember what I said about not upsetting Walter Gerrard. He won't thank you if you solve the case when he couldn't.'

'Actually, I didn't think he was a particularly nice man. I don't really care whether I upset him or not. And what's the worst he could do? Send me an angry postcard from Fuengirola?'

Chapter 7

Carole couldn't contain herself until Wednesday came around. She had blitzed the cottage and had taken the dogs out for an early morning walk to exhaust them, in the hope that they wouldn't get over excited when her visitors arrived. She had also picked up a Victoria sponge cake from the village bakery and, as soon as she got home, she unpacked her late Aunt Ellen's vintage Belleek china tea set, thinking she might use the delicate cups and saucers for her guests.

Gazing at the cream-coloured china with its decoration of little green shamrocks tugged at her heartstrings for a moment. It brought back warm memories of her idyllic Northern Irish childhood and school holidays spent with her indulgent aunt and uncle at their home on the County Down coast. However, it was also a sad reminder of the passing, a year ago, of her aunt, whose own memories were gone by then, and who no longer recognised her favourite niece. Carole hoped her aunt's dementia did not run in the family. She told herself that her new-found research projects should keep her own mind active and stave off the forgetfulness of later life.

Tom was first to arrive and he brought with him a tin of freshly baked shortbread biscuits. Carole felt a little embarrassed that her own offering was merely shop-bought. Dave was the family baker, she explained, but he had hung up his apron temporarily as he couldn't stand up for long since his accident. Daisy and Betty arrived together, as they lived near one another up on the common. Mary was next to appear, armed with a large notebook and pens, and Kitty came last, as she had furthest to come, from the neighbouring village of Chalfont St Michael.

Soon, their visitors were seated in the living room and Carole left the *Third Agers* to get acquainted with Dave whilst she made the teas and coffees. Dave explained that he and Carole, having met and married just five years earlier, at a time when they both had established careers, had each kept their own surnames. He was Dave Lloyd, he explained, a widower when he had met Carole, and she, who had not been married before, still used her maiden name of Murray. Neither of them had children, Dave said, but the recently acquired dogs were their boys.

'So, how are you both settling in?' Daisy asked. 'You've not been here that long, have you?'

'Twelve weeks,' Dave told her. 'Still got a few jobs to do around the house and garden, but breaking my ankle's slowed me down a bit. It's so quiet round here, though. I suppose we're used to London's hustle and bustle. It's taking us a while to get used to hearing the dawn chorus instead of London's commuter traffic'

'That's a shame about your ankle,' Kitty sympathised. 'I was laid up myself for weeks when I had my hip done. I was so bored. Felt like shooting myself.'

'Don't say that, Kitty. You'll put the poor man off the place,' Betty admonished her. 'Really, Dave, there's actually plenty going on. Once you're up and about, you'll see. We've had our fair share of scandals locally, you know. And, of course, there's Carole's murder.'

'Oh, it's *my* murder now, is it,' Carole laughed, as she appeared with the tray of coffees and teas.

'Carole tells us you were a murder squad detective, Dave,' Tom said, as Carole handed the cups around and offered slices of cake and Tom's biscuits. 'So, it's great that we've got the benefit of your experience and skills. It's very good of you to agree to get involved. I reckon we're very lucky to have you on board.'

'Oh, not at all,' Dave shrugged off the praise. 'No, as soon as Carole told me about the case, I was keen to be involved.

Dave probably noticed but chose to ignore the sideways glance Carole threw him. She was surprised but pleased at his change of tune.

'Yes,' she agreed, 'Dave's *very* enthusiastic about getting involved, as much as his injury will permit. Aren't you Dave?'

'So, tell us what you've found out, Carole,' Daisy urged. 'We can't wait to hear.'

'I spoke with Walter Gerrard, the detective in charge of the enquiry back then, and he told me that, despite a major search of the area, no murder weapon was ever found. They think it would've been something metal, like a tyre iron, but the killer didn't leave any physical evidence at all. Doctor Isacson was attacked from behind and he seems to have knocked her unconscious immediately then carried on beating her about the head. There were no signs of a struggle so no contact traces were left, such as fingerprints, fibres or DNA.'

'You say 'he', so you're assuming it was a man, then?' Mary queried.

'Not necessarily.' Carole said. 'We should keep an open mind on that. There was no evidence of sexual assault, though. And nothing to suggest she was robbed either. Her car keys and some banknotes and small change were still in her pockets.'

'Did Gerrard have any idea at all what the motive might have been?' Kitty asked.

'Well, he had a theory that it was a racially or religiously motivated attack. He said there'd been vandalism of some headstones in the Jewish burial ground by the Briarfield synagogue three months before the murder, but I couldn't find a single news report about that. I think either he might have been following a false lead at the time, or maybe nowadays his memory is faulty and he's mixed this case up with a different one.'

'I've never heard of any such attack,' Betty confirmed. 'And I'm sure my Jewish neighbours, the Barnets, would have mentioned it. They worship at that synagogue.'

'Someone I'd really like to have spoken to would be Emerald Isacson's sister, Euphemia,' Carole continued, 'but Gerrard thinks she quit her teaching job and moved away after the murder. He thinks she might even have gone to live and work in Israel.'

'I'm not sure that's right,' Tom said. 'I'd heard she'd been the biology mistress at Briarfield High School up until the murder, and folks were surprised when she gave up her teaching career to run a teashop somewhere around here.'

'A teashop?' Carole queried. 'Are you sure?'

'Yes, according to my neighbour, Callum Dennis. He taught at Briarfield High back then, too. He knew her. He thinks she's still running that teashop. He didn't say exactly where it is.'

'If she's still using the same surname and still living in the UK,' Dave added, 'we should easily be able to track her down from the phone book or the electoral register.'

'And if she subsequently married, we should be able to find out her married name from General Records Office,' Carole suggested. 'Isacson isn't that common a surname, surely?'

'I'll run those checks,' Dave volunteered. 'That's the only kind of running I can manage right now.'

'Does anyone know anything about the laboratories where Emerald worked?' Carole asked. 'She might have had colleagues she was particularly friendly with and who could tell us more about her. We can't rule out a work colleague being involved in the murder, either. She might have had a falling out with one of them. It could've been a case of professional rivalry, or even an affair gone wrong.'

'She worked at the Chiltern Biosciences Institute,' Betty advised. 'Back then, most of the scientists would probably have been men. So, an affair with a married colleague is certainly a possibility. Romance could have burned over the Bunsen burners. A little titillation amongst the test tubes. Passion over the Petrie dishes.'

'And what did they do there – science-wise, I mean?' Carole asked.

'I've no idea,' Betty conceded. 'And they closed down years ago. After that, the site was taken over by a medical diagnostics centre. They carried out x-rays and scanning procedures. I think they had a pharmaceutical operation there as well.'

'But that's gone now, too,' Daisy said. 'It closed down as well, five or six years ago.'

'So, who owns the site now?' Carole asked.

'Don't know,' Daisy shook her head. 'It's been unoccupied ever since. Maybe they had difficulty finding a buyer for the premises.'

'You're joking,' Dave said. 'This is the Chalfonts. We're less than half an hour from London by road and rail. Houses around here fetch silly prices. You could sell off your garden to a developer and he'd shove up a block of luxury commuter flats in it. The Gallows Hill site has acres of land and it's on the edge of scenic woodland. Surely, it would have been snapped up by developers immediately it came on the market?'

'Well, you'd think so,' Kitty agreed, twirling her short blonde curls around her finger thoughtfully. 'But there have always been unsavoury rumours about that place.'

'What sort of rumours?' Carole was intrigued.

'Was it a bordello?' Betty asked. 'Or maybe they were trafficking women for sex slavery?'

'Whoa, Betty,' Kitty erupted into laughter. 'Not *that* kind of unsavoury.'

'Well, what, then?' Betty seemed disappointed.

'The government first acquired the site during World War Two,' Kitty explained. 'They used radium up there to make luminous paint for the dials and instruments for Lancaster bombers. Obviously, you can't have a light on in the cockpit when you're night bombing. Local rumour has it there's still radioactive stuff buried in the ground up there. And if it is in the ground, it could also be in the River Misbourne. I'm on the river watch team, you know, Carole. I've always said we should test the river for chemical and other kinds of contamination.'

'But that would have been back in the nineteen-forties,' Dave pointed out. 'And if the site's been occupied by other outfits since then. Whether those were government or commercial, surely any contamination would have come to light. In any case, local councils are obliged to maintain registers of contaminated land. Any and all such sites should be listed on that register. It's an offence not to do so.'

'That would be something we could ask Councillor Kulwinder Kaur about,' Mary suggested. 'She should have access to that register, and she's also the planning advisor on the parish council. She could probably give you details of who's owned the land and why it's been empty for so long.'

'Yes,' Carole agreed. 'That's a good idea. Now then, has anyone heard about the journalist who was also found dead in Percival's Wood in the autumn of two thousand and one?'

Their astonished expressions told her no-one had. Although Carole's searches had turned up a press report of the case, because it had been deemed to be a suicide, it hadn't made the front page of *The Sentinel*, nor even the centre pages, so it wasn't surprising to Carole that nobody had heard of the incident.

'Coincidentally,' Carole added, 'though I know Dave doesn't believe in coincidences, the suicide was Charlie Herron, the freelancer who'd actually reported on Emerald's murder. He was found hanging from a tree branch in the wood some eighteen months after Emerald's death. No suspicious circumstances, apparently, and the coroner declared it a suicide.'

'Do you think *he* could have been the murderer?' Kitty asked. 'Maybe he was overcome with remorse afterwards and that led to his suicide.'

'It's a possibility,' Carole agreed. 'But I can't imagine what his motive for murder would have been.'

'Perhaps he was having an affair with Emerald,' Betty ventured. 'And maybe the poor man was heartbroken when she died. Sort of Romeo and Juliet, Home Counties style.'

'Big stories must have been hard to come by,' Tom suggested. 'Maybe he bumped her off in order to create one.'

'That's an extreme length to go to for a story though, Tom,' Mary frowned.

'Walter Gerrard told me Herron was a heavy drinker,' Carole added, 'and he'd been depressed because his wife had left him. That seems a more likely reason for his suicide. And Gerrard suggests the woods are the place to go if you want to make a good job of killing yourself. You're less likely to be found and saved. Finding Emerald's body there might have given him the idea. Once things really got him down, maybe he acted on that idea.'

'D'you want me to do some research on Charlie Herron, then?' Kitty asked. 'I could find out where he lived and maybe make some local enquiries about him.'

'Yes,' Carole agreed. 'That would be great, if you could. Maybe there was no connection between the two deaths, but it'll be interesting if it turns out Charlie Herron actually knew Emerald Isacson.'

'Right then,' Daisy rubbed her hands together enthusiastically. 'I vote we go and have a look at these woods sometime soon. We should check out the murder spot for ourselves. And, since Dave has kindly offered to trace the sister's whereabouts, what do you want the rest of us to do, Carole?'

'Wait, you're not really thinking of going into the woods, are you?' Dave cautioned.

'Oh, I'm pretty sure the killer will be long gone by now, a quarter of a century later,' Carole assured him. 'And if we go as a group, we should be pretty safe.'

'I'll be with the girls,' Tom added. 'I'll look after them.'

'So, Daisy, would you and Betty like to check out some of the local tearooms?' Carole asked. 'Maybe make discreet enquiries as to who owns them, then report back to me, if you would. Even if we do track down Euphemia Isacson, it's possible she might not want to discuss her sister's murder. But I think I have an idea for a way I might gain her trust.'

'Yes, Betty and I will be happy to undertake tearoom duties. We like a good scone, don't we?' Daisy grinned.

'Indeed, we do,' Betty agreed. 'And I could also ask the Barnets, discreetly of course, if they've ever heard of any trouble at their synagogue or cemetery. Then we can rule that in or out.'

Mary, ever the practical one, Carole thought, tore a sheet from her large notepad and placed it on the coffee table.

'Right. Let's all jot down our mobile numbers and e-mail addresses on this sheet,' she said, 'and we should each add details of the enquiries we'll be making. That'll avoid any duplication of effort.'

'Good idea, Mary,' Carole said. 'And since you know Kulwinder, maybe you and I could arrange to see her together and ask her about the Gallows Hill site. She might be able to give us an idea whether those contamination rumours are true or not. If they aren't true, she might at least know why it's been abandoned for so long.'

'Yes, I'll call Kulwinder,' Mary agreed. 'Let's not forget though, people, that we all have our other assignments for the local history project as well. Carole, you can pick Kulwinder's brains about local administrators at the same time.'

'So, Dave,' Tom said, 'you're the real detective, what are your thoughts so far on the case?'

'Well,' Dave began, seeming pleased to have been asked his opinion, 'I doubt this was an impulse act by a random killer. It doesn't sound like it was just some sick individual, hanging around in the woods, waiting for a victim to come along.'

'What makes you think that?' Tom asked.

'They never found the murder weapon, did they? And Gerrard says it was something metal, something like a tyre iron. That suggests the killer purposely took the weapon with him into the woods rather than picking up a convenient branch or a rock, as you might in a heat of the moment attack. Clearly, he was intent on killing someone. And, since it was a weekday, he could have been hanging around all day and encountered no-one. If he went into the woods equipped to kill, it's more likely he had a victim in mind. He might have followed the victim into the woods. He might even have arranged to meet her there.'

'That's a good point,' Carole agreed. 'And a metal weapon is more likely to kill than, say, an opportunist item like a tree branch. So, he didn't just intend to hurt Emerald. He meant to kill her.'

'It makes no sense that someone should take offence against a birdwatcher,' Tom added. 'Maybe the killer thought that Emerald, armed with her binoculars, was doing something else, spying on him, perhaps?'

'Possibly,' Dave agreed, 'and the absence of robbery or sexual assault also suggests Emerald Isacson was an intended victim, not an unlucky chance victim. She was targeted by someone with a specific motive. Find the motive and you'll find the killer.'

'That sounds logical,' Tom said. 'Should I speak to my neighbour, the one who worked with Euphemia? He might have kept in touch with her after she left the school. He might have known Emerald, too. He might know whether she'd ever upset anyone.'

'Yes, please, Tom,' Carole said. 'Well, I think we have all the bases covered. Would everyone be free to meet at the woods on Saturday morning? The reason I suggest a Saturday is there might be more people out walking in the woods and it should feel safer than on a quiet weekday. Don't forget, the murder happened on a Wednesday afternoon and no-one was around to witness it.'

All, Dave apart, agreed they could make it and that a Saturday was indeed a good idea. Tom advised them the small layby on the Briarfield Road would be the best place to park in order to access the woods. It was thus agreed they would meet up there at ten o'clock the following Saturday. When they had all completed Mary's contact and task sheet, they took their leave of Carole and Dave.

'There, I told you they were good people, didn't I?' she said as she began gathering up all the cups and saucers.

'Yes. I liked them. You do realise though, Love, that you've probably got a bigger team of investigators working on the Isacson case now than Walter Gerrard had twenty-five years ago?'

'Yes, I wouldn't be surprised. But even so, given the absence of physical evidence, as cold cases go, this one is positively frozen solid. It's going to take some thawing out.'

Chapter 8

Carole had a little difficulty finding a parking space near *The Elsinore*, the giftshop and tearooms in Briarfield. It had been just the third teashop Betty and Daisy had visited before they had established that this one was owned by a lady named Euphemia. The scones were pretty impressive, too, they had reported back. Carole thought it lucky that the person she was seeking had such an unusual forename. She guessed the odds against there being any other teashop anywhere in the country, let alone in the county, run by a proprietor named Euphemia, would be astronomical.

Since it was Friday and therefore market day in Briarfield, Carole was lucky to find any parking space at all. She only secured the one she did because she just happened to arrive as a car was pulling away. Parking up, she walked across the road and glanced in through the windows of Euphemia Isacson's busy establishment. All the tables were occupied but she decided to venture inside anyway and perhaps browse the gifts and trinkets she could see were arranged on the shelves.

There were two women, who looked to be in their fifties, serving behind the counter, and a younger girl who seemed rushed off her feet serving the teas and cakes. Carole could discern no resemblance between any of the employees and the photograph of Emerald she had seen in the police files. Of course, she realised Euphemia would be in her seventies nowadays and, in any case, there was no guarantee she would resemble her younger sister. Emerald had been dark-haired, but, with an Irish mother, Euphemia might just as easily have been fair.

'What can I get you?' one of the ladies asked from behind the counter.

'May one buy the cakes to take away?' she asked.

Carole thought it might be best to give them some custom before giving them the third degree. When the woman answered in the affirmative, Carole ordered two of the Danish pastries. Given the teashop owner's ethnicity, she hoped they would be rather authentically Danish.

'Is Euphemia in today?' she ventured, as the woman selected two of the pastries with her pastry tongs and deftly wrapped them in a paper bag.

'No, she doesn't come down very often these days. But you should find her at home.'

Carole hadn't been able to establish where Euphemia actually lived, since there was no Euphemia Isacson in the phone book, and Dave hadn't been able to find her on the electoral register. He speculated it might be because, for some reason, she was using a different surname these days, and yet if this was because she had married, he hadn't been able to find a marriage record either.

Carole considered there was something in the way the woman had said 'she doesn't come *down*', rather than saying 'come *in*' or 'come *over*', which made Carole wonder if Euphemia might actually be living in the flat above the tearooms.

'Is she likely to be up in the flat?' she asked, pointing towards the ceiling, 'only I said I'd call and see if she needs her library books changing.'

'Yes, I should think so. I'd use the door knocker, if I were you, though. Her hearing's not what it was and she doesn't always hear the doorbell,' the woman advised.

As Carole handed over the money for the cakes, she recalled having noticed a blue painted front door to the right of the teashop entrance and she guessed that would be the front door to the flat. Once outside, she put the pastries in her car then, approaching the blue painted door, she grasped the door knocker firmly and rapped resolutely. She could hear classical music coming from within and she had to knock twice more before the music fell silent and, eventually, the front door was opened. A woman in her seventies, short and slight of stature, with silver hair and smiling eyes, stood there.

'Euphemia?' Carole asked. 'It is Euphemia, isn't it? I'm Carole Murray.'

'Carole …? I'm not sure I …,' she began.

'No, we haven't met before, and I do apologise for calling on you unannounced, but I live just down the road in Chalfont St George and I'm a member of the U3A – the University of the Third Age.'

'Oh, yes?' Euphemia smiled back. 'Are you wanting me to join?'

'Oh, no, well, I mean, yes, you'd be most welcome to, but what I meant to say is that I'm in the U3A's local history group and we're doing a research project on some of the famous and worthy people who have lived in this area. I've been designated to research the noteworthy scientists and medics, and I understand your father was the famous medical man Professor Per Isacson.'

Euphemia seemed taken aback for a second, and Carole wondered if perhaps Euphemia hadn't wanted to be found. Perhaps she had hoped to distance herself from the murder, in which case she might not be receptive to Carole's approach. Carole began to think perhaps she should have chosen a different approach, a more subtle one. And yet, it hadn't been that difficult for Daisy and Betty to find her, so seemingly, she wasn't exactly in hiding.

'He was,' she said. 'But how did you hear about my father?'

'I'd heard he helped invent the blood pressure gauge, so I and many others have cause to be grateful to him.'

'He's no longer with us, you realise.'

'No, indeed. But I'd love to learn more about him, and about your mother, too. She was a famous opera singer, wasn't she?'

'Yes,' the older woman beamed. 'Well, fancy you knowing all that. Would you like to come up? I was just about to make a pot of tea.'

'If you're sure I'm not disturbing you, I would love to.'

Euphemia led the way up a narrow flight of stairs, apologising for her slow progress and explaining her legs weren't as sturdy as they once were. She had contemplated moving to a bungalow, she said, but she was resisting what she felt would be a defeatist admission of old age.

'A bit like me joining an organisation which tells me I'm in my third and final age,' Carole agreed.

The upstairs flat could only be described as charming. The sitting room was decorated with cream floral wallpaper and the frilled curtains and sofa cushions were in fabric of a matching design. The leaded windows with their wonky diamond-shaped panes gave the little apartment the look of a country cottage. Glancing around, Carole could see the furniture and many of the ornaments in the room were antique and she felt it reflected either the occupant's good taste or perhaps an inheritance from affluent and cultured parents. She thought it rather different from the bland and bachelor-style basic interior of Walter Gerrard's bungalow.

Whilst Euphemia made them tea, Carole glanced around at the many black and white photographs in silver frames which were displayed around the room. She guessed that those which depicted a very handsome couple, dressed in nineteen-forties' style outfits, were photos of Euphemia's parents, Per and Brigid Isacson. Everything about the flat and its contents spoke of the comfortable, upper middle-class life the Isacsons must have enjoyed.

'So, what would you like to know?' Euphemia asked as she took a seat next to Carole on the sofa and poured their tea.

'Isacson, that's a Danish name, I understand.'

'Yes. My father's family was Danish. His Jewish ancestors who settled in Denmark generations ago would have adopted the Danish way of spelling Isacson with one 'a'. You see, biblical names like Isacson, Jakobsen and Abrahamsen are fairly common amongst non-Jews in Scandinavia. The Jewish settlers in Denmark wanted to fully integrate, hence the Danish spelling.'

'And then, in the nineteen thirties, I gather your father came to England. Is that right?'

'That's right, he was a teenager, fleeing from the Nazis when they invaded Denmark, and he arrived on the *Kindertransport*. You've heard of that, haven't you?'

'I have. He must have been very frightened.'

'He was, and very wary, as a lot of Jewish refugees were. A lot of them were fearful that the Nazis would get to England. Luckily, it didn't happen. As soon as he was eighteen, he joined the Royal Air Force and flew on bombing missions to Europe. He trained as a scientist after the war. He was living in London then and that's where he met and married my mother.'

'She was Brigid Dornan?'

'Yes, and, owing to her connections in the music world, she and my father moved in rather glittering circles. In the early days of their marriage, they attended wonderful parties and they mixed with some very rich and important people. Mother became very friendly with the composer, Euphemia Allen. Have you heard of her?'

'No, I'm afraid I haven't. Did she live around here?'

'Yes, at Gaunt's Cross. She wrote many pieces for the piano, including 'Chopsticks'. I'm sure you've heard of that?'

'I have indeed. It's the only tune I've ever learned to play on the piano. Never knew who wrote it, though.'

'She and my mother became best friends after my parents moved out to Briarfield,' Euphemia continued, 'and so, when I was born, Euphemia agreed to be my godmother. That's why I was named after her.'

'Oh, I see. I'd got it into my head that perhaps Euphemia would be a Danish name,' Carole said, hoping to steer the conversation back to the

Isacson family. 'So, it wasn't an ancestral name from your father's side, then?'

'No. Sadly, my father didn't know very much about his immediate family, let alone his ancestors. They all perished in the Holocaust, you see – his parents, uncles, aunts and cousins. Teenaged boys are never interested in their family tree anyway. He would never have thought to ask his parents about that sort of thing whilst they were alive. In later years, when he got to wondering about his ancestors, there was no-one left to ask.'

'So, was he an only child?' Carole asked tentatively.

'Yes, he was.'

'And were you an only child also?'

Euphemia glanced away suddenly and her wistful gaze took in the array of framed photographs on her sideboard. Carole hoped she wasn't about to cause this rather sweet lady to re-live a painful memory.

'No, I had a sister, but, um, she passed away quite some years ago.'

Carole glanced along the collection of framed photographs but couldn't see any which might be of Emerald Isacson. In fact, she couldn't see any in which the subject resembled Euphemia either. Her host fell silent for a second or two, but then she turned towards Carole and was smiling again.

'My sister was called Emerald.'

'That, too, is a very pretty name,' Carole said, gently.

'She was named after her godmother, too. Have you heard of Emerald Cunard?'

'The shipping magnate's wife?' Carole gasped. '*That* Emerald Cunard? She was fabulously wealthy, wasn't she?'

'Yes, she was. I told you my parents moved in the best circles,' Euphemia chuckled. 'Mrs Cunard was a great philanthropist, you know. She funded the arts and gave money to all sorts of good causes. She became a sort of mentor to my mother during her singing career. Would you like some more tea?'

'Yes, thank you. I hope I'm not tiring you out with my questions.'

'Not at all,' Euphemia smiled sadly as she topped up their tea cups. 'I think it's rather nice to know my parents will be remembered, if only by your local history group.'

Carole had already decided there was no way this sweet, frail and genteel little woman could have murdered her own sister. Of course, Euphemia was getting on in years now and she would have been twenty-five years younger and a deal stronger at the time of Emerald's murder, but she really didn't strike Carole as the kind of person who would bludgeon anyone to death, especially not her own sister. It seemed rather a pity that this daughter of successful socialite parents now lived a quiet and probably lonely life in a small apartment over a teashop. Carole sensed Euphemia's sadness at remembering the past and, as much as she wanted to discuss Emerald's fate, somehow the time didn't seem right to mention the murder. She felt she had gained Euphemia's trust and that was enough. She didn't want to upset her and risk losing her trust. That burning topic could wait until another day.

'So, did you and your sister both follow your father into the field of science?' she asked.

'Yes. Although Emerald was the brainy one,' Euphemia said proudly. 'She had a degree in bio-chemistry and a doctorate in bio-sciences, you know. I just taught biology at a local school.'

'That must have been very rewarding, though,' Carole probed, 'helping all those pupils develop an interest in science.'

'Yes, but one gets tired of teaching the same curriculum, year in and year out. I received a small inheritance from our parents, and after my sister died, the house seemed very big and empty. So, I decided to take early retirement, sell off the house and invest in the tearoom. I have some dependable staff running it for me these days.'

Glancing around the room, Carole noticed a small bookcase under the window. There was a whole row of books on birds and a pair of binoculars stood on top of the bookcase. She wondered whether this might provoke just a little more information regarding Emerald's life, if not her death.

'I see you're keen on birds,' She remarked.

'Yes,' Euphemia suddenly became animated. 'Do you know, forty years ago, my sister and I used to drive out into deepest Wiltshire to gawp at the newly introduced red kites. Nowadays, they've spread into Buckinghamshire. These days, they come and gawp at me!' she laughed.

'I see you have binoculars. Do you ever go out birdwatching around here?'

'No, not these days,' her face fell again. 'Not for many years. My legs won't take me far.'

The septuagenarian drained her teacup and sank back into her chair with a sigh. Carole feared she might have exhausted her.

'Well, I think I've taken up enough of your time. Thank you so much for telling me about your parents. I shall have some interesting facts to report back to my group. Who, knows, we might even publish a book about the local celebrities one day.'

'That would be lovely, though I would prefer it if you didn't mention me in your book. I'm quite a private person and I prefer to live a very quiet life these days. I don't mind you coming here. You're most welcome, but I wouldn't want a constant stream of visitors. However, if you would like to know more about my parents, and about some of the interesting local people they socialised with, I could look out some papers for you. I have quite a lot of family papers and photos in the loft.'

'I wouldn't want to put you to any trouble,' Carole said.

'No, it wouldn't be any trouble. I'll look them out over the weekend. Why don't you call on me again next Monday morning. The teashop is closed on Mondays and it'll be easier for you to park outside.'

'That's so kind of you. Shall I call at around ten o'clock?'

'Yes, do. You know, I haven't spoken with anyone about my parents, not in a very long time. Nor have I looked through the family albums in years. It will be so nice to look back on happy times. I'll look forward to seeing you then.'

***

Back at Rowan Tree Cottage, Carole related all she had learned to Dave.

'She's the sweetest old lady, Dave. There's no way she bumped off her sister.'

'Did she have any theories about who did?' Dave asked.

'I didn't actually ask her about the murder. I thought it was too soon. Didn't want to scare her off. And that paid off, as she's invited me over on Monday morning. Says she's going to root out some family papers and photos I can have a look at. I might gently drop it into the conversation then.'

'That's considerate of you. I'm sure the memory of the murder will be painful, even after so many years.'

'Yes. Oh, and it looks like *both* sisters were into birdwatching. She has a lot of books about birds. She also has a pair of binoculars. I did wonder if they were the same pair her sister was wearing when she was murdered.'

'Well, the police probably would have returned them to the family after the conclusion of their enquiries.'

'Apparently, just like her sister, she never married. I'm surprised you couldn't find her in any of the electoral records though. There can't be many locals named Isacson – especially spelled with just the one 'a', not two.'

'One 'a'? You didn't tell me that, Carole,' Dave was deflated. 'No wonder I couldn't find her. Why only the one 'a'?'

'It's the Scandinavian spelling of the name. Did I not mention that? Sorry.'

Chapter 9

The following morning, Saturday, Carole got to the supermarket over at Gaunt's Cross before nine o'clock in order to pick up her pre-booked grocery order and drop it off at home before heading off to meet the others at Percival's Wood. She spotted a familiar face at the customer service desk. It was another of her history group members Malcom Rawlinson.

'Hello, Malcolm, are you collecting a grocery order too? She asked.

'Not groceries, no,' Malcolm said. 'Picking up a birthday gift for the missus.'

'So, how's your bit of the project going, then? I've forgotten which 'famous and infamous' folks it is you're researching.'

'The war heroes. Actually, I'm also planning on taking Dorothy for a birthday dinner soon at the *Austen Arms*. I heard that, in the bar, they've got some framed photos of the Blount family who used to live there, including the VC holder. They might let me snap some shots of those photos. Killing two birds with one stone, you might say.'

'Well done. You'll have to let me know if the food's good there. And do wish Dorothy a happy birthday from me.'

At ten o'clock, the group of *Third Agers* began to assemble in the car park by Percival's Wood. Tom was already there when Carole arrived and was changing from his driving shoes into stout walking boots. She noticed that, as well as a change of footwear, the contents of his car boot also included a large thermos and his biscuit tin.

'I thought we'd need a coffee to warm us up after our tramp in the woods,' he explained.

'How thoughtful, Tom,' Carole beamed.

Daisy and Betty were next to arrive, car sharing as per usual. They, too were wearing sensible shoes, she noted as they climbed out of Daisy's car.

'I see we're all suitably shod,' Carole remarked.

Kitty was next to arrive and she had picked up Mary, the convenor of their cohort, on the way.

'I hope we don't have to go too far into the woods,' Kitty said. 'Only I'm breaking in a new hip, you know. Don't want to overdo it.'

'I hope no-one minds me bringing our dogs along,' Carole asked as she opened the rear of her car and unharnessed them. 'Dave suggested we'd feel safer with Ronnie and Reggie.'

'Ronnie and Reggie?' Betty exclaimed. 'Really? You named them after London's most infamous gangster twins? I love it!'

'It was Dave's idea,' Carole confirmed. 'And, like the Krays, they're very naughty boys, always stealing food. But, unlike the Krays, they're very loving and they'd never hurt anyone.'

'Aw, I love greyhounds,' Daisy said as she dropped to her knees and both dogs immediately came to her and began licking her hands and face. 'They're just gorgeous. Are they rescues?'

'They are,' Carole confirmed. 'Ex-racers. They're a couple of early retirees, just like me and Dave.'

'Has anyone got a map of the woods?' Mary asked.

'I have,' Carole assured her.

'I've got one, as well,' Tom said. 'If Kitty's hip gives out before we get to the murder spot, one of us can take one of the maps to navigate back here with her.'

'Good thinking,' Carole said. 'Now, it's supposed to have happened around a mile or so into the wood, in a clearing in a copse of beech trees just a few hundred yards west of the main trail. Dave's worked out roughly where the spot is judging from the maps on the police file and he's marked it with an 'x'.'

They all had a look at the maps to orientate themselves. Whilst they were doing so, a black Citroen saloon car rolled up and slowed down to look at them. Carole realised that their four cars had pretty much filled up the little lay-by parking area and there wasn't room for any other vehicle to park.

'Sorry,' she called out to the man behind the wheel. 'Were you intending to park here? If so, we could …,' but the driver simply scowled at her and drove off. 'Oh, please yourself then,' she shrugged.

The *Third Agers* set off in twos along the path. Once they were far enough from the main road, Carole decided it was safe enough to let Ronnie and Reggie off the lead. The dogs raced ahead happily, sniffing their way along the path. The ground was dry, just as it had been on the afternoon of the murder all those years before, Carole noted, and the beech trees were all in leaf already. It occurred to Carole that, if Emerald's killer had gone into the woods ahead of her and had lain in wait for her, she might not have spotted him. Equally, though, she wouldn't have seen anyone following her either. Carole wondered whether the killer had been just lurking, awaiting *any* potential victim who might come along, or was he, as Dave suggested, targeting Emerald specifically and had he followed her into the woods?

Carole guessed it would take them around half an hour to reach the spot where the murder had occurred, that's if they managed to find it, so she took the opportunity of asking the others how their own enquiries were coming along.

'Tom, did you get a chance to ask your neighbour about Euphemia?'

'I did. She was head of the school science department when he started there straight from teacher training college in the late nineties. Says he didn't really get to know her that well, though. She could be difficult, he says, and she wasn't very sociable. He wasn't surprised she never married as she was so disagreeable. Kept herself to herself.'

'Really?' Carole was surprised. 'She's obviously mellowed with age, then. I thought she was quite nice when I met her. Did he ever meet her sister Emerald?'

'No, he says not. He did say, though, he'd once heard Euphemia complain that Emerald was their parents' favourite. Emerald was the younger and the prettier of the sisters and she was the clever one of the two. Callum had the impression Euphemia resented her younger sister's success. She used to complain that their folks had given Emerald more encouragement than they showed Euphemia. That's how come Emerald went on to get her doctorate.'

'Well, that could be a motive for murder,' Carole suggested. 'Sibling rivalry is quite a strong emotion and, over the years, it can fester. Euphemia did say she'd been left money by her parents. She didn't say whether her sister had been left more than her. I wouldn't have thought Euphemia physically capable of murder, though, but I might be wrong. And the sweet old lady impression might just be an act.'

'I spoke with the Barnets, by the way,' Betty said, catching up with Carole as they sauntered along the path. 'They've been members of the congregation at the Briarfield synagogue for over thirty years now and they never heard of any damage being caused in the cemetery.'

'Really?' Carole was surprised.

'Yes. In fact, they'd never heard of any Jewish cemetery this side of London ever being vandalised. That detective must have been mistaken.'

'That's very helpful, Betty. It's odd that Gerrard should have been so specific about when and where the vandalism happened, if in fact it didn't happen at all anywhere on his patch,' Carole puzzled. 'Mary, did you get in touch with Kulwinder?'

'I did. She's pretty busy most days and evenings with parish council meetings and stuff, but she can see us next Wednesday afternoon, if you're free. She'll be in the council offices.'

'Yes, I can make that. By the way, I'm seeing Euphemia Isacson again on Monday. She's promised to look out some family papers and photos for me to see. I saw some photos of her parents on her sideboard. The Isacson's were an attractive couple and they moved in quite grand social circles. There should be some photos taken with some local celebrities of the day. More candidates for our famous folks, perhaps.'

'This time, will you ask her about her sister's murder?' Kitty asked.

'Yes. I won't plunge straight in, though. I'll maybe wait until she produces a family photo including Emerald and I'll ask here where Emerald is these days. If she wants to tell me about the murder, then she will.'

'What will you do if she doesn't want to discuss it? Will you press the issue?' Mary asked.

'No, I don't think so. I wouldn't want to upset her. She seemed such a lovely person, not at all like Callum's description.'

Eventually, the six friends arrived at what Dave's map had identified as the locus of the murder. They filed into the clearing and stood, glancing all around them.

'It looks … spectacularly ordinary,' Mary remarked.

'I'm not sure what you expected to see, Mary,' Tom said. 'There wouldn't be anything interesting here after all these years – no bloodstains, no body, and no murder weapon. The police back then drafted in uniforms from other areas, as well as soldiers from the camp up at Dalton and even local boy scouts. They did finger-tip searches of the woods from here on outwards. They found nothing, and nor will we.'

'How's the hip holding out, Kitty?' Carole asked.

'So far, so good, thanks,' Kitty assured her.

'So, what do we do now?' Daisy asked. 'Should we take some photos?'

'Oh, yes,' Betty said, taking out her phone. 'Gather round, everyone, let's do a selfie.'

'I was thinking more of photos of the empty clearing and the view back along the path, for forensic reasons – so we can look at them in detail later,' Daisy told her.

'Oh, of course. Sorry,' Betty said. 'Today just feels like a fun group outing. You're right, though, Daisy, we should be a bit respectful. After all, someone died here. Two people, in fact.'

'No reason we can't do a selfie as well, though,' Kitty grinned. 'We could put it in the U3A's *Age Matters* magazine and caption it 'Third Agers on the Trail of a Killer'.'

Once they had all taken a variety of photos, both forensic and fun group shots, Carole walked into the middle of the clearing and glanced all about her. She then circled around the clearing and stood for a moment, thinking. Her dogs, having expended much of their energy racing up and down the paths, now settled down at her feet.

'You know, wherever you stand in this clearing, you have a pretty good view of the path. The tree canopy is quite high here and I imagine it wouldn't have been a great deal different twenty-five years ago,' she surmised. 'There aren't any shrubs a killer could hide behind, not this far into the wood. The beech tree canopy above our heads is so dense here, nothing much grows underneath it.'

'There's lots of mushrooms and toadstools though,' Kitty said, poking at one with her shoe.

'He'd have had to be a very tiny killer to hide under toadstool,' Betty chuckled. 'And the worst he could have done was tap her on the ankle with a twig, not bash her brains in.'

'What are you getting at, Carole?' Tom asked.

'Well, even though we're in the middle of a wood, from this spot you get a pretty good view all around. Even if you were standing here, looking up at the trees and bird watching, you'd probably be aware of anyone coming along the path or creeping up behind you.'

'I see what you mean,' Daisy agreed. 'It wouldn't be easy for someone to sneak up on you without being seen. In fact, it's an odd place for a killer to pounce. We passed through much denser shrubby areas before we reached this clearing.'

'What does that tell us?' Mary asked.

'That she did see someone coming,' Carole reasoned, 'but she wasn't wary or scared of him. She felt comfortable enough with him to have turned her back on him, perhaps to continue using her binoculars to watch the birds, and he struck her from behind. Perhaps she knew him.'

'Perhaps he was also a keen birdwatching friend,' Daisy suggested. 'Maybe she was expecting him. Maybe he was someone she'd arranged to meet here. Maybe she was standing here in order to show him something. Something in the clearing, or maybe up in the trees.'

'D'you think it was a secret romantic rendezvous? With a secret lover.' Betty trilled. 'A married man, most likely. D'you think they were at it, right here, kit off, down amongst the toadstools? Ooh, saucy!'

'Or maybe they came into the woods together,' Mary suggested. 'To look at birds, or other wildlife, or something.'

'That's another possibility,' Carole agreed. 'But surely, she'd have noticed if the man she either met or accompanied into the woods was carrying with him something like a tyre iron. My gut feeling is that she would have encountered him unexpectedly, and when he suddenly produced a weapon, she turned and ran, but he caught her up here in this clearing and hit her from behind.'

'If it was someone she knew, another birdwatcher perhaps, then maybe that someone really was her sister,' Tom suggested. 'It was springtime, so maybe she'd asked her sister to come to see some special bird hatching out, or a nest with young in it.'

'Maybe. But she'd surely have wondered why her sister brought a tyre iron with her. On Monday, I'll ask Euphemia whether Emerald had a boyfriend or a lover. Of course, she might not know. Even if she does know, she might not tell me. It's strange, though, that neither of them married.'

'Maybe it's not so strange,' Daisy said. 'You said Emerald was a government scientist, didn't you? Back when she would have started out, women working in government and the civil service were forced to resign on marriage.'

'Of course,' Carole agreed. 'I should have thought of that. Compulsory resignations were only done away with for female civil servants sometime in the 'sixties. If you loved your career and wanted to keep it, you either had to live in sin or stay single.'

'John and I lived in sin for a couple of years before we married,' Betty said, wistfully. 'Of course, he's no sinner these days.'

'Too much information, Betty,' Daisy rebuked her. 'I think perhaps we should head back.'

'Indeed,' Tom agreed. 'It's almost time for elevenses. I've got coffee and ginger biscuits in the car.'

At the sound of the word 'biscuits', to everyone's amusement, Ronnie and Reggie leapt to their feet, their ears erect, and promptly trotted back towards the path. Back at the layby, as the friends gathered around Tom's car boot, sipping hot coffee and enjoying the results of his early morning baking, Carole surveyed her little group of eager amateur investigators. Although she had only met them for the first time a couple of months earlier, it somehow felt as if she had always known them: Tom, with his local knowledge and unstinting culinary generosity; Kitty the perennial volunteer with a big heart and devotion to keeping the rare local chalk stream clear; Daisy with her enthusiasm and practical mathematician's logic; Betty with her wild imagination and ability to see the risqué possibilities in every situation, and Mary, their wise shepherd who tried to rein them in and keep their project on track.

It felt good to be part of a team again, Carole thought, and to have something to investigate. As she savoured the warmth of the tiny cubes of crystallised ginger in Tom's crumbly biscuits, she realised how much she was looking forward to her next meeting with Euphemia Isacson in a couple of days' time. Like Malcolm Rawlinson, she hoped to be killing two birds with one stone – gathering more interesting information about Euphemia's famed scientist father and his scientific associates, and also finding out a little more about Euphemia's murdered sister Emerald. She hoped to have fresh information to report to the group at their next meeting. Yes indeed, for Carole, Monday could not come around quick enough.

Chapter 10

'Carole, you didn't!' Dave fumed, as she knew he would when she showed him the book and the diaries she had taken from Euphemia's flat following her discovery of the woman's body that Monday morning. 'You actually took these? You've interfered with a crime scene. You could be arrested. You, of all people, should know how important it is not to touch anything at a crime scene.'

'I know, I know, Dave. Please don't shout at me. And I realise the diaries could be pertinent to the investigation, but the police didn't solve Emerald's murder, so I'm not hopeful they're going to solve Euphemia's either.'

'Maybe, maybe not, but you still shouldn't have interfered. I mean, if these do turn out to be relevant, what are you going to say to the police when you return them? How are you going to explain that you took them?'

'I thought about that. I'll just say that she gave them to me during my *first* visit to her flat and I was so shocked this morning when I found the body that I forgot to mention them to the detective.'

Dave continued to shake his head. Carole felt he was still thinking like the policeman he used to be, rather than like the intelligence officer he had become following his first early retirement from Gloucestershire Constabulary. Working for the Security Service had sometimes necessitated working around the rules in order to achieve one's goals, especially when the aim was for the greater good and to keep the British public from harm.

'Anyway,' she continued, 'I'll hand them over soon, but look, since you've obviously got your detective's head on this morning, I'd be really grateful if you would trawl through the diaries and see if there is anything in them which might be relevant to Emerald's murder.'

To her relief, Dave picked up one of the diaries from the kitchen table, sat down and began to thumb through it.

'In the meantime,' she added, pleased to have distracted him, 'I'll check out the author of the birdwatching books. It's odd that there were twelve copies of the same book. Do you think Emerald might have been so forgetful that she'd buy the same book over and over?'

'No. That does seem odd. I can't see why she would do that. Unless, perhaps, each of her friends unwittingly bought her a copy of the same book, knowing that she was a birdwatcher and that she lived in the Chilterns.'

Carole was relieved that she had steered Dave away from her transgression and had interested him in the documents instead. She opened the book at the fly leaf with the inscription.

'And what do you make of this?'

Dave read the handwritten dedication.

'Looks like she might have been in a relationship with the author. Did his name crop up in the case files?'

'No. Looks like Walter Gerrard's team didn't know about him. I'll look him up. It'd be interesting to speak with him.'

'But he might be the murderer. You really should leave him to the police, Love.'

Carole walked over to where Dave was seated and swept her fingers through his still dark, wavy hair.

'You're right, of course, Love. I'll just do a check on him to satisfy my curiosity, then I'll leave the rest to the police. I promise. And thank you for indulging me.'

She kissed his forehead. He slipped his arms around her and her and drew her to him.

'Once a researcher, always a researcher,' he smiled. 'I know you can't help yourself, Love. Investigating an historic murder was one thing. But now the second sister has been killed – twenty-odd years after the first, and just days after you visited her. That can't be a coincidence. The murderer's still out there. I don't want you to put yourself in harm's way. You're retired now, remember.'

'You're right, Love. I'll be careful. You hungry?'

'Starving.'

She made him a conciliatory cup of coffee and prepared sandwiches for them both, then she left him in peace to eat his whilst he pored over the diaries. Taking her lunch into the living room, she opened her laptop and, whilst she ate, she searched the internet for 'F.E. Cassoni author'. To her surprise, there were no results. She searched for the title of the book, in the hope that detail of the author would come up that way, but with no results again. It was a fairly old book so she presumed it would be long out of print. She checked inside the cover of the book to see if there was an author biography, but there was none. She noted the name of the publisher and typed that into an internet search, hoping to find contact details. She fully expected the publisher might be able to tell her more about the mysterious Cassoni.

She did have a little more success searching for Marwood Press. There were a lot of titles still current which had been published by that particular publishing house. Opening the link to Companies House, she searched for the company's business record, in the hope of finding their actual address. However, the company was listed as having folded in 2006. The two company directors' names and addresses, a Marlon Marbury and Francis Wood, were included so she cross checked these with the online phone directory.

Unfortunately, both directors were either ex-directory or they were not landline subscribers. For all she knew, they might live overseas or even be deceased. The only way she could contact the directors of the publishing company, she realised, would be to write to them via the address listed at Companies House. However, she knew that might cut across the police investigation. If Inspector Hogget should find out about F.E. Cassoni, and if he also contacted the publishers and found out she had already written to them, he would want to know why she was making her own enquiries. If that happened, once she handed the book and diaries to the police, her innocent sounding explanation as to why she had not done so immediately might not seem quite so innocent.

Dave seemed quite absorbed in his reading of Emerald's diaries, so Carole decided to share the tragic news of Euphemia's demise with her fellow *Third Agers*. She composed a text message to send to her little group of five.

'*Went to visit Euphemia this morning. Found her dead – murdered! Are you free to come to ours this evng 7 pm for glass of wine, nibbles and update?*'

***

By six o' clock, the heavens had opened up and released a sudden deluge of spring rain. By seven, there was a proliferation of wellingtons in Carole and Dave's porch and raincoats on their hallstand. Naturally, Carole's new friends were deeply intrigued and wanted to hear all about the latest murder. The promise of wine meant that all except Kitty had walked around to Rowan Tree Cottage. Kitty's village, Chalfont St Michael, was a mile and a half away, too far for her to walk, especially with her new hip, so she had driven over. Once they were all settled and had been furnished with drinks and hot home-made sausage rolls,

Carole recounted her experience of finding the body of Euphemia Isacson.

'That must have been deeply shocking,' Mary said.

'Well, yes, it was. I'd called an ambulance first and it took a while to arrive so I had to wait with the poor lady's body lying there. You might think what I did next was inappropriate, though,' she said, casting a warning glance at Dave in case he should say what he thought about her actions, though he simply cleared his throat. 'But I decided to have a look around whilst I was waiting.'

'Weren't you worried the killer might still be there?' Kitty asked. 'I'd have got myself out of there pretty damned quick.'

'She was so cold that I realised she'd been dead all night, so I imagined the killer would have fled the scene.'

'Carole's never heard the saying 'curiosity killed the cat',' Dave interjected.

Carole shot him another pleading glance. She decided she wouldn't mention that she had taken documents from the flat, only that she had seen them.

'If she was dead, why did you call an ambulance?' Mary asked.

'Well, I wanted to buy a little time so I could have a look around first. The police would have got there too quickly. You see, I'd noticed something odd. There were a dozen books on birdwatching in the book case.'

'The newspapers did say Emerald was a keen birdwatcher,' Daisy commented. 'So, it wouldn't be unusual that there should be books on the subject in the flat.'

'No, but these books were all duplicate copies of the same book by an author named F.E. Cassoni. Who buys twelve copies of the same book? But what was most intriguing was that one of those books included a handwritten dedication to Emerald from the author.'

'Why is that intriguing?' Tom asked.

'It read *'To EM with love from FE'*, so it looks like she knew the author.'

'Sounds like she knew him pretty well,' Betty grinned. 'I wonder if she had a secret assignation with him in the woods the day she was killed. Maybe he was her secret Italian lover. Maybe he killed her in a fit of Latin passion. What a way to go! Do we know anything about him?'

'Well, I've tried looking him up but I couldn't find anything. His book is out of print and his publisher, Marwood Press, went out of business a couple of decades ago.'

'Where else have you checked?' Tom asked. 'Have you checked with births, marriages and deaths?'

'Oh yes,' Carole assured him. 'I've done everything from a basic Google search, through all the civil registration records and I checked several genealogical sites for overseas births. He's not mentioned in any online encyclopaedia either. I also ran him through the newspaper archives but found no mention of him.'

'D'you think it was a false identity?' Betty asked, 'sort of a *nom de pluie?*'

'A *nom de plume*, you mean? Maybe. All I found, though, was that there's a variety of Italian filled flatbreads called *Cassoni*, and they take their name from another kind of *Cassoni* which are traditional carved wooden wedding chests. In olden times, they would be gifted in pairs to a bride and groom.'

'Definitely sounds like a *nom de plume,*' Tom speculated.

'Probably, but it's an odd name to choose,' Carole said.

'A bit like a Cornish writer calling himself 'pastie',' Kittie ventured.

'I did find a couple of individuals on the internet with the surname Cassoni,' Carole continued, 'but none in the UK and none with the same initials as the author.'

'So, where do we go now with the investigation?' Betty asked.

'Are you sure we should actually be continuing?' Mary asked. 'In view of what happened to Euphemia, do you think it's wise for us to carry on?'

'Well, we won't be getting in the way of the police's investigation into Euphemia's murder. But there's nothing to stop us looking into the historic murder of Emerald, is there?'

'Not unless the same killer murdered both sisters,' Tom suggested. 'We could find ourselves and the police chasing the same suspect.'

'But with twenty-five years between the two deaths, it seems most unlikely it was the same killer, don't you think?' Carole asked. 'And we're not going to drop medical scientist Emerald Isacson from our project just because she was murdered, are we?'

'Ah, now,' Mary said. 'I've arranged for Carole and me to meet with Councillor Kulwinder Kaur. Hopefully, she can tell us more about the place where Emerald worked. If Kulwinder knows anything about the biosciences centre, such as who ran it and who worked there, we might find out what went on there. There might have been more local scientists of note connected with the centre. I'm thinking more for your research for our project, Carole, rather than for any links to Emerald's murder.'

'Yes, of course,' Carole agreed, 'although, for both purposes, it would be useful to know who else worked at the centre, especially who Emerald's former work colleagues were.'

'Don't you think the police will have done all that at the time?' Dave asked.

'Yes, I'm sure they did,' Carole agreed, 'but maybe they didn't do a very thorough job. After all, they don't seem to have known about this Cassoni chap, do they?'

'Oh, I found out from the old phone directories where Charlie Herron lived,' Kitty said. 'His family home was one of those little cottages in Briarfield, in the old part of the town. I haven't had a chance to go and look at the place or speak to the neighbours, though. Here, I wrote the address down for you. Mind you, if he really had separated from his wife, like that retired detective chap said, he doesn't appear at any other address in the later phone books.'

'That's brilliant, Kitty. Many thanks,' Carole smiled as she pocketed the slip of paper with the address on. 'Anyone want more drinks?'

'The rain's getting really heavy out there, Carole,' Kitty said. 'I think I might make a move for home. Don't like driving at night, especially when it's raining. The glare from headlights reflecting off the wet road is dazzling. Anyone want a lift?'

'Yes, please,' Mary said.

The others all took it as a signal to leave, too. Coats and boots were retrieved and, having bid farewell to Dave and given Carole their thanks, the *Third Agers* departed.

'Can I get you anything else, Dave,' Carole asked as she cleared up the glasses and plates.

'That big box of chocs I saw in the kitchen, are you saving them for anything special?'

'No. Not now. Should we open them?'

'Yeah, go on.'

'You've earned a choc or two, for all the help you've given me. And thanks for not saying anything to the others.'

'About what?'

'About my having stolen the diaries and the birdwatching book.'

'Well, I can't have them thinking my wife's a thief and a despoiler of crime scenes, can I?'

'Oh God, when you put it like that, you make me feel awful! I promise I'll hand them in to the police as soon as you've finished reading the diaries. Have you found anything interesting in them so far?'

'Well, a lot of it is work-related stuff, things about chemicals and stuff. She abbreviates a lot – things like *'production quotas of five hundred gallons of RB'*. Until you find out exactly what kind of work she was doing at the centre, I can't work out what RB might be.'

'It's very good of you to help out with this, Dave. I hope you didn't mind me asking you to do it.'

'No, I suppose not. It takes my mind off the pain in my ankle. You know, if I'm honest, Love, retirement isn't working out quite how I'd hoped. I'd envisaged myself being a bit more pro-active, not sitting in my armchair watching old repeats of 'Countdown' every afternoon. Although I don't fully agree with the way you've gone about it, I suppose my helping you with your investigation into the Isacson murder is a useful distraction.'

'But you said you enjoy the afternoon episodes of 'Countdown'. You never got to watch it when we were both working. And you're very good at anagrams and crossword puzzles. Didn't you have to wrestle with some tough puzzles at your interview to join our old firm?'

'Yes, but I don't want to spend *all* my time wrestling with puzzles. When this ankle's better, maybe I'll join the U3A, too.'

Dave glanced out of the window at the heavy rain, which looked as though it was in for the night.

'Maybe I should join their swimming group,' he added, glumly.

***

Meanwhile, Malcolm Rawlinson and his wife Dorothy had braved the rain and were enjoying dinner in the restaurant at the *Austen Arms*, the popular hotel and eatery in Gaunt's Cross. Malcolm was enjoying his meal all the more for having taken advantage of the restaurant's 'midweek two for one' offer. After they had eaten, Malcolm suggested they should repair to the bar area for coffee and brandies, as he wished to check out some of the historic photographs displayed on the walls. Steering Dorothy and her walking frame to a table in a cosy corner alcove, he went to the bar to order.

The smiling barman, Miguel, appeared and asked him whether he had enjoyed his meal. Assuring him that he had, Malcolm ordered his drinks and asked Miguel if it would be all right for him to take photographs of some of the images displayed on the wall of the bar area. He explained he was interested specifically in those depicting naval men. Miguel assured him there would be no problem.

'Let me known if there's any you can't reach,' the barman offered. 'I'm a little taller than you, so I can reach them.'

Whilst Malcolm and Miguel both took turns at manoeuvring Malcolm's phone into position to capture images of some of the photos which were hanging above the bar, somewhat higher than head height, a customer who was seated at the bar swivelled around on his bar stool and watched him quizzically. Malcolm stepped back from the bar and snapped a wider shot, taking in the bar area, a smiling Miguel and the man seated at the bar. The man seemed not to wish to be photographed, however, and he raised a hand to cover his face.

'Hello,' the stranger said. 'I see you're taking pictures of the photos on display. I'm intrigued to know why?'

'They were notable locals,' Malcolm explained, pleased that the man was interested, too. 'Decorated war heroes. They used to live here, before it was a hotel. When it was a family home.'

'Ah, I see. So, what do you know about them?'

'They were a father and son, name of Blount. The father, Ernest, was awarded the VC.'

'Fascinating. And you have an interest in naval heroes, I take it?'

'Not really. Not all naval heroes, just the ones who lived here – the Blounts. I've been looking into the family and their history specifically.'

'Your drinks, Sir,' Miguel interrupted as he placed two glasses of brandy onto the bar. 'I'll bring your coffees over to you.'

'Ah, yes. Excuse me,' Malcolm said to the stranger, as he pocketed his phone, picked up the two glasses of brandy and returned to his table.

'Who's that you were talking to?' Dorothy asked.

'Dunno, Darling. Anyway, the coffee's on its way.'

By ten thirty, the hotel guests had mostly headed off to bed and the clientele in the bar had thinned out. Malcolm and Dorothy decided to call it a night, too. Malcolm moved Dorothy's walking frame nearer to her.

'Darling, why don't I escort you to the front entrance then go and bring the car around? It'll save you having to trundle across the car park in the dark.'

'Good idea. Thank you, Dear.'

Having deposited his wife by the hotel's main entrance, Malcolm exited the building and headed around to the darkened car park at the rear. He began to make his way to the far end, where he had parked his car. Turning up his coat collar to fend off the rain, he picked up his pace and felt around in his coat pocket for his car keys. A dark-coloured saloon, parked in the shadows at the far end of the car park, suddenly started up and the driver switched his headlights onto full beam, blinding Malcolm for a second. Malcolm halted as he heard the driver accelerate suddenly and all the car park's security lights came on at the same time. Malcolm turned to step out of the way of the oncoming vehicle. Before he could sidestep it, however, the car hit him head on at full speed, tossing the sixty-eight-year-old into the air like a rag doll. The driver stopped and, stepping out of the car, walked back to where Malcolm lay, motionless on the damp ground. Bending down, he quickly searched through the casualty's pockets, then calmly walked back to his car. Heading straight out of the car park exit, he disappeared into the night.

Dorothy waited and waited and, when some ten minutes had passed but Malcolm had not appeared, she feared he must be having some trouble starting their car. She set off to walk around the building to the car park. As she turned the corner, she could see little, since the car park was in darkness. With the aid of her walking frame, she began to make her way across the car park. It was when her movement triggered the security lights that she saw a crumpled figure lying on the ground. She guessed it must be Malcolm and she feared he had collapsed for some reason. Heading over to him as quickly as she could manage, she bent down. She saw he was lying quite still and his eyes were open.

'Oh, Malcolm, Darling,' she whispered. 'Darling, speak to me.'

However, it was obvious that her beloved husband of forty-three years was dead. Glancing desperately around her and realising she was all alone in the car park, she began to panic.

'Help me!' she shouted. 'Somebody, please, help me!'

Chapter 11

Weatherwise, the weekend was a complete washout, with the kind of rainstorms which often herald the arrival of April, but Carole and Dave had spent much of the time indoors reading through the late Emerald Isacson's diaries and trying to make sense of her mainly cryptic entries.

'There are a lot of bird references,' Dave announced. 'For example, she mentions the disappearance of the kingfishers. Could that be something else for you to investigate – missing birds?'

'Does she say why they vanished?' Carole asked. 'Not poachers, surely? Kingfishers aren't edible, are they?'

'Dunno. She was into trapping minnows in the Misbourne, as well. Looks like her interests weren't restricted to birds. She was fascinated by fish and other aquatic life forms, too.'

'You're right about the abbreviations,' Carole agreed as she picked up and perused one of the diaries herself. 'She uses them a lot. There's a whole string of them here. Ni, Cu, Pb, Cd, Cr, Hg, and more.'

'They're not all two letter abbreviations, though, are they?' Dave pointed out.

'No, there's some three letter ones here – PFA, PFO, and so on, then lists of measurements and percentages. Maybe I can ask if anyone in the group knows what they mean.'

'Didn't find any FEC's, though,' Dave advised.

'FECs?'

'F.E. Cassoni. The putative lover boy,' Dave grinned. 'There's no mention of him. She has check lists of birds she's ticked off, and numbers of water voles she spotted. She seems to have been more into wildlife than men. I noticed one entry where she talks about finding a kite by the river, which seems to have upset her. Tragic, she describes it.'

'I haven't seen anyone flying kites around the valley, but I found the remains of a helium balloon by the river yesterday when I took the dogs down there. And I heard that one of the local farmer's cows died when it stepped on some torn and twisted wire from one of those sky lantern things and its foot got infected. You never know what's going to fall out of the sky these days.'

'Maybe the kite Emerald found was of the avian variety. Can't see anyone getting upset over a plastic one.'

'Yes, a dead kite would upset a birdwatcher. In fact, Euphemia mentioned kites. She said she used to drive into deepest Wiltshire to see them but they've bred so successfully that, nowadays, they're out here in the Chiltern Hills, too.'

'I think we're going to need some expert help deciphering these journals, Carole. But I'm not sure who we can ask, since you don't have a legitimate reason for being in possession of them. When are you intending to give them back?'

'Um, soon. Just as soon as we've managed to make sense of them.'

'The diary entries stop abruptly in March 2000. As you'd expect, given her sudden death.'

'So, the last entries might be the crucial ones,' Carole reasoned. 'Is there anything interesting in those?'

'Just what looks like more work stuff and more initials. *MB of SPD to compare test results this lunchtime AA.* That's dated the day before she was murdered.'

'What do you suppose that means? Was she involved with Alcoholics Anonymous?'

'Or the Automobile Association,' Dave suggested. 'Who knows? One thing's for certain, the police would definitely have checked that out, given that it's the last appointment she ever recorded in her diary.'

'I'll check the photos I took of some of the minutes and statements in the police file, but I don't recall any reference to MB, or AA or SPD.'

'So, what's the next stage in your investigation?'

'It's not an investigation, Love. Not really. It's research – research and analysis. And my next stage will be to interview Kulwinder Kaur to ask what she knows about the place where Emerald worked.'

***

When Carole turned up at the offices of the parish council, Mary Keswick was sitting in the lobby area waiting for her. Mary waved Carole over and bade her sit down alongside her.

'Carole, I'm afraid I've got a bit of bad news,' she announced. 'You probably didn't get to know him that well, but our group member Malcolm Rawlinson has passed away.'

'Oh, I'm so sorry to hear that,' Carole responded, though she had to rack her brains for a second or two to recall who exactly Malcolm was.

'He was researching the, um ...' Carole clicked her fingers as she tried to remember.

'The war heroes, yes,' Mary added. 'I'm afraid he was out for dinner with his wife when he was knocked down by a car.'

'Oh, how tragic. Was his wife hurt, too?'

'Luckily, no. They'd been for dinner at the *Austen Arms* to celebrate her birthday. He'd parked in the car park around the back of the hotel. His wife is disabled and can only walk with the aid of a walking frame. Malcolm went to bring the car around to the front entrance, so Dorothy wouldn't have to walk so far. Unfortunately, another car that was parked around the back drove into him. Looks like Malcolm was killed outright.'

'Oh, poor Dorothy,' Carole sympathised. 'The poor driver must be traumatised, too.'

'Well, we don't know. He didn't stop, you see.'

'What? You mean it was a hit and run?'

'Well, it's pretty dark around the back of the hotel so maybe the driver didn't see Malcolm.'

'But he must have felt the bump, surely? He must have realised he'd hit something.'

'Apparently not. Or maybe he was drunk.'

'So, are the police investigating the incident?'

'Oh, yes. I'm sure they'll track down the driver. But, since Malcolm was one of the founder members of our local U3A branch, it would be nice if as many of us as possible could turn out for the funeral.'

'Of course. Do let me know where and when.'

The parish clerk now appeared and ushered them into the main council office. Councillor Kulwinder Kaur, a smiling woman whom Carole guessed to be of a similar age to herself, soon appeared with an armful of files. Mary made the introductions

'So, you ladies wanted to know about the occupants of the site at Gallows Hill,' Kulwinder said. 'I've dug out all the paperwork I could find on that place. You may have heard that, during World War Two, it was used by the Royal Air Force and the Ministry of Defence.'

'Do you know what exactly they did there?' Carole asked.

'Yes, the MOD had set up an operation in partnership with a local ceramics firm. Some of the civilian staff – artists who'd been decorating china before the war – were engaged in painting the luminous dials and other instruments for bomber aircraft. Another part of the site was used for training RAF ground crews, specifically their fire-fighting units. They practised setting and putting out aircraft fuel-based fires, experimenting with new kinds of fire-fighting foam.'

'And what happened on the site after the war?' Carole asked. 'Do the records show that?'

'Yes. Firstly, it became a diagnostics centre, where people were referred by their GPs for x-rays and later for ultra-sound checks. Next, it was home to a bio-medical sciences centre. They developed medical instruments and apparatus. Some of the top medical scientists would have been engaged there.'

'Would that by any chance have included Professor Per Isacson?' Mary asked.

'I'm afraid I don't have any information at all about personnel,' Kulwinder said. 'We would only hold details of the site use and any planning applications or environmental issues. You'd have to track down company records for employment records.'

'Do you know exactly what sort of medical apparatus they made there?' Carole asked.

'Yes. The post-war planning regs required full details, so … yes, here we have it, they made the kind of syringes which needed sterilising, also catheters and pace-makers for heart operations, and mesh for repairing hernias. The centre also had a pharmaceutical wing. There, they produced pills for hypertension, antacid tablets and a host of other medications.'

'You mentioned environmental issues,' Carole asked. 'Do you know if there were any such issues?'

Kulwinder flipped through all the paperwork on the file, then opened and searched through another couple of files. She shook her head.

'No, nothing on file about that. Are you thinking about the rumours that arise every now and again about the land being contaminated? Only I've heard those, too, but I've never found anything to confirm the rumours were true. And the Chiltern Biosciences Institute was a mainly government-run establishment. They surely wouldn't have moved in if they thought the land was contaminated.'

'I understand you keep a register of contaminated land?' Carole asked, 'is that right?'

'Yes, we do. Would you like me to check it?'

'Yes, please, Kulwinder,' Mary said. 'That's if we're not taking up too much of your time.'

The councillor arose, walked across to the parish clerk's office and called out to the clerk to fetch the contaminated land register. She returned and they continued to drink their coffee.

'So, is this is to do with your 'famous and infamous' local history project?' Kulwinder asked.

'Yes,' Mary said. 'Carole is researching the notable scientists and medics who lived in the area.'

'And I take it this chap whose name you mentioned was one of them?'

'Yes,' Carole said. 'His daughter, too. Doctor Emerald Isacson. Have you heard of her?'

'No, I'm afraid not. But my husband and I only moved to the village eight years ago,' Kulwinder said.

The clerk arrived bearing a thin manilla folder which she handed to the councillor.

'Ah, yes,' Kulwinder said, 'this is the register. Let's have a look.'

She flipped open the file and saw there was only one document within it. It was a tabulated form intended to take the list of all and any areas of land within the village which had been found to be contaminated in any way. She held up the file to show the form to Carole and Mary.

'Well, as you can see, there's not a single entry on the register. That's good news, isn't it?'

'That would seem to dispel the longtime rumours,' Carole agreed, as she stood up and made to shake the councillor's hand. 'Well thank you so much for seeing us, Kulwinder.'

'Aren't you forgetting something, Carole?' Mary said. 'You also wanted to ask Kulwinder about some of the more notable members of the parish council and other local administrators, didn't you? That's part of your assignment, too, isn't it?'

'Ah, yes,' Carole gave a forced smile of enthusiasm and sank back into her seat. 'Of course. The administrators. How could I forget them?'

Just then, the office door opened and a smiling lady in her seventies, clutching a cup of coffee, came into the room.

'Ah, now here's a lady who can help you,' Kulwinder said. 'Lucy, come in. Come and join us.'

The lady duly came over and sat down with them.

'Carole, this is Councillor Lucy Goddard, our current Parish Council Chair. Lucy, you know Mary Keswick, don't you? And this is Carole

Murray. She moved into Rowan Tree Cottage on Hawthorn Lane just a few months ago.'

Carole and Lucy shook hands, and Mary explained to Lucy about the 'famous and infamous' project their U3A group was pursuing.

'Carole is interested to know if there were any noteworthy councillors or other administrators locally – or disreputable ones,' Kulwinder advised.

'Well, fancy that,' Lucy smiled. 'I've been on the council for decades. No-one's ever included us in a project before. But did you notice the oak board in the outer lobby when you arrived, the one with all the names and dates engraved on it? Well, those are the names of the people who served as Council Chairmen during much of the village's history. I'm not sure any of them have been especially famous or infamous, but, since I've lived around here for much of my adult life, I can tell you all about most of them. Follow me.'

'Thank you, Lucy,' Carole forced another smile as she followed the Council Chairman out into the lobby. 'It's very good of you to spare the time.'

Chapter 12

The rain had been falling all night and there was no let up the following morning. It was around eight o'clock that morning when Carole walked slowly down the stairs ahead of Dave, whose progress, one step at a time and placing his weight on his one good foot, was slow and painful. She walked ahead so she might block his fall if he should trip. He collected his crutches which were propped against the hall stand and headed for his favourite armchair while Carole went into the kitchen to make them some coffee.

'That's the last of the milk,' she told him as she handed him his mug. 'So, rain or no rain, I'll need to venture into the village this morning for some more. I'll pop into the bakers for some of those nice soft white rolls for breakfast if you like. Anything else you need?'

'Would you call in at the library and pick up some books for me, Love. I've finished reading those diaries and if I don't have something else to read, I'll soon be bored out of my skull.'

'Okay. What should I get you?'

'I've reserved the new Lynda La Plante and I got an e-mail yesterday to say it's in. It's the last in the Jane Tennison series. A couple more crime thrillers would be good, too. You know the kind of thing I like.'

Carole fed the dogs their kibble and let them out into the back garden, then she slipped on her raincoat and wellingtons. Picking up her shopping bag, she opened the front door, only to find two raincoated individuals standing there. It was DI Hogget and his female detective. Her heart stopped briefly as she wondered whether, they'd somehow found out she'd taken items from the murder scene. Hogget flashed his warrant card.

'Morning Ms Murray. Remember me? DI Bernard Hogget and this is DS Anna Caulfield. We met at Miss Isacson's apartment the other day. We'd like another word with you.'

'Of course. Come in. Filthy weather, isn't it?' Carole said nervously, as she stepped back into the hall, put down her bag and stepped out of her wellingtons and raincoat.

'Yes, indeed,' Hogget agreed. It's absolutely persisting down out there. Were you thinking of going into the village this morning? If so, I would advise against it.'

'Oh, why? Are you here to arrest me?'

'No, not at all,' Hogget laughed. 'It's badly flooded down there, that's all. All the paths from the main car park into the village centre are ankle-deep in mud and they've closed the village off to traffic because the Misbourne's burst its banks.'

'Ah, I see. Well, do come in. I'd offer you a hot drink but we've no milk, I'm afraid.'

'Well, that's very kind of you. Actually, a couple of black coffees wouldn't come amiss,' Hogget smiled, as he and his sergeant took off their raincoats.

Realising she wasn't going to escape, Carole hung their coats and hers on the hallstand and ushered them into the sitting room.

'This is my husband, Dave Lloyd. Dave, this is Detective Inspector Hogget and DS Caulfield from Thames Valley. Dave used to be a detective, too,' Carole informed them, hopeful that this might help her case if they had somehow found out about the filched documents and decided to take action against her.

Carole quickly made coffee for the detectives then joined them in the sitting room, where they were already engaged in amicable conversation with Dave.

'I'm so glad you've called,' Carole fibbed. 'Only, what with the shock of finding poor Euphemia deceased and all, I quite forgot to tell you that she'd lent me some items on the first occasion when I'd visited her. I can't now return them to her so you might like to take them.'

'Oh, yes?' Hogget said. 'Which items would those be?'

'Well, she seemed pleased that I was showing an interest in her celebrity parents and she offered to lend me some papers she thought might provide some background. You remember I told you I'm involved in a U3A local history project? There were some old diaries which she thought her parents had kept, and also a book on birdwatching.'

'Birdwatching?' Hogget queried.

'Yes, I believe the sisters were both keen on birdwatching. I'll get the items for you.'

Carole collected the diaries and the book, placed them in a plastic carrier bag and handed them to the Sergeant.

'And were they very informative?' he asked.

'Not really. Turns out the diaries were actually her sister's and they didn't have any mention of her parents at all. It's their parents I was interested in, you know, for my assignment on local celebrities.'

'So, you're saying the diaries belonged to the sister who was murdered many years ago?' Hogget asked.

'Yes, that's why I thought you'd want them,' Carole explained, her eyes wide with feigned innocence.

'And did you read them?'

'I had a quick browse, but I could see there was no mention of her parents in them. They just seemed to be desk diaries, you know, with work stuff in them.'

'Okay, well we'll have a look at them ourselves. Now, the main reason we came was to see if you'd be willing to give us your fingerprints and a DNA sample. It's so we can isolate any prints or DNA the killer may have left from those of other recent visitors to the apartment.'

'Oh, of course. I'd be happy to do so,' Carole agreed, relieved that she wasn't going to be asked anything more about the diaries.

The sergeant opened her bag of tricks and withdrew her fingerprinting and DNA kits. Whilst she commenced the process of taking samples from Carole, the DI took out his notebook.

'Could you give me an idea of what you might have touched when you were at the scene?' he asked.

'Oh, well, let me see. On my first visit, Euphemia handed me some of the framed photos of her family for me to have a look at. My prints may still be on those. She gave me tea, but the tea things will presumably have been washed up by now. I probably touched the sitting room door, but not the handle, as the door was already ajar during both my visits. I pushed open the back door on my second visit, again not touching the handle. I can't think of anything else I would have touched.'

'Okay, that's fine,' Hogget jotted down the details in his notebook and sipped at his coffee. 'So, were you in the police as well?'

'Me? No, I was a civil servant. I took the voluntary early release package last year.'

'Which branch of the service were you in?' he asked.

'Government Communications Procurement Directorate,' she gave the standard answer which few people felt moved to query further.

'Is that part of the Home Office,' he asked.

'Hmmh. Would you like some more coffee?'

'No, thank you. You were about to leave when we arrived. I think we've held you up long enough. But how's the U3A project going?'

'Oh, I'm still managing to research the bits I've been assigned, though it's unfortunate I wasn't able to get more information from Miss Isacson before her untimely death. And now, tragically, we've lost another member of our local history group – Malcolm Rawlinson.'

'Rawlinson? The hit and run victim? He was in your U3A group, was he?' Hogget seemed surprised.

'Yes. He'd gone to the *Austen Arms* for dinner. It was his wife's birthday. But he'd told me he hoped to get copies of some photos they have on display in the bar, photos of a couple of local war heroes, for our project.'

'So, that's *two* people involved with your project who've been killed in the last fortnight. Sounds like the project's jinxed. Or maybe you're the jinx, Carole,' Hogget conjectured.

'I very much hope not,' Carole said, a little taken aback. 'But have you caught the driver who knocked him down?'

'Not yet. Seems there's a problem with the hotel's CCTV. But we're working on it. Anyway, thanks for your co-operation and for the coffee. Nice to have met you, Dave. Bye for now.'

Carole led Hogget and his sergeant into the hallway and handed them their coats. She was quite relieved to see them drive off, not least because she had found it awkward making excuses regarding the items she had taken from the murder victim's flat. She told herself it wasn't the first time she had lied to the police, but whenever she had done so previously it had been during officially sanctioned Security Service operations, when the need-to-know rule was applied, rather than to cover up her own lawbreaking. She found Hogget's suggestion that she might be a jinx somewhat unsettling. Surely, Rawlinson's death was simply a coincidence? She hoped Hogget was joking. She returned to the sitting room where Dave gave her a reproving look.

'I think you got away with it,' he said, with a sternly reproving look.

'Yes, Love. I rather think I did.'

Chapter 13

Carole was glad of her wellingtons as she plodded through the river water to get to the village baker's. The rain had eased off slightly and a weak sun was trying to break through the cloud. She could no longer see the division between river and road, as the swollen Misbourne had escaped its course and had pooled out into the high street, creating a shallow muddy pond. Its waters were black and pungent and a layer of concealed mud tugged at her boots and hindered her progress as she waded her way along the high street towards the small supermarket. A little group of villagers stood in the churchyard, peering over the railings and down into the river's murky depths.

She thought that was a very British obsession, the same obsession which drew crowds to stand and stare down into any sizeable hole in the ground whenever anyone dug one. Even in the busy capital, whenever builders were excavating down deep into the earth to sink the foundations for a new block of city apartments, they would cut viewing panels in the hoardings around the site so that the public could stand and stare into the hole. Sometimes, the builders would thoughtfully cut some at lower levels also, to allow children to peep in.

What the general public didn't realise, but she did, having once entered just such an excavation site where the body of a Russian diplomat had been discovered, was that the more artistic of the builders would often paint caricature heads and bodies around those peepholes on the inside of the hoardings. Some of the painted figures Carole had seen had depicted a portly man sitting on a lavatory, or an equally large woman with the wind raising her skirt to reveal knee-length bloomers. It caused the builders much amusement to see the faces of passers-by thrust into the peepholes and completing those caricatures. It had reminded Carole of those amusing boards with cut outs for holidaymakers' faces, as used by seaside photographers. Carole smiled to herself at the memory.

She now noticed a man who, curiously, was taking photos of the flooding using a very professional looking camera. As she drew nearer, a young woman who stood alongside him clutching a notebook, stepped forward and stopped her.

'Hi, I'm Helen Chandler, reporting for the *Bucks Sentinel*,' she said. 'I'm writing a piece on the floods. Do you live in the village? If so, I'd like to ask you what you think of the situation. Have you ever known it to be this bad in the past?'

'Oh, I'm sorry. I've only lived here for the past few months,' Carole told her. 'And I'm lucky to live halfway up the valley, so I'm not greatly affected by the floods.'

'Okay, no worries,' the reporter said, as Carole stepped around her and headed for the supermarket.

On the way back, Carole had to walk more gingerly, since she was now weighed down with her shopping, and the submerged pavement was very slippery beneath her boots. She had bought a chicken to roast for dinner and a couple of bottles of wine, as well as the much-needed milk and bread, and her bag was heavy. The reporter didn't seem to be having much luck with her interviews, so, on impulse, Carole approached her.

'Helen, might I have a quick word with you?' she asked.

'Sure, if you can put up with that stink. I think it's why no-one wants to stand here and speak to me.'

'Yes, why does it smell so bad? The river isn't normally this stinky, is it?'

'No, it's because there's raw sewage coming up with the floodwater,' the reporter explained. 'See the manhole over there. And the same's happening to the manholes all along the high street.'

Carole glanced in the direction in which the reporter was pointing and saw a small cascade of black water shooting up through the ventilation holes in the metal manhole cover.

'Oh God! Really?' Carole gasped. 'That's sewage?'

'Yes. You see, the village's Victorian sewers can't cope with the additional volume of effluent flowing down from the couple of thousand new homes that have been constructed up the valley in recent years. The river often does flood after heavy and prolonged rain, but it's getting worse year on year.'

'And that's because of over-development, is it?' Carole asked.

'Mainly. There's also the effect of climate change. We're getting more rain each year. When the river is in full spate, the water companies get overwhelmed and release raw sewage into the rivers. You said you haven't lived here long, so I guess you haven't experienced the flooding here before.'

'No. Funnily enough, the estate agent didn't mention anything about this.'

'No, and they didn't when I moved into the village two years ago. Isis Water is the company responsible. I've been chasing them for a statement and asking what they're going to do about it, but they're not returning my calls.'

'Helen, could I ask you about something else – something not connected with the floods?'

'Sure, fire away.'

'It's probably before your time, but there was a reporter who often wrote for the *Sentinel* – a chap named Charlie Herron. He was found dead in Percival's Wood. Do you know anything about the case?'

'No, I never heard of him. Was this recently?'

'No, a long time ago – more than twenty years ago, in fact. The coroner declared it a suicide, but he left no note, and a woman was murdered in the same stretch of wood just eighteen months before that. They never caught her killer.'

'And you think the two deaths might have been connected?' Helen asked.

'Well, it's possible. I called in at the *Sentinel*'s offices to ask about Herron, but nobody remembers him or the incident.'

'And who was the woman who was murdered?'

'She was a fifty-one-year-old government scientist named Emerald Isacson.'

'And you say they never caught her killer? Do you think Herron killed her and then killed himself?' the reporter began scribbling in her notebook.

'I don't know. Could be. That's Isacson with one 'a' by the way.'

'Wait a minute,' the reporter started. 'Wasn't that suspicious death in Briarfield last week a woman named Isacson with one 'a'? Were the two victims related, by any chance?'

'Yes. Sisters. And, in fact, I was the person who found the body – the recent one that is.'

'No way! Did you know the victims? Could I interview about it? You could describe the crime scene for me.'

'Oh, I'm not sure the police would want me giving out details. They never arrested anyone for the murder of Emerald Isacson, and they've not yet said if they're treating Euphemia's death as murder. Could have been an accident or natural causes, I suppose. It would be interesting, though, if all three deaths turn out to be connected somehow.'

'Yes, it would. Listen, could we get together for a coffee sometime and you could at least tell me what you know about this Charlie Herron?'

'Yes, I'd like that. My name's Carole Murray. Here, let me write my mobile number and e-mail address in your notebook. There was very little in the press about Charlie Herron's death, unlike the murder of Emerald Isacson, so if you do find out anything about Herron, I'd love to know.'

'Okay, I'll check it out and then I'll call you.'

Carole suddenly remembered her promise to collect Dave's books, so the community library was her next port of call. Once she had divested herself of her muddy boots and left them in the library porch, she saw that Kitty Walker was one of the volunteer library assistants on duty.

'Awful news about Malcolm,' Carole said.

'I know,' Kitty said. 'His widow's distraught. She waited outside the hotel for him. When he didn't appear, she struggled around to the car park where she found his body. How could anyone run someone down and then take off without helping them? What sort of a person would do that?'

'I know,' Carole agreed. 'It's awful. And I hear the police haven't traced the driver yet.'

Carole headed over to browse the crime section and selected a few thrillers she hoped Dave hadn't already read, then she queued up at the desk again to check them out and to collect the book he had reserved. A middle-aged man ahead of her seemed to be venting to Kitty about the state of the village and what he referred to as 'the effluent produced by the affluent'.

'I know, Rob,' Kitty sympathised. 'You're preaching to the converted. They're turning our villages into dormitories for London commuters. There's been far too much development, if you ask me. It's not just the sewage system, the entire local infrastructure can't cope. You can't keep throwing up new houses and not building new schools and doctor's surgeries. Things are just the same down in Chalfont St Michael where I live.'

The man suddenly became aware of Carole queueing patiently behind him and he stepped to one side.

'Sorry, I'm holding you up,' he smiled. 'Do go ahead.'

'Thank you,' Carole said and she handed Kitty the books and her library card. 'May I take these out, please, Kitty, and there's a reserved book to collect. In the name Dave Lloyd.'

'Sorry for the rant,' the man smiled at Carole whilst Kitty checked through the reserved books, 'but I run a team of volunteers who look after the river and keep an eye on the health of the water.'

'He roped me onto the river watch team, too,' Kitty grinned, as she scanned firstly the books and then Carole's library card.

The thought crossed Carole's mind that Emerald Isacson diary entries seemed to indicate she, too, had an interest in the river and the aquatic wildlife. She wondered whether the scientist might have been a member of the river squad.

'If I may ask, did you ever have a lady named Isacson on your team?'

'Not in my time,' he shook his head. 'The name's not familiar. I'm Rob Younger, by the way. Why, would you be interested in joining the team?'

'Carole Murray. I'm not sure my husband would put up with me joining another group. I'm in the U3A, you see, and that keeps me pretty occupied. We only moved here a few months ago, but we're not commuters. We've retired to the village and we'd both like to become part of the community. That is, my hubby will, too, when his broken ankle heals.'

'Okay, well here's my card,' Rob said, handing her his business card. 'Kitty and I'll be down by the old mill bridge tomorrow with another member of the team taking water samples. We get them tested to check the bacteria levels. Then I can get onto Isis Water and give them grief. If you're not busy, you're welcome to join us. We usually have a coffee afterwards in *The Whippet*.'

'Where's that? Carole asked.

'It's *The Hare and Whippet*,' Kitty said. 'That's the riverside pub. They do really good coffee in there. Do come, Carole.'

'Okay, I'd love to come along and observe. What time tomorrow?'

'Eleven in the morning,' Rob advised. 'But make sure you wear wellingtons. Oh, and do you have a dog?'

'Yes, two. Why do you ask?'

'Don't bring them with you. In fact, don't let them anywhere near the river. The sewage has contaminated the river banks and the pastureland on either side of the river. If dogs walk through it and then later lick their paws clean, they'll get sick. Several villagers have lost their pets that way.'

'Oh, how horrible. Thanks for the tip, Rob. Hopefully, I'll see you there tomorrow. Bye, Kitty.'

As she tramped back up the steep hill, stopping every now and again to catch her breath and to put down her shopping bags, the weight of which had been greatly added to by Dave's library books, she began to wonder whether she was reading too much into the deaths of the two sisters and the suicide of the journalist. Was there really any connection between the deaths of Herron and the Isacsons sisters, or was she letting her imagination run away with her? Despite Dave's cynicism on the subject of coincidence, might this really be no more than that?

On the other hand, she pondered, might Emerald's interest in the wildlife in and around the river have been connected with water pollution, and might she have been murdered for tackling the water company about it? Surely a water company wouldn't murder anyone, though? Or would they? Carole made a mental note to avoid bringing the dogs down to the river again, following Younger's advice. But she wondered whether there would even have been the same level of sewage pollution back in Emerald's time, a quarter of a century ago, as there was today. From what Rob Younger had said, it sounded as though it was the more recent and excessive development which had caused it. Carole realised she now had even more questions but, as yet, still no answers.

Chapter 14

The following morning, having first walked the dogs in the comparative safety of the warren of paths which ran behind the cottages on Hawthorne Lane, Carole took them home and gave them their breakfast before driving down to the village. At the entrance to the village, she came across a barrier and signs indicating the village was now closed off entirely to traffic, owing to the flooding. Circling around the roundabout, she headed back the way she had come but turned into the community centre car park and parked there instead.

The car park was fairly full but she managed to secure a parking space. Changing her driving shoes for the wellingtons she'd had the presence of mind to bring, she spotted Rob Younger and two members of his river group, one of them being Kitty. They were already hard at work. Rob was scooping up water samples at various points along the river's course and sealing the water up in glass vials which he handed to another middle-aged man who stood on the bank, wiping the vials using antiseptic wipes. He handed them in turn to Kitty, who dried the vials and stuck labels on them. Kitty welcomed Carole and introduced her to the third member of their team.

'Carole, this is Jaswinder Singh. Jazz, Carole is in my local history group at the U3A'

'Nice to meet you, Carole,' Jazz smiled. I believe you met my wife recently – Kulwinder.'

'Ah, of course,' Carole shook his hand. 'Councillor Kaur. So, what's your role on the river watch team, Jazz?'

'I run the village pharmacy, so Rob gets me to carry out the testing on the water samples. Whenever there's flooding, we always find a raised level of bacteria. It's important to monitor those levels.'

'And the bacteria come from the sewage, do they?' Carole asked.

'Yes,' Jazz replied as he stowed the vials in a wooden box. 'I can only test for bacteria, but there's probably a few more nasties in the water besides that.'

'Oh? What makes you think that?' Carole asked.

'D'you see that pipe over there, the one which emerges at the riverbank?'

Carole looked in the direction he was indicating and saw a concrete pipe buried in the river bank. It opened out directly onto the river and there was jet black water trickling from it.

'Yes. What is it?'

'It's part of the stormwater drainage system. It takes the runoff all the way from the top of Gallows Hill, via the road drainage system, and brings it under the main road and all the way down to here where it flows into the river. Thing is though, it picks up heavy metals along the way.'

'Heavy metals? Where do they come from?'

'Mainly from traffic sources. From car tyre wear, brake linings and engine and body wear. They all end up in the river.'

'So, what are these heavy metals?' Carole asked.

'Oh, all sorts – lead, mercury, copper, chromium, zinc, nickel, all injurious to the health of wildlife and humans. It's a crying shame, you know, because there are only two hundred and ten chalk streams like the Misbourne all across the world, and one hundred and sixty of them are here in the south of England.'

'I didn't know that,' Carole was surprised. 'In that case, why aren't we taking better care of them?'

'Good question,' Jazz agreed. 'The water in chalk streams is normally very pure, since it's filtered up from the aquifer through the chalk layer. And this here chalk stream used to have trout swimming in it. There once were extensive watercress beds along the valley, too. In fact, there was so much mineral-rich watercress grown here that it used to be carted up to London and sold in the markets. There's none growing here now, luckily, as you wouldn't want to eat it.'

'So, are you measuring all these heavy metals too?' she asked.

'No, I don't have the means to test for anything other than the bacteria. Trout haven't been found here for years, though. The only thing swimming in the Misbourne these days is *e-coli*.'

After the three river volunteers had consigned the samples to the boot of Jazz's car and had changed out of their muddy boots and wiped their hands clean with the antiseptic wipes, they and Carole headed along the riverside and into *The Hare and Whippet* where they ordered their coffees. Carole took in the pub's pleasant décor.

'Have you been in here before, Carole?' Kitty asked.

'No, I haven't. It's only just down the hill from us, though. I must bring Dave here when he's able to walk again.'

'You see that big glazed entrance?' Rob pointed out. 'That used to be open to the elements. It was the entrance for the horse-drawn coaches until a century ago. This was a major staging post on the route out of London to the West Country. The coaches would drive in here and they'd change horses. There used to be stables out the back. The tired horses would be led down to the bank to drink the river water. Of course, it was fit to drink back then.'

'Tell Carole what went on upstairs, though,' Kitty urged.

'Oh yes, have you ever heard of Hanging Judge Jeffreys?' Rob asked.

'Heard the name, yes,' Carole nodded.

'Well, he would use one of the upstairs rooms as his courtroom. He was an awful man. He'd condemn you to death just for stealing an apple. There used to be a scaffold out there on the river bank, and he liked to stand by the upstairs window and watch the condemned wretches dance on the end of the rope.'

'Oh God! That's awful,' Carole exclaimed.

'Yes,' Rob continued, 'and they say he suffered badly with kidney disease. That made him foul-tempered. It also affected his judgement. He once condemned an old lady to be burned at the stake, but the locals weren't having that. They rioted and threatened to burn his house down until he commuted her sentence. He still had her beheaded, mind.'

'Good God!' Carole exclaimed.

'He lived at Bulmer Court, a big mansion over at Gaunt's Cross, and that did burn down mysteriously not long afterwards, so he had to move temporarily to live up at *The Manor*.'

'Where's that?' Carole asked, intrigued.

'It's gone now. It was here in Chalfont St George, behind the village shops, where the big new estate is now,' Rob gesticulated with his hand in the general direction of the High Street.

'Yes,' Kitty added, 'and they say Jeffreys had a tunnel built under the pub and it ran across under Market Place and up into *The Manor*. It was so he could escape the vengeance of the mob after he'd had someone hanged. Don't know if that's true, though.'

'There is a tunnel down there, right enough,' Rob informed her. 'I saw it myself some years ago. After one of the previous big floods, it was. The pub cellars flooded and when the floodwaters receded, the landlord had to get workmen in to clear out the mud and debris. A bit of the cellar wall had collapsed and behind it they found a tunnel. The landlord invited me to have a look at it.'

'And did it go across under the road to *The Manor*?' Kitty asked.

'They never found out. It had quite a lot of rocks and rubble in it. The pub's owners at the time had to spend a lot of money on the clean-up of the cellars. They didn't see the point in paying to have the tunnel cleared out as well. They just boarded up the tunnel entrance.'

'Rob,' a thoughtful Jazz asked, 'do you think there's any truth in the rumours about the pub being haunted? Kulwinder tells me there's a whole file in the parish office containing reports about apparitions and stuff.'

'Well, lots of people have reported seeing ghosts down by the river, right on the spot where they used to hang people. Funny how they only see them when they're *leaving* the pub, though – you know, after an evening's drinking.'

'What about Gallows Hill, though?' Carole asked. 'How did that get its name?'

'Well, going back long before Judge Jeffreys' time,' Rob explained, 'there was a bigger set of gallows up there. They used to carry out multiple hangings of rioters and subversives there, and they'd leave the bodies hanging, to discourage others from rising up against government. It must have been a terrible sight, looking up at the skyline and seeing executed corpses swaying in the wind.'

'I wonder what it was called before they put the gallows up there,' Kitty mused.

'On one old map, it's shown as Saint George's Hill, which makes sense since it's situated in Chalfont St George. I supposed the locals began calling it Gallows Hill to show their resentment at the authorities executing people.'

'Just as we've got a Saint Michael's Hill over in Chalfont St Michael,' Kitty added. 'But I don't think we had mass executions up there.'

'Mass executions?' Carole grimaced. 'And I thought this was such a nice village.'

'Oh no, you scratch the surface of any really old settlement,' Rob told her, 'you just go back far enough, and you'll find a truly dark history.'

'Maybe you don't have to go back that far,' Carole commented.

'You're referring to Emerald, aren't you?' Kitty observed.

'Who's that?' Jazz asked.

'Tell him, Carole,' Kitty urged. 'Tell Rob and Jazz all about Emerald Isacson, and her sister.'

Once their coffees were drunk and Carole had finished recounting details of the murders, past and present, she and the river watch volunteers walked, and at several points waded, along the riverside, away from the almost deserted village to return to their cars in the community centre car park. As Carole climbed into her car and started up her engine, she saw Jazz carefully consign the box of water samples to the boot of his own vehicle. She also noticed a man seated in a black Citroen saloon, who seemed to be simply sitting and watching. Carole was aware that passing delivery drivers often did pull off the A413 into the car park at lunchtimes in order to rest up, eat their sandwiches and read a newspaper. But the driver of this particular car did not seem to be eating or reading. He was just watching. She felt she had seen that car, or one very similar, somewhere recently, but she couldn't recall where.

Chapter 15

When Carole arrived back at Rowan Tree Cottage Dave had just finished watching his favourite television game show 'Countdown'.

'Carole, you missed all the excitement,' he enthused.

'Why? What happened?'

'I only got today's 'Countdown' conundrum, that's all. It was a nine-letter word and neither contestant got it, but I did.'

'Go on, then, what was it,' she asked, as she could see he was dying to tell her.

'It was 'Cabriolet,' he announced, proudly.

'I don't even know what that means.'

'Cabriolet. It's a kind of horse-drawn carriage. It's where we get the word 'cab' from, you know, as in 'taxi cab'. But, nine letters, Carole. And you weren't here to witness my moment of triumph.'

'That's nothing short of brilliant, Love,' she smiled. 'You really are great at anagrams. You should apply to go on 'Countdown' yourself.'

'Don't you have some homework to do?' Dave asked, as they settled down in their armchairs, he with his crossword puzzles and she with the latest copy of *The Sentinel*.

'Homework? Oh, the administrators, you mean? Yes, you're right. I don't suppose I can put it off any longer. When I met two of the local councillors, Kulwinder Kaur and Lucy Goddard, Lucy spent half an hour giving me the rundown on some of the former parish chairmen. It was kind of her to take the time, though none of them seemed to have a history half so interesting as the Isacsons.'

'You never know until you delve into them. Remember the Krogers?'

'Who?'

'A bookseller and his wife. Boring little couple. Lived in a modest little bungalow in west London. Turns out they were Russians – members of the 'Portland Spy Ring'. Like I say, you never know what you'll find when you delve into the lives of ordinary people.'

Carole nodded resignedly. She put down her newspaper and reached for her laptop instead. She scrolled through the recent images until she found a photograph she had taken with her camera phone. The photo was of the carved wooden board which hung in the parish council offices. Lucy's account of the previous councillors and their achievements didn't suggest either fame or infamy, but Carole ran some of their names through the online newspaper archives anyway.

Her supposition was largely correct. She checked the name of each parish council chairman in turn, working backwards from Lucy, the present incumbent, and found lots of results for each one, mainly for their involvement in planning applications and appeals, in press interviews regarding plans for re-routing heavy traffic in connection with the construction of a major new railway line through the district, and regarding their presence at interminable openings of new shops, care homes and community projects. It occurred to her that voluntary service by parish councillors, as laudable and civic-minded as those councillors were, must also be extremely tedious.

Having ploughed through articles on the very similar service and achievements of ten of the men and women who had chaired the council, but having found nothing of interest, she decided a slightly different approach was called for. Checking the dates on which each individual chair had served, she identified the person who had held that office twenty-five years earlier, at the time of Emerald Isacson's murder. She expected the chair of the parish council back then would have had something to say to the press about such a brutal murder occurring in the village.

She was right. Chairman Andrew Maudsley had been most vociferous on the subject. He had called for lighting and closed-circuit television cameras to be installed in the car park at Percival's Wood. Such installations, he had argued, would dissuade anyone with evil intent from venturing into the woods and would make it a safer leisure amenity for dog walkers and bird watchers. It would attract even more locals to use the woods, he said, especially since enthusiasm for the spot had dropped away alarmingly following the murder.

Carole couldn't recall having seen streetlights or cameras on her recent trip to the woods and indeed, the press articles from several months further down the line reflected the fact that Maudsley's recommendations had not been carried out. As with most local initiatives, it had come down to the thorny issue of whose budget would provide the funding for this. No-one had been able to agree on whether this should come under highways, or parks and leisure, or parish council, and so nothing had been done. Clearly, the woods were no safer now than they had been a quarter of a century ago.

Carole continued to follow Councillor Maudsley's career as reported by the press, and unexpectedly came across his obituary. He had died suddenly and tragically at the age of fifty-eight, apparently. Amongst the litany of his achievements, both as director of several health and fitness companies, and as a long-serving parish councillor who had served several times as chairman, was an account of his untimely death. Seemingly, having been an enthusiastic supporter of the village's leisure centre and indoor swimming pool, Maudsley's own efforts at fundraising had seen the centre opened back in the nineteen-seventies. Thirty-odd years later, he had raised further sponsorship money from his own company and from some other local companies to effect improvements to the centre and bring it up to date and into the twenty-first century.

Tragically, however, in May two thousand and one, whilst on a late-night impromptu visit to the centre to inspect the progress of those improvements, Maudsley, who held his own key to the premises, had slipped and fallen into the swimming pool. Being a non-swimmer, and having apparently knocked himself unconscious by banging his head on the poolside as he fell, he had drowned. His lifeless body had been found early the next morning by the centre's cleaning contractors.

The articles reflected the fact that the centre's insurers had not been happy about his having paid a solo visit to the centre late at night, and without telling anyone else he intended to do so. Maudsley's shocked and grieving widow had told *The Sentinel*'s freelance reporter Charlie Herron how proud her husband had been of the centre. Seemingly, he had regarded it as his pet project and so he had wanted to reassure himself that the quality of the work the building contractors were carrying out was of the high standard he expected.

'*Hmm,*' Carole thought. '*Charlie Herron again,*' since she realised it would only be a few months later that Charlie Herron, too, would be dead.

The death of Councillor Maudsley did seem an odd sort of accident, but an accident it was deemed by the local coroner. One of the centre's swimming instructors, interviewed by Herron, had told the reporter that Maudsley had been especially excited by the planned installation of new Olympic standard diving boards and that, despite being a non-swimmer himself, Maudsley was in the habit of standing by the deep end of the pool, his palms placed together, poised as if intending to dive in. He had even adopted such a pose for a publicity photograph for *The Sentinel*.

The instructor thought Maudsley might have been doing that very same thing on that fatal night, when he must have overbalanced and toppled into the water. Herron's interview for *The Sentinel* included that very photo.

Carole thought how unfortunate and senseless the councillor's death had been. Good works and good intentions aside, though, did Maudsley qualify for inclusion in the catalogue of famous and infamous residents? She wasn't sure. As interesting as his tragic demise might be, she wasn't sure it made him either famous or infamous. She decided she would devote her time to checking out more local scientists and medical people instead, since there seemed to have been a handful of those who had chosen to live locally. She felt Mary Keswick would understand and might let her off the task of researching the local government administrators.

Closing her computer, she went into the kitchen and switched on the oven, then began preparing vegetables to go with their chicken for dinner. Running tap water onto the potatoes, she found herself thinking back over the morning's events and the abysmal condition of the local chalk stream. The more she considered the bacteria-laden River Misbourne, the more she wondered how far back in time the leaching of sewage into the river occurred and whether any of the village's many scientists had taken a stance on that. Yes, she decided, the scientists should prove to be a far more interesting bunch to research than the administrators.

Chapter 16

At eleven o'clock the following morning, Carole made her way to meet up with Helen Chandler at the reporter's invitation. Carole had suggested they met at *The Whippet*, since the coffee there was indeed good, and she chose a quiet alcove in the bar in which she and the reporter might discuss the murders without being overheard.

'Sorry I'm late,' Helen apologised when she arrived. 'Been on the blower to CID, trying to find out what progress they've made on a hit and run death in Gaunt's Cross. Let me get us some coffee. What'll you have?'

'A latte, please.'

Carole decided she wouldn't volunteer the information that she was acquainted with that victim, too. Hogget's suggestion that Carole might be a jinx still rankled with her. In any case, she knew nothing more about Malcolm's death that the reporter probably did.

'So, did you find out anything about Charlie Herron?' Carole asked as Helen returned from the bar with a caffè latte for each of them.

'Well, I found out his widow still lives in the area. In fact, she still lives in the same cottage in Briarfield which she shared with her husband at the time of his death. I have the address.'

Carole took a look at the address the reporter had written on a page torn from her notebook. It was the same address Kitty had found.

'Wait a minute, though,' Carole was puzzled. 'I understood Mrs Herron had left him and that was the cause of his depression.'

'No, I found nothing to suggest that. I got my information from the local undertaker who confirmed that the funeral party had left from the Herrons' home, and that those who attended the cremation were invited back to the house for drinks afterwards. Not sure that would be the case if they'd split up. Who told you that?'

'A retired police detective. Mind you, he's in his seventies now and I've found his memory to be a bit faulty on at least one other issue, so maybe he was mistaken. So, if Herron wasn't depressed over a marriage break-up, I wonder why he killed himself?'

'Don't know. The undertaker had a bit more information about the family,' Helen said, referring to her notebook. 'The widow paid all the funeral expenses – three Bentleys and top-quality floral tributes. She sent him off in style, apparently. They had two sons. One was nineteen and the other twenty when their father died. Both were at university at the time.'

'The former detective I spoke to thought Herron was an alcoholic. That might have made him depressed. I don't suppose there's any way we could confirm that, though,' Carole pondered.

'No. But it's a bit of a cliché, isn't it, the hard-drinking journo who spends his life hanging around bars hoping for a scoop, ends up inventing the news and succumbs to alcoholism? It's a very old-fashioned stereotype. An early twentieth century trope, you might say.'

'Is it?'

'Oh yes. You can't succeed like that in journalism these days. Couldn't twenty odd years ago, either. You have to be alert and anticipate where the next story's coming from. And you have to be fit enough to travel to where it's happening. Anyway, tell me about the Isacson sisters. What's the story with them?'

Carole took a deep breath and considered carefully what she would say. During her MI5 career, speaking with journalists was absolutely *verboten*. Any pearls which needed dropping to the press would be dropped by Security Service officials far more senior than herself. One or two people, who sat at a higher point on the pay scale, had a mutual understanding with certain newspaper editors, but no-one, not even a senior analyst such as herself, would ever be sanctioned to divulge as much as the time of day to a reporter. Carole reminded herself that, although she was no longer employed by her old firm, she was still subject to the Official Secrets Act, and always would be. She still didn't feel comfortable speaking with a journalist.

'Well, they were both unmarried. They were the daughters of a prominent medical scientist, a Dane named Per Isacson. Their Irish mother was a well-known opera singer in her day. But the sisters' deaths occurred twenty-five years apart, so it's not clear whether they're connected.'

'But *how* did Euphemia die?' Helen asked. 'Did she have her head stoved in, same as her sister? I checked out the press reports on Emerald Isacson and I understand she was beaten about the head.'

'Yes, she was. But the police haven't told me what caused Euphemia's death. We won't know the cause for certain until the post mortem has been carried out, will we?' Carole replied, guardedly.

'But you saw the body, didn't you? You must have an idea what killed her.'

'No, I *found* the body, but I didn't examine her. I'm not a medic. I'm just a retired civil servant.'

'But was there a lot of blood, consistent with a head wound?' the reporter pressed.

'I really couldn't say. Just from standing in the doorway, I could see she was pale and lying very still so I called an ambulance. I didn't spend long in the flat. It was the paramedics who established that she was deceased.'

'So, regarding the earlier death of her sister, the only thing which links the deaths of Emerald Isacson and Charlie Herron is the location in which they died.'

'Yes,' Carole agreed. 'Though it seems Herron was the first journalist on the scene very soon after a dog walker reported finding Emerald's body, and so he got the scoop on the murder. And it was his report for *The Sentinel* which was picked up by the nationals.'

'I wonder how he beat the others to the scene. Perhaps he had a tame policeman in the local squad and they called him out first,' Helen speculated.

'I wouldn't know.'

'How come you know so much about the Isacsons, then?' Helen asked.

'Oh, didn't I mention? I thought I did. I'm researching some of the well-known scientists and doctors who've lived around here over the years. It's for my U3A local history group's project. I was looking into Per Isacson – he helped develop the blood pressure gauge, you know – and I discovered that, although one of his daughters was killed all those years ago, the other one still lived around here. So, I called on her to get more information about their father. She gave me some details about the lives of her parents and invited me to call again. I did and that's when I found she had passed away.'

'Passed away, or was murdered?'

'I don't know, Helen. Thus far, I believe the police are simply treating it as an unexplained death, pending the autopsy. But Euphemia was in her seventies. It's not unusual for people in their seventies to die. And it's twenty-five years since her sister died. Seems unlikely the deaths will be connected.'

'Hmm. You're right,' Helen sighed with disappointment. 'I suppose I won't start getting excited until we know the cause of death.'

Carole felt relieved that the reporter wasn't too pushy. She had wanted to pump the reporter for information, not to be pumped by her. She wondered if she might be able to get a little more information from her.

'As I said, I'm looking into famous local scientists for this project, but I've also been tasked with researching local government officials and other administrators, and I've found another suspicious death.'

'Oh, yes?' Helen again looked interested.

'Well, it's probably not that suspicious a death, more an odd one, really – Andrew Maudsley, who was chairman of the parish council back in June two thousand and one. He drowned in the swimming pool here at the village's leisure centre.'

'He … drowned,' Helen repeated, her interest seeming to wane again.

'Yes. It was odd that, as the owner of several health and fitness centres himself, and having raised money to build the village's leisure centre, he'd never learned to swim.'

'Odd, maybe, but not everyone is confident in the water. Didn't they have life guards on duty in the pool, though?'

'Not when he died. It's also odd that he let himself into the centre late one evening to inspect some modernisation work which was being carried out, including the installation of new diving boards. It's thought he was standing at the edge of the pool down by the deep end, making motions as though he would dive in, when he slipped and fell in. That's an odd thing to do, isn't it?'

'Oddly idiotic, more like. If you're a non-swimmer and you're in a leisure centre all by yourself, why would you go anywhere near the edge of the pool, especially at the deep end, and why would you be larking about pretending to dive in?'

'Well, exactly,' Carole agreed and she produced her mobile phone. 'Look, I have a photo of Maudsley in just such a pose. I took this pic from a newspaper article. He posed for this shot to get publicity for fund-raising purposes.'

Helen gazed at the photo for a few seconds.

'It's not surprising he fell in, leaning over like that, pretending he's about to dive.'

'Yes, but he also hit his head as he slipped, and they think that contributed to his drowning. If he hadn't knocked himself out, he might just have managed to grab onto the rail at the side and pull himself out. I'm just wondering how easy it is to overbalance and fall face first into the water but still crack your head on the side of the pool.'

'I see what you mean. Maybe ..., maybe his feet slipped out from under him and he fell backwards and banged his head that way.'

'But would that have caused him to fall into the water, or just to land on his back on the side of the pool? And, surely, if he had been leaning forward, with his hands clasped together in a diving attitude, wouldn't he be more likely to fall forwards into the water?'

'I see what you're getting at,' the reporter nodded. 'Did he fall, or was he smacked on the head and pushed in? So, this could have been another suspicious death, but what's the connection between Maudsley and Emerald Isacson?'

'Hmm. I'm not sure. As chairman of the parish council, Maudsley had called for lighting and CCTV cameras to be installed in the car park up at Percival's Wood after Emerald's murder, not that they ever were. But that's the only connection I could find. I suppose it might help to know whether Maudsley's injury was to the front, side or back of his head. If it was to the front, he might just have plunged head first to the bottom of the pool where he might have banged his head on the bottom, but ...'

'But if it was to the back of the head,' Helen said, following Carole's thinking, 'he might have been attacked in the same way Emerald Isacson was – bashed on the back of the skull. But there's no way I could get hold of the pathologist's report. It's not a public document.'

'I'm not sure I could either,' Carole said.

'Hmm,' Helen deliberated. 'I suppose I could have another talk with Mister Levitt, my friendly local funeral director. His is the biggest undertakers in the area and he might just have arranged Maudsley's funeral, too. If he did, he might be able to tell me more about the condition of Maudsley's body.'

'Is that the sort of thing you mainly report on? Sudden deaths?' Carole asked.

'Seems like it, just lately. Sudden deaths and floods.'

'So, what've you heard about this hit and run, then?'

'Happened in the *Austen Arms* car park. Late Monday night. Some old chap heading back to his car when he was knocked down and killed.

The driver didn't hang about to see if he was okay. Probably had too much to drink,' Helen explained, and she flipped back a page in her note book. 'A Mister Malcom Rawlinson.'

'Poor chap. Did they get the driver?'

'No. And according to the barman, Rawlinson's wife is disabled. She was in a dreadful state. They had to send her home in a taxi. Goodness knows how she'll manage on her own. They didn't have any children, apparently. The hotel manager was more concerned about who would be collecting their car, since it's taking up a space in their car park.'

***

Having picked up a few bits of food shopping, Carole called in at the pharmacy. She could see Jazz Singh was busy in the back of the shop making up prescriptions. She asked the assistant for a pack of antiseptic wipes, suitable for cleaning her dog's feet after their walks, given the amount of sewage sloshing around the river area. She also asked for some latex gloves and some medical specimen containers.

'For wet or dry specimens?' the assistant asked.

'Er, wet,' Carole told her.

The assistant handed Carole wipes and gloves and showed her a plastic specimen container with a screw-on cap and an adhesive label.

'Yes, this is fine,' Carole confirmed. 'But I'll need three of these containers.'

The assistant gave Carole a bemused look and commented that her GP must be a most thorough individual, since most only required patients to fill one bottle at a time with urine. Carole simply shrugged. She wasn't going to explain that she needed the bottles because she intended to take her own samples of river water. The assistant would almost certainly want to know why and Carole didn't want to start a panic by explaining she suspected there might be worse things in the river than e-coli. Carole's next stop was at the bakery, where she picked up a crusty farmhouse loaf for lunch.

Dave was seated in his armchair, trying to perform some leg raises and other exercises when Carole arrived home. He arose and hobbled into the kitchen in anticipation of lunch. Carole dropped two fresh eggs into boiling water for their lunch and began slicing and buttering some of the crusty bread.

'So, did you have a busy morning?' Dave asked, as he sat himself down at the kitchen table lunch.

'It was an interesting one. I met with Helen Chandler. She's a local reporter who lives here in the village and she's going to do some digging for me. How was your morning?'

'I spent the morning with Jane Tennison,' Dave informed her.

'Who?'

'DCI Jane Tennison. *Prime Suspect*. You know, the character in the Lynda La Plante detective novels.'

'Oh, your library book,' Carole smiled, as she lifted their eggs out of the water and placed them in egg cups. 'Here, soft-boiled, as you like it.'

'Tell me something,' she asked as she watched him deftly smash the top of his egg with his spoon, as he had done since boyhood in order to let the witch out. 'D'you think it's possible for someone to dive forwards into a swimming pool and at the same time suffer concussion by smashing their head on the concrete edge of the pool?'

'I should think that's pretty much *im*possible,' Dave said.

'Well, alternatively, if he dived into the deep end, into, say, at least eight feet of water, do you think he would enter the water with sufficient force to bash his head on the bottom of the pool?'

'No, I don't think so. Even if he dived off a diving board head first, he'd be unlikely to hit his head on the bottom. That depth of water would slow him down. Why? Who's dead now?'

'A parish council chairman. Back in two thousand and one. The year after Emerald Isacson died.'

'And you're thinking it was another murder?' Dave said, as he scooped out a spoonful of soft-boiled egg and popped it into his mouth. 'Pass the salt, would you.'

'It's just possible.'

'Where did he hit his head? Front or back?'

'Dunno. I'd need to see the autopsy report. Any idea how I'd get hold of it?'

'Ah, so that's what this conversation is about. You want me to use my police contacts to get you someone's autopsy report? Why not just come straight out and ask me?'

'Well, I wanted your opinion as well – your expert opinion as a former murder squad detective.'

'It was the major incident team actually, and there's no need to butter me up. Why not just call Geoff Jackson at the TVP's unsolved case unit? Pass the salt, Love.'

'Of course. I hadn't thought of him. I'll give him a call right now.'

Carole abandoned her egg and raced off to the phone, leaving Dave to struggle to his feet and hop awkwardly on one foot around the table to reach for the salt.

Chapter 17

Dave Lloyd had been wearing his boot-style foot brace for what seemed like an eternity, and Carole noticed a distinct uplift in his mood as the date approached for his next GP appointment when he was to have his ankle assessed and, they both hoped, the brace removed. Carole drove him down to the surgery. The waiting room was full and there was a queue of people in front of reception, mostly trying to make appointments. Carole recalled what Kitty had said about there being insufficient medical centres to cope with the number of newcomers settling in the village.

There was a rather frail-looking elderly lady at the head of the queue. Carole recognised her. Esme Bickerstaff was a member of the U3A's textiles group. Carole had seen some of Esme's rather beautiful embroideries and patchwork quilts displayed at the U3A Open Day and had felt moved to approach the lady at her group's stand and congratulate her on the neatness of her handiwork. Carole and Dave couldn't help overhearing Esme's exchange with the somewhat po-faced receptionist.

'Could I make an appointment to see Doctor … Battery Charger?' the lady asked.

'Doctor … *Bhattacharya*,' the receptionist said, fixing her with a coldly withering look, 'has no appointments this week. D'you want to see someone else or to come back next week?'

Carole and Dave tried to conceal their mirth as the lady was quickly fixed up with an appointment to see a locum, whose name she might more easily pronounce. Soon, it was Dave's turn to see Doctor Bhattacharya with whom, fortunately, Dave did have an appointment. To Dave's satisfaction, the GP removed the medical boot and replaced it with a lightweight neoprene splint. His crutches were also exchanged for a strong, tubular steel walking stick. Armed with this and the doctor's warnings that he should exercise the leg but 'go easy' on it for the next couple of weeks, and definitely not climb any trees – ever, Dave left the surgery a happier man. Since the high street was still closed to traffic, Carole had to drive the long way around the village, to the outskirts of Gaunt's Cross.

'You do realise you've just overshot,' he pointed out, as Carole drove him away from the surgery. 'You've missed the turn off for the village centre.'

'Deliberately, so, Love. I'm afraid the village is still awash with sewage and the high street is still closed,' Carole explained. 'If we're to keep your nice new splint dry, we have to turn off the bypass here, drive towards Gaunt's Cross and double back on ourselves.'

'What a pain. Is this what you've been having to do to get to the village shops?'

'Yes. They say that, even when it stops raining, if it ever does, they'll still need to keep those tankers continually draining the excess out of the sewers in the village for a few more weeks yet.'

'I hope they get it sorted by the time I'm able to drive again. I don't fancy having to drive a mile or two just to pick up a loaf of bread from the bakers when it's only an eight-minute walk from home.'

'Like I've had to do for the past few weeks, you mean?' Carole griped. 'I hope you appreciate the lengths I've had to go to just to get you your favourite bread. Tell you what, Dave, since we're almost in Gaunt's Cross, why don't we treat ourselves to lunch. How about a bar snack at the *Austen Arms*. Let's celebrate your big boot coming off.'

Carole parked in the car park to the rear of the hotel and, whilst helping Dave clamber out of the car, she glanced around and noticed there were a couple of security cameras trained on the car park. She thought it would be odd if both of them had been out of order when Malcom Rawlinson had met with his death there. Once inside, she found a small table in a quiet corner of the bar and left Dave seated there whilst she went to the bar to order a coffee for herself and a beer for Dave and she picked up a couple of bar food menus. She spotted the photographs of the naval war heroes immediately. The barman, whose name badge indicated he was named Miguel, seemed very friendly, so Carole decided to engage him in conversation.

'Hi, Miguel,' she said, bestowing on him her broadest smile and brandishing her mobile phone, 'would anyone mind if I used my camera phone to photograph those pictures you have on the wall. They're some local war heroes and my local history group is running a project on famous people who lived locally.'

The barman seemed surprised but he smiled back, 'of course not. But they're a bit high. I can do that for you, if you like.'

He put out his hand to take the mobile from her and, holding it on a level with the framed photographs on the wall behind him, he focused carefully before taking several shots, then handed back the phone.

'There was a man in here just a few nights ago who also asked me for copies of those photos,' Miguel said, as Carole tried to place his foreign accent.

'Yes. That was Malcolm Rawlinson. He was in the local history group, too. I suppose you heard what happened to him?'

'I did. The police were here. It's an awful thing to happen. Do you know if they caught the driver?'

'I don't believe so. I heard the security cameras in your car park were out of action.'

'Oh, no,' he protested. 'There's nothing wrong with the cameras. The police asked to check the recordings but there was no DVD in the machine.'

'Oh, dear,' Carole said, thinking that must have been an unbelievable stroke of luck for the hit and run driver that night. 'That's unfortunate. Did someone get in trouble over that?'

'I was on duty that night. It was my responsibility to change the DVD at the start of my shift, and I know I did so. Someone must have stolen it.'

'Really? Who would do that? Do they think the hit and run driver took it? I mean, how would he even know where to access the machine?'

'That's what I don't understand. The machine is in the manager's office behind reception. The office isn't kept locked when the manager's not on duty, but there's usually someone on the reception desk most of the time. They only leave it unattended for short periods in the evenings when they take their meal break. Maybe whoever took it guessed where the machine would be. But it's very strange.'

'Was anything else taken?'

'No. Just the CCTV recordings.'

'So, I suppose the police will be interviewing everyone staying at the hotel, and the staff too?' Carole reasoned.

'No, they didn't do that so far. I think they decided it was a drunk driver who didn't even realise he'd hit someone. I was disappointed that our manager didn't believe I'd changed the DVD. I expected him to stand up for me, however he and the police accepted the lack of CCTV footage was my fault. But I know it wasn't.'

Carole was shocked to hear this. The barman seemed genuinely upset. She ordered their drinks and took the menus back to Dave.

'You took your time,' he said. 'You and that good looking barman seemed to be getting on well. I thought you and he were about to get a room together.'

'Don't be daft,' she chided him. 'I was just picking his brains about the hit and run accident which happened here the other night. Only it's not sounding like an accident to me.'

'Oh no. Not another murder. Please tell me you haven't found another one to investigate.'

'No, Love. It's nothing to do with me. Anyway, I've ordered you a beer, so then, what would you say to a juicy steak sandwich?'

Carole was pleased to see Dave enjoying his lunch. He definitely seemed much more cheerful for having ventured out of the house. They passed an enjoyable hour at the *Austen Arms* and agreed they would return another time and try the restaurant menu. Carole remembered she hadn't left out any food for the dogs' lunch so they headed home. On their return, as they pulled into the driveway, they were surprised to find the dogs were out and were pacing about nervously in the front garden.

'Did you leave the back door open?' Dave asked.

'No, I know I locked it, and the dogs were definitely indoors when we left.'

At Dave's insistence, Carole remained in the car, her mobile phone at the ready, whilst Dave, firmly clutching his stout walking stick, let himself in via the front door and checked to see how the dogs had got out. Just moments later, he re-emerged, shaking his head ominously. Carole got out of the car.

'Looks like we've had a break-in,' he told her. 'The glass in the back door's smashed.'

'Oh, no,' Carole's heart sank as she followed him back in.

Carole experienced what was almost a sense of *déjà vu* as she stepped over the papers and books which were strewn over the sitting room floor. Every desk drawer and even the kitchen cupboards had been left open and most of their contents tossed out. The scene was reminiscent of the state in which Euphemia Isacson's killer had left her flat, although this time, mercifully, there was no dead body lying amongst the mess.

'The first time I venture out of the house in weeks and this happens,' Dave said. 'We'd best check to see what's been stolen. If you check upstairs, I'll have a look down here.'

As she turned back towards the stairs, Carole immediately spotted the twenty-pound note and three one-pound coins she had left on the window ledge by the front door to pay the window cleaner who was expected the following day. The money was lying exactly where she had left it, so she supposed the burglars must have overlooked it. After a thorough search of the house, however, they came to the conclusion that, in fact, nothing was missing.

It struck them as most odd that neither the few bits of cash, nor any of Carole's jewellery had been taken, and their television and other items of undoubted value to an opportunist burglar were left untouched. It appeared that someone had smashed the glass in the back door to access the lock, letting themselves in, and had rifled through all the paperwork in the house then had simply left, apparently empty-handed, leaving the backdoor open.

Just then, the doorbell rang. Carole went to answer it and saw a uniformed policeman standing on the step. She spotted Mrs Edmonds, their next-door neighbour standing at the front gate.

'Is everything okay?' The policeman asked. 'Only your neighbour here gave us a call. She said your dogs were barking fit to burst, and she realised you were out as your car wasn't there. Seeing your dogs were loose in the garden, she thought you might have had an intruder.'

'She was right,' Carole gave a wave of thanks to her neighbour and ushered the constable in. 'We've been burgled, all right, but it doesn't look as though anything's been taken.'

She led the policeman into the kitchen where Dave showed him the damage to the back door.

'This is how they got in but, like Carole says, nothing's missing.'

'I imagine the dogs barking probably put them off,' the policeman opined.

'You'd think the presence of two barking dogs would have put them off even *trying* to break in,' Dave said. 'But they've clearly come in and turned the place upside down, both down here and upstairs.'

'Like all greyhounds, though, Ronnie and Reggie are gentle souls,' Carole explained, as she stroked her still nervous pets. 'They'd bark at an intruder but they'd never attack him.'

'Ronnie and Reggie?' the policeman laughed. 'Like the Krays? I like it. Of course, the real Ronnie and Reggie would have taken a shotgun to your burglar. Well, I'll let CID know and they might send someone around to dust for fingerprints – eventually. I wouldn't hold your breath though. If nothing's been stolen, it was probably just kids who broke in.'

'You're probably right,' Dave agreed. 'And it's probably not worth sending anyone around. I'll get a glazier over soonest to repair the window. In fact, I might just get the door replaced with a more solid one.'

'And we thought this was such a nice neighbourhood,' Carole lamented, as she showed the policeman out.

'It is a nice neighbourhood, Carole,' Dave said as she closed the front door. 'I checked the crime stats before we even put in an offer on this place. Apart from a few opportunist thefts from unlocked car boots and a bit of petty shoplifting, there isn't a lot of crime around here.'

'So why …,' Carole began.

'I think whoever broke in did so because they were looking for something.'

'D'you think this might have something to do with my research?'

'You mean your investigation? Well now, I wonder who it is you've upset.'

Carole looked thoughtful for a few moments, then, on impulse, she headed into the kitchen.

'Dave,' she called out, moments later.

Dave followed and was surprised to see Carole on her hands and knees, searching through the under-sink cupboard.

'Dave, did you move that old red tartan biscuit tin that was in here?'

'No. What would I want with that?'

'Then the intruder must have taken it.'

'Why? What was in it?'

'Three little containers of river water. I was planning to take them to that forensics lab down near Abingdon where one of the scientists, Doctor Reid. has agreed to test the water for me.'

'Why?

'Because he owes me a favour. You remember we helped him out when they had that break-in by those Russians who were trying to access the nuclear reactor on the same site?'

'No, I mean why do you want the river water tested? Doesn't someone already test the water? The Isis Water Company, for example?'

'No. That's just it. They don't. Jazz Singh, he's one of the river watch group, he tests it for bacteria, and he and Rob Younger, he runs the group, he says there's probably heavy metals and all sorts of nasties in it. And Helen, who writes for *The Sentinel*, she's doing a piece on the river, and then there's …'

'All right, okay. Enough about river people and sentinels. I'm sorry I asked,' Dave held up his hands and, exasperated, limped off back to his armchair in the sitting room.

Later that afternoon, whilst Dave interrogated the Yellow Pages, seeking a replacement door company, Carole drove the long way round to the village again and called in at the pharmacy once more.

'Three *more* urine specimen bottles?' the startled assistant exclaimed. 'That must be one *hell* of an infection!'

***

At the next meeting of the U3A local history group, the talk was all about Malcolm's tragic death. Mo Durrani, a close friend of Malcolm's, said he had been to see Malcolm's widow and, having obtained her husband's car keys, he had collected their car and driven it back to the house. Social services were trying to organise some residential care for Dorothy, he explained, since she wouldn't be able to manage on her own. Mary asked Mo to liaise with Dorothy regarding funeral arrangements, since many of the U3A members would wish to attend.

'Don't you find it odd that the hotel's CCTV footage went missing on the evening he was killed?' Carole asked.

'Did it?' Mary was surprised. 'Wait a minute. You're not suggesting it was deliberate? Haven't the police decided it was an accident? You're surely not suggesting it was murder?'

'Who would want to kill Malcolm?' Mo asked. 'He was a delightful man. A real gentleman. Didn't have an enemy in the world.'

'Well, the barman at the hotel swears he'd put a new DVD into the machine, but when the police got to the hotel, there wasn't one in the machine. So, there were no CCTV images from the car park.'

'I would think it more likely the barman is lying to cover his mistake, rather than someone killed Malcolm deliberately then went into the hotel and stole the CCTV footage,' Mo said.

'We'll need someone to take over his research into the war heroes,' Mary said.

'I'll do that,' Mo volunteered. 'I would have volunteered to take on the war heroes myself rather than the vicars, especially since my own ancestors fought with the Baluchistan Infantry in Mesopotamia during

The Great War, but Malcolm beat me to it when Mary asked for volunteers.'

'I did think it odd that you were doing the vicars, Mo.' Carole added. 'I'm guessing from your name you would be Muslim?'

'That's right. But I didn't mind really. I'd never actually set foot inside a church before. The local parish churches are actually quite nice – historic and serene. Not knowing anything about Christianity, it's been a learning experience for me.'

'Do you think you'll be able to pick up where Malcolm left off?' Mary asked.

'I think so. Dorothy told me Malcolm had used his phone's camera to snap the photos of the Blounts in the bar at the *Austen Arms*. Unfortunately, they haven't yet found his phone. He must have dropped it in the car park. Dorothy asked me to have a look for it when I went to get the car but I couldn't see it. Maybe it will turn up.'

'I took some shots of those photos, too, Mo,' Carole said. 'I'll ping them over to you if you let me have your e-mail address.'

'So, everyone,' Mary moved them on. 'How are we all getting on with our research? Anyone got anything to report?'

Carole informed Mary that she had pretty much drawn a blank when it came to researching the local administrators, with the exception of one council chairman whose efforts had seen the construction and subsequent updating of Chalfont St George's Leisure Centre.

'Never mind the boring old administrators,' Daisy urged. 'How's the murder investigation going?'

'Well,' Carole said, 'I discovered, from a non-disclosable source, that Emerald Isacson's interests weren't confined to birdwatching.'

'Really?' Betty asked.

'Yes. It seems she also took a keen interest in the wildlife in and around the Misbourne.'

'Oh, how boring,' Betty exclaimed. 'I half expected you were going to tell us she'd been running a house of ill repute, or something equally scandalous.'

'Oi!' Kitty objected. 'There's nothing boring about our river and its fauna. It's one of the world's rarest chalk streams, you know.'

'It's one of the world's rarest open toilets at the moment,' Betty responded.

'Yes, well,' Carole interjected, 'as I'm sure Kitty will concede, the river water is badly polluted at the moment, and I have reason to think it was twenty-five years ago, too.'

'It's true, the Misbourne's always been subject to seasonal flooding and sewage contamination,' Tom agreed. 'I blame the Victorians. They didn't make the sewage pipes big enough. And they didn't bury them down far enough.'

'I don't suppose their planning took into account future expansion of the villages along the river,' Daisy added. 'They couldn't have imagined there would be this much development in our beautiful valley a century and a half down the line.'

'I blame Isis Water,' Mary chipped in. 'They don't want to spend the money to fix the problem. But those tankers must be costing them a fortune.'

'I think you'll find it's costing *us* a fortune,' Tom corrected her. 'That's why our water charges are so high, and they're set to increase further still.'

'Yes, well, that aside,' Carole said, 'I understand from speaking to Jazz, the local pharmacist, that he regularly tests the river water for bacteria, but, as far as he knows, no-one's ever tested it for the presence of other nasty things, you know, chemicals and stuff.'

'Yes, that's true,' Kitty confirmed, 'at least our river watch group hasn't.'

'Well, here's the thing,' Carole informed them. 'I took some samples of the water myself, intending to send them off to a forensic lab where I know one of the scientists, and he'd agreed he would run a whole range of tests for me.'

'Oh, brilliant!' Kitty enthused. 'Our little group doesn't have a budget and we could never afford those sorts of tests. They're very expensive. Rob did look into it.'

'Yes, but the thing is, our house was broken into and, oddly enough, the only thing the intruder stole was the water samples.'

'That *is* odd,' Mary agreed. 'Why would they take those? How would they even know you'd taken samples?'

'That's more than odd, Carole' Tom said, gravely. 'That's quite worrying. You know what that means, don't you?'

'No, what does it mean?'

'It means someone's been watching you.'

Chapter 18

Carole returned from the post office, having despatched her latest river water samples to the lab near Abingdon. Given Tom's suggestion that someone might be watching her, she had decided to post the samples, rather than risk being followed to the laboratory and perhaps even being robbed of her samples on the way. She had just pulled into the driveway when her mobile phone rang. It was Geoff Jackson from Thames Valley Police.

'This is highly irregular, you know, Carole,' he began. 'I'm not actually authorised to give out information from pathology reports to a civilian. I could get into trouble just for calling up the file. However, since it's you …,'

'Geoff, I'm very grateful to you. If this should help identify Emerald Isacson's killer, then you'll get the credit for solving the case. I promise you.'

'Fair enough. What was it you wanted to know?'

'Charlie Herron hanged himself from a tree branch – allegedly. Does the pathologist's report describe any other injuries he might have had, say, something which might suggest he was murdered, or that he might have been restrained in any way prior to death?'

'Let's see …, no, there's no injuries listed which are described as *pre-mortem*.'

'No? Nothing at all?'

'No, although there was a severe skull fracture, but the report suggests that could have happened when he was cut down. The report adds that he was a tall man and he weighed sixteen stone. He would have been a dead weight when he fell – no pun intended, I imagine – and there were rocks and logs lying around on the ground in the clearing where he was found. The pathologist suggests his head might have landed quite heavily on one of those and that might have done the damage.'

'I see. And did the pathologist definitely conclude the fracture occurred *post-mortem*?'

'Well, it says there was some blood found in the tissues beneath the scalp and surrounding the site of the fracture, which could suggest the heart was still beating *after* he sustained the injury to his skull. However, the pathologist states the bleeding could equally be the result of *petechiae.*'

'What's that?' Carole asked.

'Says here they would be blood vessels which had burst due to asphyxiation during the hanging, leaving blood trapped under the scalp, and the coroner suggests the blood could have been suffused more widely under the skin if the dead man's head impacted on a rock when he was cut down.'

'But it is just possible he was hit on the head with a rock and rendered unconscious, and then someone strung him up.'

'Yes, that would seem to be a possibility, but it looks like the pathologist dismissed that option. I guess he knew best. So, what's the connection between this man's death and that of the Isacson woman?'

'I don't know, yet, Geoff. But you might want to keep a copy of that pathologist's report handy, in case I do manage to establish a connection. I'll keep you informed of anything else I find.'

'Cheers, Carole. But if anyone asks, you didn't get this information from me. Okay?'

***

The following morning, Carole drove over to Briarfield and parked up in front of a row of quaint little cottages. She sat silently in the car for a few minutes, working out exactly what she would say to Charlie Herron's widow. Even assuming Mrs Herron still lived at the same address, she might not wish to be reminded of the manner of her late husband's death. Carole would have to handle this enquiry with the utmost tact. Eventually, she summoned up the courage to get out of the car and go and knock on the door.

The seventy-something lady who answered the door seemed friendly enough and confirmed she was Mrs Herron.

'I do hope I'm not disturbing you, Mrs Herron, but my name's Carole Murray and I'm researching some of the famous and infamous people who have lived around this area in the past. It's for a project the members of my U3A local history group are putting together.'

'Oh? Well, I don't think I qualify as either famous or infamous, Dear,' Mrs Herron laughed.

Carole felt it was a good sign that, despite the tragedy which had entered the woman's life, albeit twenty-odd years ago, she had a sense of humour.

'The person I'm researching at the moment, well, it's three people, actually, is a famous scientist who lived here in Briarfield with his equally famous opera singer wife and his daughters, one of whom also went on to be a successful scientist.'

'Oh, and did they live here in my little house?'

'No, I haven't yet housed them,' Carole bit her tongue, realising she had inadvertently used a term more commonly used by police and intelligence staff to describe the act of establishing where a suspect lived.

'I mean, I'm not exactly sure which was their house, but the daughter of the family, the scientist daughter, she was tragically murdered.'

'You're talking about the Isacson woman, aren't you? The body in the woods case. My late husband found the body, you know.'

Carole was relieved that Mrs Herron had recalled the case and had mentioned it first. She felt this made things a little easier. However, it looked as though Mrs Herron's memory might not be that dependable, since, according to the police files, it was a dog-walker who had found the body in the woods.

'Yes, that's her, and I understand it was your husband who wrote the press story about the case. It was an excellent article. All the nationals picked it up.'

'That's right. My Charlie was so proud of that scoop.'

'Well, the members of my group are thinking they might turn our project into a book and I thought the Isacson murder would be an interesting inclusion. I was hoping you might just have kept some of your husband's notes on the case and that I might be able to see them.'

Mrs Herron seemed thoughtful and Carole hoped she hadn't caused the lady to recall a truly upsetting time in her life. It was a few moments before she replied.

'Well, I might be able to help you. Would you like to come in?'

Over a cup of tea, the journalist's widow explained what had happened to her late husband's papers.

'As you can see, this is a rather small house, and Charlie used the little back bedroom as his study. He had a desk in there and shelves for all his box files. His brother and family flew over from Canada for the funeral and I needed the space to put them up. I got my son Raymond to clear out the study so we could use it as a bedroom for my nephews.'

'Ah, so I imagine you threw away your husband's papers?'

'Oh no, Dear. Ray took them away. Not sure whether he'd have kept them. He followed his father into journalism, you know. He's a political correspondent, though. Works mainly in radio and television. He's not really interested in crime stories.'

'Ray Herron? Of course, I've heard of him. Does he still live locally?' Carole asked, hopefully.

'Not round here, no. He's up in Hertfordshire. It's not too far way, mind. I could give you his phone number and you could give him a call. He'll be able to tell you if he's kept the papers on that murder case.'

'Thank you. I'd appreciate that. You say Charlie actually found the body? That must have been upsetting.'

'It didn't seem to affect him at the time, but it must have preyed on his mind, I suppose. I mean, there wasn't any other reason why he … you do know he killed himself, don't you?'

'I did hear that, Mrs Herron. And I'm so sorry. It must have been a terrible shock for you.'

'It was. So unexpected. I never understood why he did it. He didn't leave a note or anything. At the inquest, the coroner asked me if he'd been depressed. But he hadn't. He was always so upbeat about everything, my Charlie. And he was so proud of our boys. He'd never have left them without their daddy.'

'If you don't mind me asking, on the day he found Miss Isacson's body, do you know why he'd gone to the woods?'

'Not really. He'd been working on some story or other. Don't know what it was, but he seemed pretty excited about it. I got the impression he was expecting to meet someone up there. When he came back, he looked … shaken. He didn't talk about it much. The awful thing is that he didn't go into those woods again, not until the day he died. That day, he told me he was going up there again and I made some pathetic little joke, like 'don't go finding any more dead bodies', but he didn't. That day, *his* was the dead body that was found in the woods.'

'In his article he wrote for *The Sentinel*, he said it was a dog walker who found the body of Doctor Isacson.'

'Yes, he did write that. I've always wondered why. When he came back from the woods, he told me he'd stumbled across the body himself and he'd called the police. Maybe he said it was a dog walker because finding the body had upset him so much. If that were the case, though, you'd think he'd never want to go near those woods again, wouldn't you?'

'I'm so sorry, Mrs Herron. I hope my asking my silly questions hasn't upset you.'

'No, you're all right, Dear. It's all so long ago. It's just water under the bridge now. Let me write down our Ray's number for you.'

'Thank you for your time, Mrs Herron, and for the tea,' Carole said as she headed out of the cottage. 'And I do apologise if my questions were intrusive. I didn't mean to get you talking about the time you lost your husband.'

'No, you're all right, Dear. It was the most awful time, heartbreaking. You know, it's bad enough burying your husband, the father of your boys, and him only in his forties. But to have someone burgle your house whilst you're at the funeral, that was the absolute pits.'

'I'm sorry?' Carole pulled up short. 'You were burgled? On the day of the funeral?'

'Yes. The police said the burglar would probably have read the funeral announcement in *The Sentinel* and knew there'd be nobody home. That's what they do, apparently. No scruples some people.'

'Oh, that's truly despicable. Did they take much?'

'No. We didn't have much to take. They must have been disappointed. Goodness knows, though, they searched the place hard enough. Left a right mess.'

As she drove home, Carole considered all she had learned and she tried to make sense of it. It might have been a dog walker who had discovered Charlie Herron's body but, if his widow was correct, it was Herron himself who had discovered Emerald Isacson's body and not, on *that* occasion, a dog walker. Even though, for whatever reason, Herron had claimed someone else had found Emerald's body, surely Walter Gerrard would have known the truth. Why would he maintain the story about a dog walker having found it? It seemed he'd also been wrong about Charlie Herron's wife having left him, and he was probably wrong about Herron being an alcoholic. Was his memory faulty, though, or was he lying? Was he guilty of mis-remembering, Carole wondered, or was it … misdirection?

Carole wondered how Herron had managed to be first at the scene of Emerald's murder. His widow suggested he had gone to the woods to meet somebody on the day Emerald died, so had that somebody been Emerald? Had Charlie Herron met and killed Emerald? That seemed unlikely, since he had immediately reported finding her body. Perhaps he had witnessed the murder, though? But surely, he would have told the police that? Did Emerald's killer know Charlie had seen him and had he later lured Charlie into the woods in order to kill him, too? But why would he wait eighteen months to do so? Why would Emerald even want to meet with a reporter? And why there, in the middle of woodland? Maybe Charlie had arranged to meet Emerald there for some reason but had arrived after the killer had left? Once again, there were more questions than answers.

Then, there were the break-ins. Charlie Herron's house had been burgled whilst his family members were attending his funeral, albeit that, apparently, nothing was stolen. Presumably, the intruder was looking for something specific. But did he find it? If he'd been looking for something contained in Herron's papers, then he wouldn't have found it, as his widow had already cleared his papers out before the funeral.

Euphemia Isacson's flat had been ransacked by her killer, too, and now Carole and Dave had been visited by an intruder, but nothing of any value had been stolen. She didn't need her sceptical husband to tell her these were not coincidences. The fact that the only thing stolen from Carole and Dave's house was the samples of river water, told her that the answer to all her questions was quite possibly to be found … in the Misbourne.

Chapter 19

It was half past four in the morning when Carole suddenly awoke and sat bolt upright in the bed.

'Oh, God!' she exclaimed.

Instantly, Dave was awake, too. He flung back the duvet and thrust his good leg out of the bed and onto the floor.

'What is it? Did you hear something?' he asked, as he wiped the sleep from his eyes and grabbed his walking stick from the bedside rug. 'If those intruders are back ...,'

'No, it's not that,' Carole said. 'I've just had a terrible thought.'

'A terrible thought? You mean a nightmare or something? You were dreaming?'

'No, Love. It's just occurred to me. Something Tom Sharples said.'

Dave blinked at his wife in disbelief.

'Something Tom Sharples said to you has just occurred to you, at God-knows-what-time in the morning, and you woke me up to tell me?'

'No, what I mean is, Tom pointed out that the only way the intruders could have known about the river water samples I took is because they've been watching me. And if they've been watching me, they might have followed me to Mrs Herron's house. Someone broke into her house twenty-odd years ago, while she was at her husband's funeral. And, just days after I visited Euphemia Isacson, someone broke into her house, ransacked it and killed her. If it was the same person, and if they know Mrs Herron's been speaking to me, they might break into her house again and this time they might kill her, too. I've got to warn her.'

'What? No, wait a minute. Let's think this through first,' Dave switched on his bedside lamp, glanced at the clock and, on seeing the time, did a double take. 'Oh, God, it's half past four. So, look, we think they broke into Euphemia's because they were looking for something, right?'

'Right.'

'And maybe they killed her because she wouldn't, or couldn't give them what they were looking for. Right?'

'Right.'

'And we think they broke in here because they were looking for something, which they did find, and they took it away. Right?'

'Yes, that's right.'

'So, if they didn't find what they were looking for the first time they broke into the Herrons' house, why would they have any reason to break in again now, twenty-odd years later? Why would they think they'd find it now, when they didn't find it back then? And what do we think *it* is, anyway?'

'Well, I don't know, Dave. But I suspect it's something to do with the river. And what if they don't like the fact that Mrs Herron has been speaking to me? What if they decide to kill her just *because* she's been speaking to me?'

'Why would they do that?'

'Well, because of what she might know.'

'And do you know what it is she might know?'

'No.'

'So, why would they wait till now to kill Mrs Herron?'

'Well, why did they wait till now to kill Euphemia?'

'As it happens, I've been giving that some thought. And I think I might know why?'

'Why?'

'Look, I'm never going to get back to sleep now, so let's get up and you can make us some coffee and we can talk this through. Okay?'

'Okay, Love. Thanks.'

The rain was still falling outside and so they took their coffee into the sitting room and curled up together on the sofa under a warm woollen throw.

'So, what's your theory, then, ex-detective Dave?' Carole asked.

'Supposing Euphemia Isacson *wasn't* Euphemia Isacson.'

'What? Well, she *said* she was Euphemia Isacson. If she wasn't Euphemia, who else would she be?'

'Supposing she was Emerald Isacson,' Dave suggested.

'But Emerald died twenty-five years ago.'

'Did she, though? What if, all those years ago, the killer had murdered Euphemia by mistake, thinking she was Emerald? I mean, you said both sisters were into birdwatching. The killer might have followed the sister he *thought* was Emerald into that wood when she was birdwatching and killed her, but it was actually Euphemia he killed.'

'But, why would he want to kill either of them?'

'Maybe he thought the sister with the binoculars wasn't birdwatching, but observing something else. Perhaps he thought she was spying on him. Or maybe he wanted Emerald dead for some reason, but mistook Euphemia for her. And supposing Emerald guessed the killer had meant to kill *her*, not Euphemia, then perhaps she reasoned that, once they realised their mistake, they'd come after her again. So, perhaps the best way she could think of to protect herself was to pretend to be her sister.'

'You think, maybe, that's why she quit teaching right after the murder?'

'Yes. It's unlikely she could have fooled the other teachers into thinking she was her sister. And maybe that's why she buried herself away in that little flat over the teashop.'

'Well, that seems a bit of a far-fetched idea, but what made you think of it?'

'You told me one of Euphemia's teacher colleagues described her as difficult or unpleasant or something, and he said she'd been quite jealous of her sister Emerald.'

'Yes. That's what Tom told me he heard from his neighbour. But I didn't find Euphemia at all unpleasant. In fact, she was rather sweet.'

'So, maybe that's because the sister you met was Emerald, not Euphemia.'

Carole considered this for a few moments. It certainly did seem an outlandish suggestion, but it was at least a possibility. However, something else occurred to her.

'But if Emerald was worried the killer might come back for her, why didn't she tell the police?'

'Maybe she doubted the police would be able to help her,' Dave suggested, clearly still thinking it through himself. 'I mean, maybe she knew who the killer was but couldn't prove it. Maybe he was someone powerful – someone high up. Maybe someone in the police. Or in government. Her boss, or someone.'

'But, why didn't she just move away? She could have changed her name and moved somewhere safer?'

'It's not that easy for an individual to change their identity and their location. Not if they want to sell a property or to receive their pension. We, of all people, know that. Even when, as a powerful organisation, we had to re-locate some of the agents I used to handle, giving them new identities and a new location, we weren't always successful. It wasn't always possible to keep them safe forever. Remember Ivan Vasilevsky? They got him with a car bomb.'

'That's true,' Carole shuddered at the memory of Dave's first case with the firm, and the awful sight they both witnessed of the aftermath.

'If she had run away,' Dave continued, 'her killer might have guessed she was Emerald and would have tried to find her. But the killer had no reason to kill the woman he *thought* was Emerald's sister. By taking on her sister's identity and staying put, she was able to hide in plain sight.'

'Hide in plain sight? Yes, I can see that would work. And it looks like it did work for her – until now. But now that she's dead, too, I don't suppose there's anyway of proving she was really Emerald.'

'Dental records might prove it. We should probably do a little more digging before we speak to DI Hogget about this, though.'

'Yes, but if we wait too long, Hogget will have to do some digging, too. Once they bury her, he'll have to dig her up to check her teeth against Emerald's dental records.'

'That's true. So, what do you plan to do next?'

'I've arranged for us to drive up to St Albans later this morning. I called the Herrons' son and he says he's kept a lot of his father's papers. I think we might just discover what's behind the murders if we can have a look at those papers. We might find a link between Charlie Herron and Emerald Isacson. We might also find out who he was planning to meet up there in the woods on the day he died.'

'Actually, if it stops raining, that could be a nice little run out into Hertfordshire for the two of us. We could treat ourselves to lunch at a nice country pub.'

'Four of us.'

'Eh?'

'I've asked Daisy Cooper and Kitty Walker to come along, too. Reason is that Raymond Herron reckons his father left twenty years' worth of paperwork. I thought we'd need some help going through it all.'

'Okay. Well, if you're dragging me off to deepest Hertfordshire in this rain to sort through some mouldy old paperwork, I'm going to need a decent breakfast first.'

'A full English?'

'The works.'

***

They set off after breakfast, collecting Daisy and Kitty on the way. During the forty-minute drive along the A404, Carole explained Dave's theory to their incredulous passengers.

'That sounds a bit far-fetched,' Daisy declared.

'That's what I said,' Carole agreed. 'But then again, I asked myself why anyone would murder a seventy-odd-year-old teashop proprietor.'

'So, even assuming Euphemia *was* really Emerald,' Kitty reasoned, 'that means it's taken the killer twenty-five years to realise his mistake.'

'Possibly,' Daisy agreed. 'But why did he come after her now? *How* did he find out she was Emerald?'

'Oh, God! I was hoping you wouldn't ask that. D'you think it might be my fault?' Carole asked. 'I mean, Euphemia, or Emerald, or whichever sister she was, was killed after I visited her. D'you think my researching the original murder has stirred things up?'

Nobody answered. Carole guessed they'd all been thinking that but hadn't wanted to say so. She began to feel awful. Eventually, it was Dave who sought to reassure her.

'Not necessarily, Love. I mean, you don't know who else this Miss Isacson had been speaking to. And we don't absolutely know for sure that she was really Emerald, or, if she was, that the killer found out she was. It might be a simple case that she disturbed a burglar. Her death might have nothing to do with her sister's death all those years ago.'

'But both sisters were hit over the head. Both were attacked from behind and smashed on the back of the head, weren't they?'

'Yes, but that might just be a …,' Dave began.

'A coincidence?' Carole interjected. 'You don't believe in coincidences, though, do you?'

'No, but if I was going to murder a sweet little old lady – not that I ever would – I'd probably hit her over the head from behind. That way I wouldn't have to look her in the face. Maybe anyone wanting to kill a sweet little old lady wouldn't want to see her face as they did it.'

'You're only saying that to make me feel better.'

'What? That I wouldn't murder a little old lady?'

'No, that her murder might not be my fault.'

'Who else knows you're investigating Emerald's murder, Carole?' Kitty asked.

'Apart from our fellow *Third Agers*, there's Geoff Jackson in TVP's unsolved crimes unit.'

'He's a good bloke,' Dave assured her. 'I worked with him.'

'And there's Walter Gerrard,' Carole continued, 'the retired detective who investigated the murder twenty-five years ago. Then there's Helen Chandler, a freelance reporter, and now Mrs Herron, and her son that we're going to see today.'

'Anyone else?' Daisy asked.

'And Justin Buchanan at the *Sentinel* knows I've been enquiring about the death of Charlie Herron. And his assistant, Trudy. I think that's about it.'

'Jazz Singh knows,' Kitty corrected her. 'And Rob Younger. You told them when we were in the pub. And I expect Jazz's wife Kulwinder knows, if Jazz has mentioned it to her. But Rob and Jazz and Kulwinder are good people. They wouldn't murder anyone.'

'No, they wouldn't,' Daisy agreed. 'But you don't know who else they might have told. The fact that Carole is investigating a murder is hugely interesting. It could be all round the village by now.'

'Researching,' Carole corrected her, 'not investigating.'

'Same thing,' Dave said. 'Especially the way you go about researching things. Talk about a dog with a bone. But what we haven't considered in all this is motive. Why was Emerald Isacson targeted in the first place?'

'I've a feeling we might find the answer to that in Charlie Herron's papers,' Carole said. 'At least I hope we do.'

'Carole, you just passed the turnoff for St Albans,' Dave warned, as Carole continued along the route to Hatfield.

'It's okay, I meant to take this road,' Carole advised, as she turned left into a quiet narrow farm drive and pulled up. 'I just wanted to make sure we're not being followed.'

In the back seat, Kitty glanced slowly and ominously across at Daisy. Daisy returned her alarmed look.

Carole waited for a few minutes, until, gazing into her rear-view mirror, she saw three or four cars driving past on the road to Hatfield, then she reversed back out of the farm drive and headed back the way they had come before taking the turnoff to St Albans.

'Just a small precaution,' she reassured them. 'Can't be too careful with a murderer around.'

Dave glanced over his shoulder at Daisy and Kitty. They didn't look the slightest bit reassured.

Chapter 20

The six huge tea chests which confronted them when Raymond Herron opened the automatic gates of the double garage adjoining his five-bedroom Arts and Crafts style house presented a formidable challenge.

'I did tell you there was a *lot* of paperwork, didn't I?' Andrew said, apologetically. 'But it's all in box files and they're marked alphabetically. So long as you know what you're looking for, it might not take you too long to find it.'

'That's just it, though,' Carole said. 'We don't really know. But how did all this stuff fit in the boxroom in your parents' little cottage?'

'It didn't. Dad rented a lockup garage where he kept most of this. After he died, I just cleared out what was in their box room and took it to the lock-up. Eventually, when I bought this place, I gave up the rental on the lock-up, hired a van and brought all Dad's papers here. I'm sorry to say they've been sitting here in the garage all these years gathering dust. I'd been meaning to sort them all out and get rid of them, but every time I came in here and looked at the papers, the sheer size of the task overwhelmed me. My plan was to wait until the day we ever decide to move house again and to have a really big bonfire.'

The four friends stood and stared at the tea chests as the enormity of their task overwhelmed them, too.

'Let me get you some garden chairs so you can at least sit down on the job,' Ray offered. 'And I expect some tea would be welcome, too.'

'I know,' Carole said, when she had peered into the chests. 'Since they're alphabetically arranged, why don't we take six box files each and go through them. Daisy, you take, A to F, Kitty, you take G to L, then if Dave takes M to R, I'll take the rest?'

'That means you get eight box files, Carole,' Daisy, the mathematics whizz, pointed out.

'That's okay. It was my daft idea to drag you all down here. In any case, I don't suppose there'll be too many papers in the X, Y and Z box files.'

Three hours and two rounds of tea later, Dave suddenly brandished a thick manilla folder in the air.

'Bingo! I think this must be it.'

'What is it?' Carole asked excitedly.

'It was in the 'M' box. It's a file marked 'Misbourne'. Just flicking through the papers inside, I see the name Isacson mentioned numerous times.'

'Does that mean we can stop looking now?' Kitty asked wearily.

'I'm not sure,' Carole said. 'There might be more stuff that's relevant in the box files we haven't checked yet.'

'Judging by how long it's taken me to go through three of my six boxes, and that's about an hour a box,' Daisy said, looking at her watch, 'if I have to go through the remaining three, we'll still be sitting here after dark.'

'I agree with our mathematician friend's calculations,' Kitty said. 'And besides, I'm getting cold. And hungry. You did promise us lunch, Carole.'

'Okay, well, who checked the 'I' box? Were there any papers in it marked 'Isacson'?' Carole asked.

'I just did, and there weren't,' Kitty said. 'Haven't come across anything at all mentioning the Isacsons.'

'Okay, then let's call it a day. Let me have that Misbourne file, Dave. I'll call at the house and ask Ray if it's okay to take it away. I'll take the tea things back, too. Whilst I do that, will you put all your box files back in the tea chests? Then we'll go and find somewhere nice to eat. Lunch is on me.'

Although Carole was very eager to begin perusing the 'Misbourne' file as soon as possible, Dave told her it would be unwise to get the file out in the pub restaurant. He urged her to wait until they got home. She could hardly contain herself, but she knew Dave was right.

***

'You don't really think we were followed to St Albans, do you?' Carole asked as they let themselves into Rowan Tree Cottage that evening. 'I'd hate to think we might have put Ray Herron and his family in any danger.'

'No, I didn't notice anyone on our tail,' Dave assured her. 'And I was keeping an eye out via the car's vanity mirror. I'm used to checking behind me when I'm driving. It was necessary whenever I'd meet up with agents for the firm. Old habits die hard.'

'That's true. Should we crack open a bottle of wine whilst we look through Charlie's file?'

'Good idea. And we'll need to think of a really safe place to keep the file. Don't want it to go the way of your water samples. I don't think Ronnie and Reggie's nerves would stand another break-in.'

Carole fetched a bottle of red wine and two glasses and they settled down on the sofa to begin perusing the fruits of the late Charlie Herron's research. Since the papers in the file were neatly arranged in date order, the oldest at the back, Dave suggested unlacing all the documents from the file, placing them upside down on the coffee table and each taking one document at a time to read, so they'd be perusing the oldest first.

It was almost midnight by the time they had devoured and discussed the entire contents of the file and had finished the wine. Dave turned to Carole, his face grave.

'This is dynamite, Love,' he said. 'And, like dynamite, it's dangerous to keep it in the house. We'll need to work out what to do with it. It's not safe to keep it here.'

'I think we should sleep on it.'

'You're right. Things should seem clearer in the morning.'

'No, Dave. I mean *literally* sleep on it. I'm going to tuck the file under our mattress for tonight. And, yes, we can work out what to do with it tomorrow.'

It took Carole a long time to fall asleep. She couldn't relax as her head was full of the concerning facts she had read in Charlie Herron's 'Misbourne' file. The information kept going around and around in her head. When, finally, she did nod off, she began to dream a strange dream. She was floating along very slowly in the inky and stinky black waters of the Misbourne. As she meandered along with the flow, passing through meadows and pastureland, she glimpsed terrible sights on each river bank. There was a flock of freakish two-headed sheep, a cow which was a kind of push-me-pull-you creature with a head at each end of its body, and there were some giant hens which squawked alarmingly as they galloped alongside her, pausing only to lay huge and oddly luminous eggs on the river bank.

Eventually, Carole's hallucinatory 'Alice in Wonderland' journey came to an abrupt end when she was confronted by a massive crustacean swimming upstream towards her, waving huge and threatening claws in her direction and making a strangely incongruous squeaking sound. Mercifully, she awoke with a start before the fearsome aquatic monster actually devoured her whole. She sat upright, breathing heavily, but relieved to find she was in their own cosy dry bed and not in the cold and sewage-laden river.

Dave lay sleeping peacefully beside her, so she laid her head back on her pillows again. Then, she heard it again. It was the same squeaking noise the monster lobster creature had been emitting in her dream. However, she now realised it was a familiar squeaking sound. It was the sound their kitchen door made whenever it was opened or closed. Of course, the kitchen door was usually left open during the day, mainly because it was the most used room in the house. The kitchen door was only ever closed at night or when they were out, and that was to stop Ronnie and Reggie going in and foraging for food. Greyhounds, Carole had discovered, were incorrigible counter surfers. She feared it was only a matter of time before they worked out how to open the refrigerator.

Realising Dave must have failed to close the kitchen door properly and the dogs must have got in there, Carole climbed out of bed intending to go down and close it. She checked herself for a second or two, however, and wondered whether the noise might have been caused by the intruders again. She told herself that was most unlikely, since the dogs hadn't barked. However, though she felt it was probably an unnecessary precaution, she picked up Dave's walking stick from the bedside rug. She descended the stairs into the darkened downstairs hallway – mentally cursing the fact that their old cottage did not have a light switch on the upstairs landing connected to the downstairs hall light. That was another of the little jobs Dave had planned to organise before he had broken his ankle. As she reached the bottom of the stairs, she realised the squeaking noise had stopped.

She headed for the hall light switch but was suddenly aware of a draught coming from the direction of the front door. Dave must have left the front door open as well, she supposed. It wasn't like him to be that careless, however, and she froze and listened. Suddenly, she was aware of movement in front of her. She glimpsed the outline of a man in the darkness, a shadowy figure emerging from the dining room and standing still just a few feet in front of her. His shape was outlined against the dim moonlight which shone in via the open front door. Startled, she raised the walking stick and took a couple of steps back.

That was when she fell backwards over a sleeping dog. To her surprise, the dog did not stir. However, Carole did. Letting out a blood-curdling scream, she leapt to her feet again and struck out with the walking stick. She felt it connect with the side of the intruder's head.

Immediately, he fled out via the front door. Seconds later, the upstairs landing light was switched on, enabling Carole to locate the light switch and turn on the hall light. Dave came rushing downstairs, as fast as his still healing ankle would allow.

'Carole, are you okay?' he gasped. 'What is it? What happened?'

'The intruder. He came back,' she panted, and she crouched down to check on Ronnie.

To her surprise Ronnie was still sleeping soundly. Dave took the walking stick from Carole and hobbled past her to the front door. At the sound of a car driving away, he came back and the couple began to hunt around for Reggie. They found him, also sound asleep, in the kitchen. Neither dog could be roused from their deep slumber.

'They've been drugged,' Dave announced as he closed the front door and bolted it. 'I think we're going to need a new front door as well as a back door. They got through this one too easily.'

'I'll put the kettle on,' Carole offered. 'I think we need some hot, strong tea.'

'Good. And then, as soon as it's light, we're going to the police. We're going to give them the file and we're going to hand the investigation over to them. Okay?'

'I suppose so.'

'I mean it, Carole. You need to let this go now.'

'Hmmh,' Carole nodded.

Chapter 21

Carole couldn't tell whether or not DI Bernard Hogget was buying their story. His expression was one of polite scepticism as Dave outlined his theory regarding Euphemia having been killed by mistake and Emerald having assumed Euphemia's identity. When Dave had finished his explanation, Hogget sat back in his chair and took a deep breath. Eventually, he spoke.

'But why, Dave? Why would anyone want to kill Emerald in the first place?'

Dave produced the 'Misbourne' file and slid it across the table towards the detective.

'This makes grim reading,' he warned. 'But it's all in here. What Emerald had discovered was a huge cover-up by the authorities.'

'What sort of cover-up?' Hogget asked, without even glancing at the file.

'Emerald Isacson, the scientist sister, had long suspected the River Misbourne was being polluted,' Dave said.

'She wasn't wrong,' the detective said. 'It's full of sh...,'

'Yes,' Carole interrupted, 'but it wasn't just sewage. She tested the water and found even worse pollutants than e-coli. She found heavy metals – just about every kind of heavy metal, and in really high concentrations. There was cadmium, chromium, nickel, arsenic. A whole cocktail of deadly poisons.'

'That's right,' Dave added. 'She also found some other nasties, substances called PFOs.'

'Not to be confused with UFOs, I suppose,' the detective said, his expression now one of incredulity.

'You really should take this seriously, Bernie,' Dave urged. 'I looked them up. PFOs are perfluoro-octane sulphonates. They're known as 'forever drugs' because, once they get into the ecosystem, they hang around forever, in the soil, in the groundwater and in the organs of animals and humans.'

'Yes, and they're highly carcinogenic,' Carole added.

'If they're so dangerous, who's putting them out there, and why?' Hogget asked. 'Where do they come from?'

'I looked that up, too,' Dave explained. 'For decades, they've been used in the manufacture of a huge range of goods. They're in paper, in the plastic laminate in your passport, in the household polish you spray on your dining table, and even in the stain repellent spray you use on your upholstery. From there, they get into the air you breathe and the water you drink. They're everywhere, but the dangers they present to wildlife and to humans wasn't known until Emerald Isacson tried to tell the world twenty-five years ago.'

'That's right,' Carole agreed. 'It's all in Charlie Herron's file. Emerald realised the PFOs were also used in really high concentrations in fire-fighting foam. She realised there was a link between PFOs and the high cancer rates found amongst fire-fighters, including the RAF's wartime fire-fighters who'd trained up at the site where her laboratories were.'

'Is there such a link?' Hogget asked. 'I didn't know that.'

'Yes,' Carole continued. 'Once she discovered that link, Emerald tested the soil in the grounds up at the Chiltern Biosciences lab where she worked. She found huge concentrations of PFOs there. She realised that was because, during the war years, the estate had been a training centre for RAF ground crews. They'd been continually drenching the grounds in foam as they practised putting out aircraft fires.'

'Yes, and the PFOs soaked into the soil there and slowly leached down the hill into Percival's Woods, and into the storm drains. It's been pouring downhill into the River Misbourne for years,' Dave added. 'Emerald Isacson found out it was harming the local wildlife. It was killing the fish in the river, and the birds who ate the fish, and it was also harming adults and children in the community.'

'Harming them how?' Hogget asked, his expression reflecting a greater interest now.

'She persuaded the children's clinics in the villages along the river to begin routinely testing children's blood, and the doctors discovered local children had higher than average levels of lead and other poisons in their blood,' Dave explained. 'Many of them were suffering from rickets and restricted growth. Rickets hasn't been common in this country since the war.'

'Yes, and exposure to cadmium is a major cause of osteomalacia – that's the adult form of rickets,' Carole chipped in. 'It also causes lung cancer. The chromium in the river can cause liver and kidney damage and it affects the central nervous system.'

'And were there cases of those conditions in the villages, too?' Hogget asked, pulling the file across the desk towards him and opening it tentatively.

'Yes,' Carole replied. 'Emerald got the parish council chairman, Andrew Maudsley, to trawl through the records of fishing licenses issued locally and she visited all the anglers on the list. For decades, they'd been fishing the Misbourne for signal crayfish and trout, and eating them. She found half the anglers had died prematurely and they'd all been suffering a variety of cancers she believed were caused by the toxicity of the water.'

'Good God!' Hogget exclaimed. 'I used to catch fish in the Misbourne when I was a lad. I caught many a tasty trout down there.'

'Emerald tested locally produced hens' eggs and also local honey,' Carole continued, 'and she found those products were heavily contaminated, too. So was the water cress growing around the river.'

'So, what did she do with this information?' Hogget asked.

'She and Maudsley contacted the Ministry of Defence,' Dave explained. 'They were the owners of the land the labs were built on, and they still own the land today. The MOD agreed to conduct their own tests, but *their* test results showed very low levels of metals and no PFOs.'

'And you're thinking the MOD's test results were doctored?' the detective asked.

'That's what Emerald thought,' Carole agreed. 'The MOD must have known her findings were right. That's why, after the war, they leased out the land to a radiochemical company which was producing large quantities of radium from concentrates and using it for medical diagnostic purposes. It's not clear whether MOD told the company the land was contaminated.'

'That company produced, amongst other things, isotopes for use by medical radiographers,' Dave added. 'When that company left the site – for reasons which were not recorded – it was next leased to the Chiltern Biosciences Institute, the outfit Doctor Emerald Isacson worked for. She also found high levels of radioactive substances in the soil, presumably left by the previous occupants. Her own company left the site around five years ago, since which time it's been abandoned. It's still a toxic wasteland. The MOD knows the land is heavily contaminated. If it wasn't, they'd have sold it off to developers long ago, and for megabucks.'

'That's right,' Carole agreed. 'With all the facilities of Chalfont St George nearby and a fast rail link to London from Gaunt's Cross, it'd be prime building land, but for the contamination.'

'So, this Maudsley chap, the councillor, what did he do about it?' Hogget asked. 'Didn't he report Doctor Isacson's findings?'

'Apparently, he tried to,' Dave said. 'There are copies in this file of letters he wrote to the local MP and to the defence minister. But no-one would listen. He and Doctor Isacson then spoke with a journalist about it. The journalist, Charlie Herron, put together this file with all their evidence. He was planning to go public with the scandal.'

'So, why didn't he?'

'Because,' Carole explained, 'before he could do so, he died. Although the verdict was suicide by hanging, he had what seems to me to be a *pre-mortem* skull fracture to the back of the head, just as both Isacson sisters had. Herron was probably alive but unconscious when a rope was tied around his neck and he was suspended from a tree – in the same wood where Isacson met her death.'

'Good God! That's awful. So, I suppose his death dissuaded Maudsley from speaking out?'

'No,' Carole said. 'He died prematurely, too, several months *before* Herron died. Maudsley drowned – allegedly.'

'In the Misbourne?' Hogget asked.

'No, in the swimming pool at the leisure centre,' Carole advised. 'Apparently, he made an unauthorised visit on his own to the swimming pool late one night and he went too close to the edge, fell in and drowned. I've got someone checking the undertaker's records to see whether he also had an injury to the back of his head, like the others. I'm pretty certain he will have done. If so, then that makes four potential murders.'

'This is a lot to take in,' Hogget said. 'I'm sure there's some sort of register of contaminated sites, though. We should check that out.'

'Carole already did that,' Dave said. 'It's a file in the parish council offices. But it's blank. According to that file, there's no contaminated land anywhere in the parish.'

'So, maybe we should get the ground tested independently. And the river water, too,' Hogget suggested.

'I've already got someone testing some river water samples for me,' Carole advised. 'A government scientist I know and trust. I'm just waiting for the results.'

'But there's one thing I don't understand,' Hogget frowned. 'One of the Isacson sisters, and the journalist and the parish councillor all died twenty-five years ago. But the subject of my investigation, the other Miss Isacson, was only killed a couple of weeks ago. Why now?'

Dave glanced sideways at Carole. He didn't want to alarm her unduly, but he guessed she already realised how much danger they were in.

'I think someone knows Carole and I have been looking into the original murders. Someone found out Carole had visited the surviving Miss Isacson. Days later, *that* Miss Isacson was murdered, too. If they still believed the surviving sister was Euphemia, they might have thought she actually knew what her sister Emerald had known about the contamination and that she was telling Carole. Or, they might have worked out for themselves that she really was Emerald but they'd left her alone so long as she kept silent about what she knew. In either case, someone doesn't want us digging up their dirty secrets. And they're prepared to break into our home to stop us.'

'You've been broken into?' Hogget seemed surprised.

'Yes. Twice. The first time, we were out, and all they stole was a first set of water samples Carole had taken from the river. The second time was just last night, whilst we were asleep. And we think they were after this file. They probably slipped something through our letter box, too, something which drugged our dogs. Knocked them out for hours. Ronnie and Reggie will eat anything.'

'This is very worrying,' Hogget said, gravely. 'I know you're an ex-detective, Dave, but I think you need to back off. Leave the investigation to us. Meanwhile, I'll keep this file in my safe. I'll also increase the night patrols in your area, as a precaution.'

Hogget pushed his notebook and pen towards Dave.

'I have your home address already, but write down your landline and mobile numbers. I'll put them on our system. Any nine-nine-nine calls from your numbers will elicit an immediate response.'

'Thank you, Bernie,' Dave wrote down their numbers. He rose and took the detective's outstretched hand.

'My thanks to you both for this information,' Hogget said. 'Look, you won't be surprised to know I checked you both out on our systems. I know you both worked for the Security Service, and I'm grateful for what you've turned up so far. But now, you need to exercise the utmost caution. So, please, leave the investigation to us now.'

Dave and Carole drove home in complete silence. They hadn't had a great deal of sleep the night before, and Carole felt both physically and emotionally exhausted. She felt a great sense of relief, though, at having offloaded their suspicions of a conspiracy behind the killings, and having left the file, with all its disturbing information, in the DI's safekeeping. Dave had been right when he had described it as dynamite.

'Why don't I make us both a bacon sandwich?' Dave asked as they entered their kitchen.

'Oh, yes please,' Carole sighed, as she filled the kettle. 'Oh, d'you think this water's safe to drink?'

'Yes. Our drinking water doesn't come from the Misbourne.'

Dave took a packet of bacon from the fridge and placed several rashers under the grill.

'Oh, the man from the door company's coming this afternoon,' he said. 'He's going to measure up for a couple of those composite jobs. Seems they'll withstand anything, even an attack by a hatchet-wielding maniac. You can choose the colours.'

'We'll certainly feel a lot safer with axe-proof doors. Maybe we should consider one of those letterbox baskets, too. You know the kind I mean? They catch the mail as it comes through the door. They might catch drugged meat, too. Look at our poor boys. They're still pretty groggy.'

'Yes, silly buggers. I'm disappointed they didn't bark when the intruder stuffed whatever it was he stuffed through the letterbox.'

'Trouble is, Dave, we've trained them not to bark when the postman comes. They probably thought the postman had brought them a treat, even if it was the middle of the night when the treat was delivered.'

'Yes, how *do* you teach a dog that not everyone is who they pretend to be?'

After lunch, Carole stretched out on the sofa to have a snooze, whilst Dave switched on the television for his regular dose of 'Countdown'. It was around two-thirty when a knock at the front door disturbed their afternoon.

'That'll be the man about the doors,' Dave said and he went to answer the door.

To his surprise, however, there were two young uniformed police officers standing there. They had respectfully removed their caps and placed them under their arms.

'Mister Lloyd?' one of the policemen asked, as he checked his notebook.

'Yes,' Dave replied.

'CID tell us you had another break-in last night. They asked us to call and take some details.'

'Goodness, that was quick,' Dave exclaimed. 'We only left the police station an hour and a half ago.'

'You're a priority response case,' the officer said. 'I understand they managed to get through your front door. Just the Yale lock, is it?'

Before Dave could answer, the dogs appeared in the hall. Ronnie began to growl at the officers. Reggie looked unusually wary, too.

'Oh, sorry, Officer,' Dave apologised as he grabbed Ronnie's collar and ushered both dogs into the dining room, closing the door on them. 'The break-in has unsettled them. No point growling at visitors now, Ron. You should have barked at the intruders last night, silly sod. Do come in, Lads.'

Dave led them into the living room.

'This is my wife, Carole. Love, these officers are here about last night's intruder.'

'Ah,' Carole stretched. 'Do have a seat. Would you like some tea or coffee?'

'No, thank you, Ma'am,' the officer said. 'We won't keep you long, we just wanted to see if you had a description of the intruder and maybe a list of what was stolen.

The officer went to sit on the sofa and, whilst reaching into his pocket for a pen, he dropped his notebook. As he stretched out an arm to retrieve the notebook, he lost his grip on his cap. Dave reached out and took hold of the cap, at which the officer immediately snatched it from him and stuffed it back under his arm again. Dave glanced from one of the officers to the other and back again. He now noticed that the one who had dropped his hat had a purple bruise on his temple.

'Which station did you say you were from, by the way?' Dave asked. 'Only I heard the Briarfield nick closed down a few months ago.'

'Gaunt's Cross,' the officer said. 'So can you tell me what was stolen, Sir?'

'Nothing at all. My wife disturbed the intruders. They fled empty-handed.'

'That's right,' Carole agreed, 'but what we think they were after was …'

'Jewellery,' Dave interrupted, and he threw Carole a warning glance. 'My wife has some nice bits of jewellery she inherited from her aunt. We kept it in a safe in our previous home, but we've only lived here a few months and we haven't yet got around to installing one here, have we, Love?'

Carole was puzzled. She realised Dave didn't want her to tell the police officers about the file. She didn't know why that should be, but she knew Dave would have his reasons.

'That's right,' she nodded. 'It's not particularly valuable, but my aunt passed away last year, so it's of great sentimental value. Luckily, they didn't take it.'

'And we've got a man coming over any minute now to measure up for some more secure doors,' Dave added, 'Front and back. I think they do safes, too.'

'That's good, Sir. The doors you've got at the moment wouldn't stop a determined thief. As you found out.'

'We're also getting CCTV installed and better security lighting. Front and back. The bastards won't get in here again.'

Carole was a little taken aback by Dave's language, but, again, she guessed he had his reasons. He seemed angry. She imagined the break-in had unsettled him, as much as it had Ronnie and Reggie. He hadn't previously mentioned he intended to install CCTV and lighting, but then he didn't always tell her what he was planning.

'That's a good idea, too, Sir,' the constable said. 'So, Mrs Lloyd, did you get a look at the intruder?'

'It's Miss Murray, actually,' Carole corrected him. 'I've kept my maiden name. It was easier for professional reasons.'

'And what profession were you in, if I may ask?'

Carole was aware of Dave giving her a sideways glance. She took this as a warning.

'Secretarial,' she fibbed, except that it wasn't a total fib, as she had indeed been a secretary before she had joined the Security Service and trained as an intelligence analyst. 'And, no, I didn't get a good look at him. I only saw his outline, as it was fairly dark. But he seemed a weedy sort of a guy, and the moment I clouted him across the side of the head with my husband's walking stick, he turned tail and ran way.'

Carole noticed the second officer, who hadn't spoken a word so far, smirk slightly. Suddenly, the penny dropped. Carole now grasped the reason for Dave's reticence. She also realised why Ronnie had growled at the officers. The man seated in their armchair, this polite young man in police uniform, was very likely their intruder from the previous night. She felt her heart begin to pound as she realised, to her horror, that Dave had unwittingly let their intruder back into their home. She felt her hands begin to shake, so she clamped one of them firmly over the other. She wondered how they would get the men to leave.

Suddenly, there was another loud knock at the door. Dave leapt to his feet.

'Ah, that'll be the men from the security company,' Dave announced. 'Well, I'm sorry we couldn't be more help, Lads. But thank you for calling.'

The two uniformed men followed Dave to the front door and left, to the din of now frantic barking from the two dogs still shut in the dining room. Dave ushered in the next caller. After a brief chat in the hallway, during which Ronnie and Reggie calmed down noticeably, Dave left the man measuring up the front and back doors, whilst he went into the kitchen to make him a cup of tea. Carole followed him.

'They weren't real policemen, were they?' she hissed.

'Yes, Love. They were. But not the kind of policemen they'd have us believe.'

'What on earth do you mean? Either they were policemen or they weren't.'

'I thought it was odd the way they kept their caps under their arms. And when that lad dropped his and I tried to pick it up for him, he snatched it off me pretty quick. He didn't want me seeing his cap badge.'

'Why not? Was it a fake one?'

'No. It was an MDP badge. There is no nick at Gaunt's Cross, and they haven't closed Briarfield nick. We were in there just yesterday, weren't we?'

'MDP? What's that?'

'Ministry of Defence Police. That's who broke in here last night.'

'Oh my God!'

'Did you see that lad's bruise? I expect he's the one you clouted. They were almost certainly our intruders. They wanted to know how much we knew. They probably hoped we'd show them what they'd broken in hoping to find – the Misbourne file. Well, like I said, the bastards won't get in here again. Now, let me give this nice chap his tea whilst you browse his catalogue and choose us some nice new doors.'

As Carole released the now calm dogs from their captivity in the dining room and brought them back into the sitting room, it occurred to her that actually they had no need of instruction in how to recognise people who were pretending to be someone they weren't. Her beloved Ronnie and Reggie had that ability already.

Chapter 22

The following day, Carole arose early. She still hadn't slept well and she had the distinct impression Dave had lain awake a long time, too, before, eventually, sleep had overtaken him. She left him sleeping and came downstairs to make herself a strong coffee. She normally preferred tea first thing, but this morning she definitely needed a stronger hit of caffeine than her favourite brand of Earl Grey tea could provide.

Switching on her laptop, she curled up on the sitting room sofa to check her e-mails. There was a message from Kitty, asking if she would be attending the next local history group meeting the following Tuesday, since they were all keen to know what had been in the 'Misbourne' file. Carole decided she would have to give some thought to how much she could actually share with her fellow *Third Agers*. She didn't want to put them in any danger.

The next e-mail she opened was from Doctor Reid, the scientist at the Police Forensic Laboratory near Abingdon. At last, it was the results of the tests he had carried out on the water samples she had sent. She ignored the text of the e-mail for the moment and went straight to the attachment which comprised a very long list of elements, each with columns of figures for parts per cubic litre and parts per million. Alongside these figures was another set of figures which were listed as the safe levels given in parts per million, for comparison with the quantities found in the samples. The figures didn't mean a lot to Carole. Although some of the substances listed were familiar to her from her research, such as nickel, chromium, cadmium, lead and arsenic, there were a number of other items she hadn't heard of before.

She spotted the perfluoro-octane sulphonates or PFOs in the list, from which she deduced the water was still the same toxic cocktail it had been when Emerald Isacson had tested it all those years ago. From this, she guessed that, either the ground was so heavily drenched in toxins that they were still leaching out, a quarter of a century later, and cascading downhill and into the river every time it rained heavily, or someone up at the abandoned site was still dumping chemicals.

There was also a footnote to the report, which footnote was in a stark red font, warning of the radiation levels in the water and referring her to the important notice in the accompanying e-mail. Flipping to the text of the e-mail, she read that Doctor Reid, having tested the samples, had found the level of radioactive substances in them to be of a sufficiently dangerous level that he had been obliged to report this to the UK Atomic Energy Authority. The e-mail urged Carole to contact the UKAEA herself, quoting the reference number assigned to the test results and advising the authority of the exact location where she had obtained the samples. This, he stressed, should be done as a matter of urgency.

For the first time since she had started poking her nose into the question of who had killed Emerald Isacson, Carole began to regret having got involved. Dave hadn't yet said 'I told you so' but she knew he must be thinking it. And now, having the UK Atomic Energy Authority on one side, wanting to know where the water samples had come from, and the Ministry of Defence on the other side, sending their police to break into her home, she realised things really were getting out of hand. However, as she sat for a while, sipping her coffee and thinking things through, she began to wonder whether she and Dave might actually be able to slip out from between the two powerful organisations and let them battle it out. In fact, there might be another fairly powerful organisation which could help them.

When, eventually, she heard Dave getting up, she made more coffee and started to make toast. Dave always said there was no more cheering aroma to wake up to in the morning than the aroma of freshly brewed coffee and toast. If he came downstairs to those aromas, she thought, it might put him in a positive and receptive mood. Soon, he was seated at the kitchen table, reading the newspaper and tucking into his breakfast.

'Dave,' she began tentatively, 'd'you know what I think we should do?'

'No, Love,' he mumbled from behind his newspaper, as he chewed his toast and marmalade. 'What do you think we should do?'

'I think we should go and see Adrian.'

Dave lowered his paper, 'Adrian Curtis?'

'Yes. I was thinking it wouldn't hurt to have our old firm on our side. Just in case things should get a bit more dangerous. I'll bet you think that's a bad idea, though, eh?'

'No. In fact I was thinking the same thing myself. Between us, we gave a few good years of our lives to the Security Service. Maybe the Service could provide *us* with a bit of security now when we need it.'

'Should I give Adrian a call and see when would be convenient for us to call on him? Would your ankle be up to travelling up to London?'

'Yes, I think so, especially if you fancied driving us up. Adrian could probably arrange a parking pass for us. It shouldn't involve too much walking.'

'Good, I'll give him a call after breakfast.'

Just then, Carole's mobile phone rang. She saw it was the journalist Helen Chandler calling.

'Hi. How are you?' she asked of the caller.

'Can't speak for long, Carole. I've managed to get an appointment to speak to the CEO of Isis Water this morning. Before I do, I just wanted to let you know that Levitt's the undertaker's called me back.'

'Oh, yes?'

'They've kept all their old records but the really old files were in their storage facility. Anyway, they did arrange Andrew Maudsley's funeral. They managed to find the relevant paperwork and they say there *was* an injury to the back of his head. In fact, his skull was badly fractured. There's no way that was caused by falling face first into a swimming pool. I think Maudsley was murdered, too. Anyway, I'll leave that with you for now. Gotta go, now. Speak soon. Bye.'

'Bye, Helen.'

'Who's that?' Dave asked, again from behind his newspaper.

'Oh, … just the hairdressers. Confirming my appointment for next week.'

Carole didn't think it would be a good idea to mention the reporter's news about Maudsley. Not just now. Not when she and Dave were trying to extricate themselves from the very sticky situation Carole had got them into. And, as for the results of Doctor Reid's tests on the water samples, she wouldn't mention those either. Not just yet. She decided she would simply forward the scientist's e-mail to DI Hogget and suggest he might care to let the atomic energy people know the water samples had come from the road run-off pipe in the River Misbourne at Chalfont St George.

***

Adrian Curtis, head of MI5's Counter-Espionage Section, Carole and Dave's former unit, agreed to see them the very next day. He gave them a very warm welcome when they arrived at the Thames House reception. Relieving them of their mobile phones, which he placed in the security lockers, he escorted them upstairs into their former office. The first few minutes were taken up with greeting their friendly former colleagues and reassuring them that quiet retirement was wonderful, if not actually as quiet as it had seemed at first. They also got to meet the new staff who had replaced them. Coffees were produced and then Adrian managed to steer them into his office.

'So,' Adrian began, 'Carole tells me you're having a bit of bother with MOD. I appreciate you weren't able to say too much over the phone, Carole. Perhaps you'd better tell me the whole story.'

Between them, Carole and Dave recounted the whole sorry tale, beginning with the historic murder and suspected murders, then the more recent murder of the surviving Isacson sister and Dave's theory of sister substitution, plus the two break-ins they had experienced, the visit by the MOD police and the shocking contents of the dead journalist's report about the contamination. Carole now had little option but to mention she had received the scientist's report and that, in addition to the chemical and heavy metal toxicity, the radioactive nature of the water sampled had been so dire that it needed to be reported to the Atomic Energy Authority.

When they had finished outlining the situation, Adrian sat back, sucking in his breath through his teeth.

'This certainly sounds like an almighty cover-up at the highest level. The question is, what are we doing to do about it?'

'I think Carole and I rather wish we could wash our hands of it,' Dave said. 'What started out as a bit of intrigue over an unsolved historic murder has snowballed into something huge and rather frightening.'

'It's true,' Carole added. 'I simply got involved in researching some notable scientists to include in my U3A local history group's project on famous and infamous locals. That should have been a safe and fairly innocuous pastime. But it's all got out of hand, somehow.'

'What do you think was the trigger point in all this, Carole?' Adrian asked. 'I mean, who do you think tipped off MOD that you were looking into Emerald Isacson's murder?'

'I've given it a lot of thought and I'm sure it wasn't Geoff Jackson at TVP's unsolved case unit. He was extremely helpful. He put me in touch with Walter Gerrard, the retired detective who was SIO in the Emerald Isacson murder case. I went to see Gerrard at his home. He's a grumpy, misogynistic old sod, and he threw me a couple of red herrings.'

'What sort of red herrings?' Adrian asked.

'I thought at first his memory might be faulty. He said he thought Emerald's murder was down to antisemitism. He told me there'd been at attack not long before on the local Jewish burial ground. But that wasn't true. It never happened. He assured me he'd been able to rule out any connection between the Isacson case and the apparent suicide of Charlie Herron, the journalist who was found hanging from a tree in the same wood where Emerald died. He said Herron had been an alcoholic who had separated from his wife. Both of those statements were untrue as well.'

'Yes, and it was shortly after that that you tracked down the surviving Isacson sister, wasn't it?' Dave added, 'and just two days later, she was murdered, too. Adrian, we think Carole must have been followed.'

'Gerrard knew I'd been with The Firm, too.' Carole added. 'He'd checked up on me before I visited him and he challenged me about it. He seemed uneasy that there might be Security Service interest in the Isacson case. I think he must be involved somehow.'

'Okay,' Adrian nodded determinedly, 'we'll start by having a look at this Walter Gerrard. If you let me have his address and phone numbers, Carole, I'll pull his phone records and see who he's been in touch with since your visit. We'll get an association chart drawn up. That'll be a good starting point.'

'Oh, Adrian,' Carole reflected sadly. 'That used to be *my* job.'

'I know, Carole,' Adrian said softly, 'and pretty damned brilliant you were at it, too. But we have a new senior analyst on the team now. She'll take this forward. You need to let it go. For your own safety, you both need to take a step back. I promise I'll let you know what progress we make. And good luck with your local history project.'

'Thank you, Adrian,' Dave said, as he rose and shook his former boss's hand. 'Come on, Carole. I'll treat you to a bespoke sandwich from our favourite Italian sandwich shop. For old time's sake.'

'Oh, if you mean Sartori's, it closed down,' Adrian informed them. 'He went back to Italy.'

'Oh, of course he did,' Dave tutted. 'I'd forgotten that. Well, we'll just head straight home, then. It'll have to be a pie and a pint at *The Hare and Whippet*.'

'Well, it's been so lovely to see you both again. I hope you'll both come up to town for our Christmas drinks do.'

'I expect we will,' Dave said as he shook his former boss's hand. 'And many thanks for your help, Adrian. We appreciate it.'

On the drive back, Carole was quiet and thoughtful.

'You okay, Love?' Dave asked.

'Oh, I suppose so. I was just realising how much I enjoyed working with The Firm. They say it's always a mistake going back to places where you've been happy.'

'Oh, Sweetheart, we are happy though, aren't we? We've got a delightful cottage in a lovely village, and two daft dogs for company. You've made some nice new friends, and we've got each other, haven't we.'

'Yes, you're right. Of course we're happy. Mind you, I'll be happier when they drain the toxic swamp out of the village and we can sit and eat our pies in *The Whippet*'s riverside gardens.'

Chapter 23

Tuesday came around and Carole headed off to the community centre for the monthly meeting of her U3A interest group. She was still undecided as to how much information she would share with her fellow local history enthusiasts. As soon as she entered the meeting room, however, she found herself bombarded with questions.

'So, what was in it, Carole?' Kitty asked.

'In what?'

'Don't be coy. What was in the 'Misbourne' file. We're dying to know.'

Carole thought they might end up dying if they *did* know. The information in the file had likely caused the murders of four people already, and Carole couldn't shake off the feeling that the most recent of those was her fault. She was even beginning to wonder whether Malcolm Rawlinson's hit and run accident had been connected. She had dragged Dave into this business, and that was bad enough, but she didn't want to involve her new friends any further and put them at risk, too.

'Well, there wasn't a lot, really. Doctor Isacson had concerns about the levels of bacteria and other possible contaminants in the river and she'd been conducting tests. Her tests were looked at by government officials, but it seems the results were fairly inconclusive.'

'So, you're saying that had nothing to do with her murder?' Daisy asked.

'Possibly not,' Carole replied, avoiding direct eye contact with Daisy.

'But what about the journalist?' Kitty asked. 'Are you saying there wasn't anything in his file that would have got him killed?'

'Well, according to the now retired detective who led the Isacson investigation, Charlie Herron was a depressive alcoholic, and the coroner concluded he'd committed suicide,' Carole explained, satisfied she was being truthful, in so far as Gerrard had indeed told her this, even if she knew his explanation to be a lie

'So, do the police know who killed Euphemia Isacson and why?' Tom asked.

'I don't know. They're not likely to tell me about the progress of their investigation.'

'Then why were the police at your house the other day?' Tom asked. 'I saw them leaving. Two uniformed officers, wasn't it?'

'Oh, that. We had another break-in.'

'Oh, Carole, not again,' Mary sympathised. 'Was much taken this time?'

'No, nothing, actually. I think the dogs scared them off. We're getting our front and back doors replaced, though.'

'So, all that sorting through Herron's box files was a waste of time, then,' Daisy remarked.

'Yes, I'm sorry about that. Sorry to have dragged you all over there.'

'Still, we had a nice lunch, didn't we?' Kitty consoled.

'Oh, how disappointing,' Betty sighed. 'Well, I still think that Cassoni chap was the killer. I've been giving it some thought. I wouldn't mind betting the Italian Mafia's behind all this. What do they call themselves, the Cosy Nostril?'

'The *Cosa Nostra*, I think you mean,' Daisy laughed. 'But why would the Italian Mafia come to Briarfield, and why would they murder a nice old lady who owns a teashop?'

'Carole,' Tom began, his face a picture of serious determination, 'I think you're holding out on us. I'm sure there was something much more dangerous in that file – something which got Emerald killed and is still dangerous enough today that it got her sister killed, too. Look, we're big boys and girls. We can handle the truth.'

Carole desperately wanted to share her knowledge with the group, but she still had serious misgivings about compromising their safety.

'If there really were something dangerous, as you put it, in that file – though I'm not saying there was – and if my stirring it up is what got Miss Isacson killed, then it would be dreadfully irresponsible of me to endanger all of you by sharing that knowledge with you, wouldn't it?

'I knew it!' Tom exclaimed. 'That file is the key to the murders. And you've just had another break-in, as well. That's too much of a coincidence, Carole. If you and Dave are in danger, then we want to help. You should tell us what you know.'

Carole was flummoxed. She knew she had to say something, if only to persuade her friends to take a step back too.

'All I can say is that there may be a … conspiracy of some kind at work here. There might be someone big behind it all, someone … a greater power than we would want to tangle with. So, I think we need to let Detective Inspector Bernard Hogget and the authorities deal with it.'

'I think I know what you're saying, Carole,' Tom persisted. 'You've stirred up a hornet's nest and it's something to do with that place where Doctor Isacson worked, isn't it? If there is some kind of conspiracy afoot, then the more people who know about it, the safer you will be. If only you, Dave and DI Hogget know about it, then you three are in danger.'

Carole hesitated. She was bursting to tell them what she knew, but she couldn't.

'Listen, there's another authority, headed by someone I trust, and they're taking an interest now, so we can step aside and let them get on with it. I would just say that, whilst Hogget's investigation is on-going, we should all keep away from Percival's Wood, and from the site of the former labs. And, as Kitty will no doubt agree, we should avoid walking with our dogs anywhere near the river.'

'Well, I have to say I'm disappointed, Carole,' Betty complained. 'I still think we should be looking for that Italian stallion.'

'Good,' Mary interjected. 'Now, can we get back to the business in hand – the project? How are we all progressing? Does anyone have anything to report? Elaine, how are you getting along with stars of stage and screen.'

Carole breathed a sigh of relief. It was good that their convenor had changed the subject.

'I've found nineteen actors and actresses so far,' group member Elaine Quinn advised. 'There were so many film studios west of London, three of them here in Buckinghamshire, and the stars found it convenient to live over this way, so I'm sure I'll find more.'

'That's great, Elaine,' Mary congratulated her.

'In fact,' Elaine continued, 'one of them, Joss Conroy, still lives locally. He's in his eighties now but he has so many anecdotes to tell about his days in film and the pop industry that I thought I'd ask him if he'd come and give our U3A a talk.'

There was a ripple of enthusiasm from the group at the prospect of this former heartthrob coming to the village to speak.

'Oh, but I've got him in my list, too,' Kitty said. 'I'm doing the musicians.'

'Well, I'm sure you can share notes on him,' Mary told them. 'He was a big star in his day. I'm sure there's enough of him to share. Any other well-known musicians, Kitty?'

'Yes, Carole gave me details of one. Anyone ever learned to play 'chopsticks' on the piano?'

There was a murmur of assent around the room. It seems everyone was familiar with the starter piece.

'Well, Euphemia Allen, who wrote it, she lived in Gaunt's Cross, too. I've found an original score and some of her personal correspondence up for sale as a job lot at one of those online auction sites.'

'Are you intending to buy it?' Carole asked. 'Only her letters might have something in them about the Isacson family. She was Euphemia Isacson's godmother, you know.'

'I thought you were going to leave the Isacsons alone, Carole,' Mary warned.

'The murder, yes, but I'm still interested in the scientist Per Isacson – for the project.'

'The papers are horribly expensive though, Carole,' Kitty said. 'You can view them online, but I won't be buying them. Not unless they drop the price by a massive amount.'

***

Back home, once she and Dave had finished their lunch, Carole thought she might take a look at the auction site where Kitty had found Euphemia Allen's correspondence, so she opened her laptop and logged on to the site. To her mild disappointment, only one of the letters was still actually visible at the site, and it was heavily watermarked to prevent anyone downloading a copy of the image. However, she was able to read much of the text. The letter was one from Euphemia Allen to her music publisher in London and it referred to an accompanying copy of a musical manuscript. Carole thought that, whilst this might indeed be worth the asking price to a collector, it wouldn't be to a *Third Ager* with no more than a casual interest in the author's friends.

'What are you researching now?' Dave asked, peering over her shoulder. 'Nothing to do with the murders, I hope?'

'No, Love. It's purely for my part of the project. Kitty spotted some correspondence for sale on the internet. It's letters from Euphemia Allen, that friend of the Isacsons who was godmother to their daughter Euphemia.'

'Ah, and does she mention Per Isacson in the correspondence?'

'No. I'd hoped she might, but all I can access here is a letter to her music publisher. See?'

Dave squinted at the image of the letter on the screen.

'Ah, now that's interesting,' he pointed to the image.

'What is?'

'See how she signs herself off at the end of the letter?'

'She writes *'Yours, Effie'*. Yes, so?'

'Well, 'Effie'. That's like FE when you say it, isn't it? FE – as in F.E. Cassoni.'

'I don't understand,' Carole puzzled. 'Are you saying Allen was Cassoni?'

'No. I'm saying it looks like Effie could be the nickname for anyone called Euphemia.'

'So?'

'So, if Euphemia Allen was known as Effie, then perhaps her goddaughter, Euphemia Isacson, was also known as Effie. And, now I come to think about it …,' Dave paused, resting his chin in his hand. 'Yes, of course. I should have seen it before.'

'Seen what before, Dave? What are you seeing that I'm not?'

'Cassoni. It's an anagram of Isacson, isn't it? So, maybe F.E. Cassoni was really Effie Isacson.'

Carole's jaw dropped as she mentally ticked off the letters in Cassoni to assure herself they did, indeed, spell Isacson.

'You're suggesting Euphemia Isacson wrote the birdwatching book? That might explain the multiple copies of Cassoni's book. And so she was FE, and she gave a copy to her sister Em, with love? Yes, I see. You could be right. How clever of you to spot that, Love. Oh, but Betty will be disappointed. She's got it into her head that fifty-one-year-old spinster Emerald was having a torrid affair with an Italian stallion, as she put it.'

'I suppose I ought to let Bernard Hogget know. No point in him looking for an Italian lover, too, if I'm right about that being Euphemia's *nom de plume*.'

'You're so good at anagrams, Dave. But I thought we were going to keep our noses out of the case?'

'Yes, Love, and we are. But this could be important. I'll just pass it on, then that'll be our involvement over and done with.'

Dave retrieved the business card Hogget had given him and he called the detective's mobile number. He outlined his latest theory, that F.E.

Cassoni was possibly Effie Isacson. When Dave had finished explaining his reasons for thinking that, Carole saw his face drop. There was a protracted silence before Dave spoke again.

'No, Bernie. I'm afraid we didn't. That's strange, though. Did they say why they wanted it?'

When Dave eventually finished the call, Carole realised there was something wrong.

'What's happened?'

'Hogget wanted to know whether, by any chance, we'd made a copy of the Misbourne file.'

'But we didn't. Why did he want to know that?'

'Because the original file is no longer in his possession.'

'What? But he said he was going to lock it in his office safe.'

'He says he did. But he says two men from the Security Service called on him and asked to see the file. They insisted on taking it away with them.'

'So, Hogget hadn't made a copy of the file either?'

'He says not. I suppose he saw no need, since he had the original. The men from our old firm wouldn't let him make a copy before they took it. I suppose they'll have had their reasons.'

'Well, that's okay, isn't it? If Adrian's arranged for it to be collected, then it'll be in safe hands, won't it?'

'Yes, you're right, Love. Seems Adrian was as good as his word. He's on the case. We can forget all about it.'

Chapter 24

The following morning, Carole drove Dave into the village to visit the library for himself. He needed to change the crime thrillers which Carole had selected for him but which, with the exception of the latest Lynda La Plante, he had already read. Kitty Walker was on library duty and was at the library counter chatting with a smartly dressed young woman. Whilst Dave browsed the crime books, Carole went over to say hello to Kitty.

'Oh, Carole,' Kitty smiled. 'Let me introduce you to Sally Grey.'

The young woman shook Carole's hand and gave her a beaming smile.

'Sally, this is Carole Murray from my U3A group. Carole, Sally is our local Member of Parliament. Rob got in touch with Sally and she's come down to speak with our river group about the pollution in the Misbourne.'

'So, you're the sleuth Kitty was telling me about,' Sally grinned. 'And you've been investigating some murders, I hear.'

'Oh, not investigating,' Carole found herself blushing. 'Just researching. I used to be a full-time researcher. Anyway, it's lovely to meet you, Ms Grey.'

'Sally, please. Rob Younger filled me in on some of the problems the village has been having with the sewage pollution in the river. As it happens, we have at least half a dozen wonderful chalk streams in my constituency alone. They provide a habitat for such rare creatures as the kingfisher, the Green Drake Mayfly and the endangered water vole, and yet the streams all seem to be threatened in one way or another.'

'Really?' Carole asked. 'So, it's not just the Misbourne?'

'No, mainly they suffer from high levels of phosphates and nitrates, mostly from agricultural run-off. These chalk streams are precious resources. They are amongst the rarest fresh water habitats on earth. I'm trying to get them special protections. In the case of the Misbourne, effluent discharge is a serious public health crisis.'

'Sally's trying to push a private member's bill through Parliament to get our chalk streams deemed sites of special scientific interest,' Kitty said. 'She has the support of the Chilterns Chalk Streams Project.'

'Well, that's truly heartening,' Carole smiled. 'Would you kindly let me have your contact details, Sally. I may have some more information regarding some additional and far more dangerous sources of pollution in our river – some substances far more serious than sewage.'

Over in the crime section, meanwhile, Dave had selected some detective novels he was fairly certain he hadn't already read. Whilst he was browsing, his mobile phone rang suddenly, so he slipped into an alcove between two of the bookshelf units where there was a little reading nook with three comfortable bucket chairs, and he sat down to take the call. It was from Adrian Curtis.

'Hi Adrian. How's it going?' he asked.

His face fell as he heard what Adrian had to say.

'No, Adrian. They were nothing to do with us. Hogget told us *your* chaps had collected the file… So, you're saying they weren't sent by you? … No, absolutely nothing to do with us at all. Like we told Hogget, *we* didn't make a copy of the file, and I gather he didn't either. So, is there anything you can do, without the file, I mean?'

Dave finished his call with his former boss and slipped the phone into his pocket whilst he absorbed the bad news.

'Is that the Misbourne file?' a voice asked from behind him.

'Kitty, I didn't see you there.'

'Sorry to eavesdrop, Dave. I didn't mean to. I was sorting books back onto the shelves. Couldn't help overhearing. Has someone stolen the Misbourne file?'

Just then, clutching a couple of library books, Carole appeared behind Kitty.

'What's that?' she asked. 'Someone's stolen the Misbourne file?'

'Shh,' Dave urged. 'Come here. Sit down, both of you.'

Carole and Kitty joined Dave in the reading nook and they sat down.

'Yes, I'm afraid so.'

'So, Tom was right,' Kitty said. 'The file *was* important.'

'Yes, Kitty,' Carole admitted. 'Sorry I misled you. I didn't want to put you good people in any danger.'

'Yes,' Dave explained, 'it seems a couple of men turned up at Briarfield nick, claiming to be from the Security Service and flashing some official looking warrant cards. They took the file into their safekeeping. And, citing national security, they wouldn't let the detective take a copy of it. Adrian called Hogget this morning hoping to make an appointment to view the file, only to be told the file had been collected by two of his officers. Which, of course, it hadn't.'

'Oh, no,' Carole exclaimed. 'So, the evidence is gone?'

'Who's Adrian,' Kitty asked.

'Oh, he's a Security Service contact of Dave's – from his time in the police force,' Carole added, diplomatically.

'So, what do we do now?' Kitty asked.

'*We* do nothing, Kitty. There's nothing for us do,' Dave said. 'It's up to Bernie Hogget and Adrian Curtis to sort this one out.'

'But if whoever took the file has destroyed it, then the murders of the Isacson sisters and Herron and Maudsley might never be solved,' Carole said.

'Maybe not, Love, but that's not our problem. Kitty, will you check my books out for me, please?'

Kitty took charge of Dave's selection of books and he and Carole accompanied her to the desk.

'Is there a local history section here, Kitty?' Carole asked, as Kitty scanned Dave's books onto the computer system. 'I'm still looking for local scientists and medics of note.'

'Yes, it's over there. But there are more books on the local area upstairs in the reference section. Do you want me to show you where they are?'

'Yes, please.'

Kitty handed Dave his checked-out books and then led Kitty upstairs, where she directed her attention to an array of local history and travel books, including several volumes of the county histories.

'If you're free tomorrow,' Kitty whispered, 'why don't you come over to my house for coffee?'

'That would be lovely. Thanks,' Carole agreed. 'I'm doing my supermarket collection at nine, but I should be free from around nine-thirty. Is, er, anyone else coming?'

'Well, I thought I'd invite Betty and Daisy, and Tom and Mary. We could discuss local history and our project, couldn't we?'

'Yes, we could,' Carole agreed. 'Nothing to do with the murders, though.'

'No, indeed,' Kitty smiled mischievously. 'Nothing to do with the murders.'

***

The following morning, Carole collected her groceries from the supermarket at Gaunt's Cross and headed home. Once she had arranged her purchases in her refrigerator and larder cupboard, she prepared a sandwich for Dave's lunch, wrapped it in clingfilm and left it by the kettle.

'Your lunch is by the kettle, Love,' she told him.

'Oh, where are you off to, then?'

'Over to Chalfont St Michael. Coffee morning at Kitty's house. Whilst I'm over there, I might pop into the butchers. I hear they do very good local sausages. 'Bucks bangers' they call them. We could have some for breakfast over the weekend. I picked up some fresh fish at the supermarket for tonight, since it's Friday.'

'Won't you be back for lunch, then?'

'Not sure how long the coffee morning will go on, but I can always make myself a sandwich when I get back.'

When Carole arrived at Kitty's house and parked up, the others were already there, and Kitty's husband Neil was in the kitchen making the coffee for everyone.

'Did you bring your wellies?' Kitty asked Carole, as she ushered her into the hallway.

'Yes, they live in my car boot. But why? Is your roof leaking?'

'No,' Kitty laughed. 'But Tom suggested we might go out for a walk after we've had our coffee and cake.'

'Nice idea. A walk … anywhere particular?'

'He suggests we could drive in a couple of cars back over to Chalfont St George and have a walk up to the site of the former Chiltern Biosciences labs, just to walk around the perimeter and look in. Just to see what we can see of the place. But shh, not a word in front of Neil. He wouldn't approve.'

'Nor would Dave – if he knew,' Carole whispered. 'I know I said we shouldn't go anywhere near the place, but just looking in at the place from outside, that shouldn't cause us any problems, should it? I mean, no-one's going to worry about a handful of retired folks out for a morning stroll, are they?'

'No. Of course they won't. It's not like we're going to break into the place or anything.'

Once Kitty had poured their coffees and teas, and cake had been sliced and served, Kitty's husband announced he was off to his walking cricket group.

'Now then, we can get down to business,' Kitty announced as soon as she heard the front door close behind Neil. 'Carole has something to tell us.'

'Do I?' a baffled Carole asked.

'Yes. You know. About the Misbourne file, and the fact that it's now been stolen.'

'Oh, good grief, Kitty! I didn't intend that *everyone* should know. It's enough that *you* overheard Dave's phone call. He and I wouldn't want to put everyone here in danger.'

'What's this?' Tom demanded.

Carole wondered whether in fact she ought to explain what had happened. It might be better for the group to hear it from the horse's mouth, she thought, than to get half the story from Kitty. It might be the best way of ensuring damage limitation.

'Okay, well, you know some of us went to the home of the dead journalist's son and he let us look through his late father's papers.'

'Yes,' Tom nodded. 'And I hope now you're going to come clean and tell us what you found.'

'There was a file indicating Doctor Emerald Isacson had taken samples for analysis from the Misbourne and from the surrounding land, including the site where she worked, and also from Percival's Wood which, as you know, runs down the hill below the site.'

'And what did *she* find?' Tom persisted.

'Well, there were indeed some dangerous substances in the ground and in the river, even back then, twenty-five years ago. She confided in the chairman of the parish council, a man named Andrew Maudsley, and he tried to take it up with the owners of the land, the Ministry of Defence, but he couldn't persuade them there was anything wrong. The MOD's own tests came back negative for the kind of toxic and radioactive substances Emerald had found. Naturally, Maudsley and Emerald suspected a cover-up.'

'So, what did they do about it?' Mary asked.

'Maudsley and Emerald went to see a journalist about it. That journalist was Charlie Herron. He created a file with all Emerald's information in it, and copies of the correspondence with MOD and the local MP. But soon after that, Emerald was murdered. I suspect she had arranged to meet Herron in the woods to show him something connected with the contamination.'

'What do you think that was?' Tom asked.

'I don't know for sure. But his widow says it was Herron and not any dog walker, who found Emerald's body. He and Maudsley continued to write to people about the issue, but then Maudsley died three months later. Herron also died the following summer, and all of them in what now looks to be suspicious circumstances.'

'But you have the file, don't you?' Daisy asked.

'We did, but, having been broken into – twice – we handed it over to Detective Inspector Hogget. He put it in his safe. However, two men who claimed to be with the Security Service called on him at the police station and demanded he hand over the file, which he did.'

'And I take it they *weren't* with the Security Service?' Tom guessed. 'They were impostors.'

'So, our work in going through Herron's files wasn't a waste of time,' Daisy said.

'Well, in a way it was,' Carole said, 'because those impostors have probably destroyed the file.'

'But you took your own water samples for testing, didn't you, Carole?' Betty asked.

'Yes, I did. And the results of the tests Doctor Reid carried out are horrific. They show the water is still highly toxic with chemicals, and it's also radioactive.'

'So, we could present those test results to the authorities, couldn't we?' Mary asked.

'Already done so,' Carole assured her. 'That is, I've e-mailed the test results to DI Hogget. He can take that issue up with the atomic energy people and also the relevant environmental agencies. At least Doctor Reid's e-mail can't be made to disappear. It's out there in the ether.'

'So, the information contained in Charlie Herron's Misbourne file is probably an indication of the motive for the historic murders of the first Isacson sister and Maudsley and Herron,' Daisy surmised.

'But Hogget isn't looking into those deaths, is he?' Tom pointed out. 'He's only investigating the more recent murder of Euphemia Isacson. Are the test results on your samples going to be helpful to him in that investigation?

'I wouldn't have thought so,' Daisy reasoned. 'Not if Euphemia wasn't involved in investigating the contamination scandal. Unless her sister shared her suspicions with Euphemia, there's no reason why she would even have been aware of it.'

'Well, actually,' Carole began, 'Dave and I think maybe the recent murder victim *was* aware, because, in fact, we don't think Euphemia was who she claimed to be.'

'I don't understand,' Betty queried. 'If she wasn't Euphemia Isacson, who was she?'

'Well, it's only conjecture at the moment – just Dave's hypothesis,' Carole began, 'but we think the killer murdered Euphemia twenty-five years ago by mistake, thinking she was Emerald. Someone involved in the MOD cover-up might have decided to kill Emerald and shut her up, but seeing Euphemia heading into the woods with binoculars, thought it was Emerald going to spy on them or gather more evidence of contamination in the woods.'

'That sounds logical,' Daisy agreed.

'So,' Carole continued, 'when the body was found in the wood and the police found a car registered to the sisters' address parked nearby, naturally, they called at the sisters' home to tell the sister they saw there what they had found. Emerald must have instantly realised *she* was the killer's intended target and that they'd mistaken Euphemia for her. So maybe, in order to protect herself, she identified the body as being that of Emerald. She then took over her sister's identity and had been living quietly ever since as Euphemia. Dave calls it 'hiding in plain sight'. What do you think?'

There was a stunned silence as the *Third Agers* took it all in.

'But why did the killer come back and kill Emerald now, if he'd been believing all these years that she was Euphemia?' Daisy asked. 'I mean, did he only just find out? How *did* he find out?'

'I have a horrible feeling that was my fault,' Carole confessed. 'I can only think he found out I'd been making enquiries and so he followed me to Euphemia's flat – that is, Emerald's flat.'

'But why would he follow you? I mean, how would he even find out you were making enquiries?' Tom asked.

'I think he might have been tipped off by someone. That someone might have been Walter Gerrard, the original detective on the case – the one who, for one reason or another, failed to solve the case first time around.'

'Do we know why Gerrard failed to solve it?' Tom asked. 'Was it just incompetence?'

'Maybe, or maybe he was coerced into letting it go. Perhaps he was threatened or even paid off by MOD,' Carole suggested.

'But how did you and Dave work out that Euphemia was really Emerald?' Kitty asked.

'You helped us with that, Kitty,' Carole said.

'Me? How did I do that?'

'I had a look at those papers you'd found on the internet, you know, the letters from Euphemia's godmother, Euphemia Allen. She signed herself 'Effie'. I had no idea Effie was short for Euphemia. But if Euphemia Allen used the nickname Effie, then probably her goddaughter did, too.'

'I'm still not with you,' Kitty frowned.

'That inscription in the birdwatching book, remember? It was 'to EM with love from FE'. Which we believe was F.E. Cassoni.'

'The Italian stallion,' Betty enthused.

'Dave worked it out,' Carole explained. 'Cassoni is an anagram of Isacson. So, Euphemia, or Effie Isacson, probably wrote that book using the pen name F.E. Cassoni, F.E. being 'Effie'. Get it? If Dave worked it out, then maybe the killer did, too – eventually.'

'But how? Daisy asked. 'Could he have seen the book, as well?'

'It's possible. He was in her flat, so he could have done,' Carole reasoned. 'Maybe, when he ransacked the flat, he saw the dedication in the book and worked it out for himself. Hmm, but then, why would he leave the book behind for others to see? Alternatively, maybe he still believed she was Euphemia but, after being tipped off by Gerrard, then having seen me collecting water samples and then visiting her, he thought she might know something of what Emerald had discovered all those years ago.'

'Carole, I think Dave's hypothesis is correct,' Tom exclaimed. 'It makes perfect sense to me that Emerald would assume her sister's identity. I wonder, then, whether Emerald was even interested in birdwatching at all. Maybe her only interest in the birdlife and other wildlife was in how it was affected by the toxins in the river. And, maybe …,'

'Maybe what, Tom?' Carole asked.

'Maybe someone from the labs was burying chemicals or isotopes in the woods, as well as in the grounds around the labs. Maybe Emerald had been borrowing her sister's binoculars and spying on them. Perhaps, when she'd been snooping around someone saw her. That may be why, when Euphemia went into the woods innocently birdwatching with the binoculars, she was killed in Emerald's stead.'

'Yes, that's very possibly what happened,' Carole agreed. 'It may also be that Emerald had gone into the woods that day to meet with Charlie Herron and show him what was going on. Maybe she did meet with him, but they found Euphemia dead and guessed what had happened. Although Emerald must have been deeply shocked and upset, she was an intelligent woman, and she must have quickly thought of a way to protect herself.'

'I think you're right,' Tom agreed. 'And after Maudsley's death, Herron must have been continuing to investigate. He may have gone into those woods again, all those months later, either to see for himself what was happening, or to meet someone and confront them with what he knew. That someone must have killed him, too.'

'I imagine we'll never know the truth, though,' Daisy said. 'Not now both sisters are dead.'

The friends fell silent for a few moments whilst they took in what Carole had said and considered all the possible scenarios.

'There's something I don't understand, though,' Daisy said. 'That site's been closed down for the past five years or so. Any contamination still leaking down into the river would surely have been greatly diluted over the years.'

'Well, not according to the test results I got from the government science lab. Those toxins are still pouring into the river in dangerously high concentrations.'

'But how is that possible?' Mary asked.

'Well, finish your coffee and cake everyone and let's take a walk up there and have a look for ourselves,' Tom suggested.

'But that could be dangerous,' Mary warned.

'It could,' Tom agreed. 'In fact, it probably will be. So, anyone who doesn't want to come doesn't have to.'

'I'll get my coat,' Mary responded.

Chapter 25

Back at Rowan Tree Cottage, whilst engrossed in reading one of his crime thrillers, Dave was disturbed by a knock at the door. It was the man from the replacement door company. In view of the break-ins and the visit by the bogus local police, Dave was cautious.

'Here to install your doors, Mister Lloyd,' he announced.

'Already?' Dave queried, naturally suspicious in the light of recent events. 'I thought you said it would take six to eight weeks.'

'Normally, it would, but I was told yours is a priority job.'

'Really, who told you that?'

'The gaffer. Seems he was contacted by another of our customers. We done a lot of security work for him and he contacted my gaffer to ask if you could be made a priority.'

'May I ask who that customer was, since I ought to thank him, as well as your gaffer?'

'Yes, it was a Mister Curtis. We done his house doors and put in a home safe for him, and he got us quite a few more orders from other people he works with. He's one of our best customers is Mister Curtis.'

Dave smiled to think Adrian was looking out for him and Carole.

'Well, that's very kind of Mister Curtis. So, do come in, and let me get you some tea and biscuits.'

Meanwhile, the group of six intrepid *Third Agers*, clad in raincoats and boots, on the recommendation of Mary who had checked the day's weather forecast, reached the lane at the top end of the abandoned laboratories site and they stood looking in via the chain-link fence.

'Why have we approached it from this side, Tom,' Mary asked. 'Wouldn't it have been better to have a look from the lower side, where it joins the wood?'

'We need to keep ourselves safe,' Tom advised. 'And, no matter how heavily contaminated groundwater might be, it never runs uphill. That's why we're starting from the uphill end of the site. We don't want to pick up toxins as we tramp around.'

'But we're not going into the site, are we, Tom?' Kitty asked. 'I mean, it's all padlocked, isn't it?'

'Well, let's start by having a look in. Depends what we can see. I heard the original lab buildings have been demolished anyway. There may not actually be anything to see.'

'Yes, and the house which once occupied the site, that was knocked down just after the war,' Mary added.

'So, what d'you think those buildings over there are?' Carole asked, pointing at a cluster of structures just visible a few hundred yards into the site.

'Judging by the corrugated tin roofs, I'd say they're probably storage sheds or barns,' Tom said.

'I wonder why they're still standing?' Mary thought aloud, 'given that the site's been unoccupied for five years now.

'Only one way to find out,' Tom said.

'You're not thinking of going in, are you?' Mary asked, alarmed at the thought.

'I can't see any security cameras, and the site's deserted,' he replied. 'Doesn't look like anyone's around. Anyone who's not happy about coming in with me can stay here.'

'But the gate's padlocked,' Carole pointed out.

'The place doesn't look as though it's been particularly well maintained, though. Let's check out the fencing,' Tom urged.

They tramped around the perimeter fence and processed along a narrow, tree-lined path which led downhill along the east side of the site, until they came to a rusted and partially collapsed section of the chain link fence. Tom pulled it apart and flattened some of it down with his boot.

'I think we could all get through here,' he said.

No-one objected. They were all overcome with curiosity now and, in any case, it was abundantly clear there was no-one around. One by one, they all squeezed through the gap in the fence, and Tom led the way across the abandoned grounds which were uneven beneath their feet, owing to the tussocks of dock and thistles and the clumps of purple loosestrife and buddleia. Eventually, they came to the sheds which also were padlocked.

'That's odd,' Tom said.

'What's odd?' Carole asked.

'Well, although the fabric of the sheds is pretty shabby – see the corrugated panels are rusty and the wooden framework is rotting – yet the padlock looks fairly new and shiny. Don't you think that's strange, for a place that's been abandoned for the past five years?'

'What does that mean?' Mary asked.

'I think it means someone's been using this shed more recently. Someone's secured the shed doors since the last site occupants moved out. I'd really like to take a look inside,' Tom said, pushing his shoulder against one of the rusting, creaking shed panels.

'Won't that be breaking and entering, though?' Betty asked.

'Only if we have to break something to get in. Otherwise, it might just be trespassing,' Tom said. 'That's probably just a slap on the wrist.'

Tom began to walk around the shed, pushing on the various panels until, eventually, he saw one of the lower panels at the rear of the structure had rusted from the ground up. Bending down, he pushed at it and it gave way. He kept pushing at it until the entire panel was persuaded to fold inwards and upwards on itself.

'I think one of us should keep watch out here whilst the rest of us have a look inside,' he said.

'I'll stand guard,' Kitty volunteered. 'In any case, I don't think my hip would let me limbo my way in under there.'

'I'll be a second sentry,' Mary said. 'Only, if we're caught, since I'm your group convenor, I might be held responsible for leading you all astray. I could get drummed out of the U3A.'

Tom bent double and pushed his way into the ramshackle shed. He held the panel up to allow the others to follow. Carole crawled in next, followed by Daisy and Betty. It was fairly dark inside, there being just a few slim shafts of daylight which pierced their way in via numerous cracks in the roof and sides, where wood had rotted and panels rusted. There was, however, a strange, greenish, almost phosphorescent glow coming from the floor area at the far side of the shed.

As their eyes gradually adjusted to the dim light, they became aware of a huge stack of metal drums which took up much of the interior. Tom produced his mobile phone and switched on its torch facility. Shining it on the drums, he spotted faded lettering. He moved nearer to the drums to see if he could read the lettering.

'Anyone know what 'RB' is,' he asked. 'Some of these drums are marked 'RB.'

Carole remembered Dave saying he had seen numerous references to 'RB' in Emerald Isacson's diaries. What she couldn't remember was whether she had mentioned to the group having 'borrowed' the diaries.

On balance, she thought she'd better not mention that. She didn't want her new friends to think her a thief or a looter of crime scenes.

'Some of these other drums are marked with 'Co-60' and 'Po-210', Tom announced, as he shone his torch over the drums. 'What d'you suppose these letters and numbers mean?'

'I hope they're not what I think they are,' Daisy replied. 'But nobody should get too close or touch anything.'

'Why, what do you think they are?' Carole asked.

'Well, they used to paint luminous bomber aircraft dials up here, I believe.'

'Yes, that's what Kulwinder told me,' Carole confirmed.

'Well, my degree was in maths and chemistry and, if I remember correctly from my chemistry studies, in the early days, they would have used radium bromide in that particular manufacturing process. That might be what's in the drums marked RB.'

'What's radium bromide?' Betty asked. 'Is it dangerous?'

'It's *incredibly* dangerous. It's highly toxic and highly soluble in water. And if it gets hot it can explode. And there seems to be an awful lot of it here.'

'And what's the other stuff?' Tom asked. 'That 'Co' and 'Po' stuff?'

'Cobalt and Polonium,' Daisy said. 'They were used in the radiopharmaceutical industry. They're highly radioactive. Listen, I think we should get out of here right now.'

At that moment, there came a fierce rapping on the side of the shed. They all jumped.

'Tom!' Kitty called from outside. 'Somebody's coming. Come out now!'

They didn't need telling twice. Tom rushed to the broken panel and held it up as he ushered Carole, Daisy and Betty out ahead of him. Once outside, they heard a vehicle approaching and spotted Kitty and Mary beckoning to them from a clump of shrubbery over by the fence. They dashed across to join their 'sentries' just as a vehicle pulled up by the front entrance to the shed which they had just exited. They couldn't see the vehicle, but they could hear the doors opening and men's voices. Tom signalled to them to crouch down and keep silent.

They heard the clanking of a chain as the padlock on the front gate of the shed was opened and the shed doors creaked open. The men's voices were now echoing from inside the shed. Tom turned to Carole.

'You and the others go back through the hole in the fence and walk away down the path,' he whispered.

'Why, what are you going to do?' Carole whispered back.

'I'm going to get the index number of that vehicle. Then I'll follow you.'

'Be careful, Tom. Those men could be the killers.'

'Go, Carole! Now!'

Carole had a little difficulty at first finding the gap in the fence through which they had entered the site, since the grass and weeds were so high, but eventually she found the spot and pushed the others through.

'Head on down to the main road,' she urged. 'I'll wait here to make sure Tom gets back here okay then we'll follow you.'

'What'll you do if he doesn't come back?' Kitty asked.

'I'll ring Dave, and he'll call someone we know. Someone appropriate.'

'His contact in the Security Service?' Kitty asked.

'Just go, Kitty! Fast as you can.'

Carole's heart was pounding with the realisation that Tom had put himself in danger and just to satisfy her curiosity. Then she told herself it was actually to satisfy the curiosity of all of them. They had all been given the option of remaining behind, but they had all wanted to come. Of course they had. Yet, she still felt guilt over the possibility that it might have been her actions which led to the death of the surviving Isacson sister. Suddenly, Tom was alongside her. They both squeezed back through the gap in the fence and followed the others as quickly as they could back down the path towards the village.

They soon caught up with the others. The path was edged by tall and overhanging trees and as the group of friends passed through a fairly dark section of the path, Mary turned around to make sure Tom and Carole were still following. Suddenly, she stopped dead in her tracks.

'Tom,' she said, pointing at his feet. 'What's happened to your boots?'

They all turned and looked towards Tom's feet. To their collective consternation, his boots were giving off a green luminescent glow in the shadows.

'Oh, my God!' Daisy exclaimed. 'You've got that stuff on your boots!'

Everyone checked their own footwear but it seemed to be only Tom's boots which were giving off an obvious glow.

'Good grief!' Tom said. 'What should I do?'

'Step out of the boots right now,' Daisy ordered;

'Here? But the ground's wet. I'll get my socks soaked.'

'If you don't take them off, you'll be leaving a trail of contamination all the way back to Kitty's car.'

'She's right, Tom,' Carole said. 'This is a popular dog walking path. If that stuff gets on the dogs' paws …'

Tom didn't need telling thrice. He promptly stepped out of his boots.

'Just hold them by the tops,' Daisy instructed. Hold them out away from your clothes. Kitty, do you keep plastic carrier bags in your car?'

'Yes, I've lots in the boot.'

'When we get back to the car, Tom, you'll need to put the boots in some of Kitty's bags. Your socks aren't glowing, too, are they? It hasn't leaked through the boots?'

'No, I don't think so,' Tom said, lifting each foot in turn and inspecting the soles of his socks.

'You'd best take the socks off anyway, just to be safe, and stuff them into the boots. Be careful not to contaminate your clothing or your hands. You'll have to walk barefoot back to the car.'

Tom complied with Daisy's urgent instructions, though he didn't look too happy about it.

'The ground's really cold and it's wet. So are my feet now. But what will we do with my boots?' Tom asked. 'Will I have to dump them?'

'Not in the ordinary waste,' Daisy said. 'They're too toxic. We should double bag them and put them somewhere safe until we can hand them over to the authorities for testing. Even a small amount of radium bromide getting onto your skin, or into the soil or the water supply could have dreadful effects on anyone who comes into contact with it.'

'Sounds like we'll need all of your bags, Kitty,' Tom said, turning pale.

'Are you feeling okay, Tom?' Carole asked, as he squelched along behind them.

'No, my feet are really wet and cold. I'll probably catch pneumonia. Don't know what my missus'll say when I arrive home barefoot.'

'I do,' Betty said. 'She'll say *what on earth have you been up to with those U3A women?*' That's what I'd be asking if John came home barefoot.'

'You can have a hot shower when you get in. Give your feet a really good soak in a basin first, though. Use three or four changes of hot soapy water,' Daisy recommended. 'I'll take charge of the boots. I'll keep them in my garage until we decide what to do with them.'

'And I'll take charge of that car number when you've got a free hand to write it down, Tom,' Carole said. 'I'll get it checked out.'

Chapter 26

It was two o'clock that afternoon when Carole arrived home and the rain had begun to fall yet again, just as Mary had forecast. Pulling into their driveway and climbing out of the car, she was distracted by the day's events as she walked up the path to their cottage. She suddenly stopped dead as she thought, for one brief moment, she had pulled up at the wrong house. Instead of the old, dark brown, varnished front door, there was a new, French grey door with double-glazed, stained-glass panels and shiny chrome fittings. She recognised it as the model she had chosen from the catalogue, but she couldn't believe it had been fitted already.

The door was ajar, which was fortunate since she didn't have a key to open it, and she could hear the sounds of hammering coming from within the house. Dave met her in the hallway.

'What do you think of our new front door, Love? And the lads are fitting the new back door right now.'

'But I thought …,' she began.

'Yes, me, too. Six to eight weeks they'd said. But Adrian Curtis pulled a few strings with the company and got us a priority fitting. Do you like it?'

'I love it. It's really smart. And we'll feel much safer now. Axe-proof they said, didn't they?'

'It'll withstand axes, crowbars, even MOD policemen's boots. Did you have any lunch?'

'Not too hungry, to be honest. I need to talk to you about something.'

'Okay, let's put the kettle on. I said I'd make the lads another cuppa anyway.'

Dave made tea for all of them, whilst Carole kicked off her boots and scrubbed her hands. She and Dave took their own tea into the sitting room. Carole closed the door behind them.

'Dave, d'you remember those references to RB that you saw in Emerald Isacson's diaries?'

'Yes. Why?'

'Well Daisy Cooper thinks it might refer to Radium Bromide. She's got a degree in maths and chemistry and she says that stuff's often referred to as RB?'

'Did you tell her you'd nicked Emerald's diaries, then?'

'Borrowed them you mean, and no, I didn't tell her that.'

'So how did you get to discussing RB?' he asked, suspiciously.

'Well, it seems, um, Tom Sharples was having a look around up at the site of the labs where Emerald used to work, and he saw some old sheds. He looked in and saw loads of oil drums. Some of them were marked RB. They were all corroded and they were leaking a sort of greenish glowing substance. He asked Daisy what it might be and she said RB might stand for radium bromide.'

'It could equally stand for a few other things, though, couldn't it?'

'It could, but Daisy says radium bromide was used for painting luminous dials. That's what Kulwinder told me they were doing up at the site during the war. And the spilt stuff Tom saw was glowing in the dark. But Tom also saw some other barrels. He described the markings on the labels to Daisy and she said they were polonium and cobalt.'

'I quit chemistry in third year,' Dave said, 'but I'm pretty sure those are radioactive elements, aren't they?'

'Yes. And Kulwinder had told me the medical supply company which had the site post-war used to produce radio-isotopes for medical x-rays. That might explain why that stuff is there, too.'

'So, these sound like pretty dangerous substances.'

'According to Daisy, they're *incredibly* dangerous. Radium bromide is highly toxic and it dissolves in water. The sheds it's kept in have rainwater leaking in through the roofs ... Tom says. Daisy said it can also explode if it gets too hot. And Tom said there was an awful lot of it – dozens of drums of the stuff. And it's all stacked in the same shed as the radioactive stuff.'

'Thank goodness you weren't with him when he went exploring. It really does sound dangerous.'

Carole felt her cheeks redden and she avoided eye contact with Dave. She hated lying to him but she knew there'd be a fearful row if he thought she, too, had let herself be exposed to contamination when poking about on the site. What he didn't know wouldn't cause him consternation.

'What do you think we should do about it?' she asked.

'I think we should enjoy our Friday night fish supper tonight. I've put a couple of bottles of New Zealand *Sauvignon Blanc* in the fridge to chill. Then tomorrow, you can call DI Hogget and tell him what Tom and Daisy think is in that shed, and I'll call Adrian, to thank him about the doors and to let him know what it is we think the MOD are covering up. How does that sound?'

'That sounds good, oh Wise One,' Carole smiled, and she kissed him on the cheek.

It was as they were finishing off their supper and contemplating opening the second bottle of wine, that Carole remembered the other thing she needed to tell Dave.

'Oh, I almost forgot. Tom said that whilst he was up at the laboratory site, a vehicle rolled up. Two men got out and they had a key to the padlocked shed. They let themselves in so Tom skedaddled, but not before he took down their vehicle number.'

'Did he tell you what sort of vehicle it was – a saloon car, or a commercial or military vehicle? And did he get a look at the men?'

'I don't think he saw the men. He just heard their voices, and he thought the vehicle was some sort of heavy-duty vehicle – a Land Rover or an offroad vehicle. But he wrote down the number and gave it to me.'

'Okay, I'll pass it on in the morning. I don't know about you, Love, but I think I'll sleep more soundly tonight, knowing our new doors are as secure as they can be.'

'I think I'll sleep like the dead if I have another glass of wine, Love,' she said, and she held out her glass for a refill.

***

The following morning, Saturday, they both awoke refreshed. After breakfast, Dave rang Thames House. He was told that Adrian was off duty over the weekend, but he spoke with his former colleague Harry Edwards and passed him the vehicle number. Harry agreed to check the vehicle's registered owner and to leave the results for Adrian to see on Monday. Dave assured him Adrian would know to which enquiry it was connected. To his surprise, Harry called Dave back just half an hour later.

'Dave, that vehicle index number you gave me. I thought you ought to know, it's not registered to an individual. It's listed as a government vehicle and it has one of those markers that stipulates no details about the owner or keeper should be disclosed. It's one of those 'hush-hush' numbers.'

'What does that mean?' Dave asked.

'It means we're not supposed to divulge details of it to anyone. However, Adrian has instructed me to give you any and all co-operation you need. So, I can tell you the vehicle is registered to MOD.'

'Why the special marker, Harry? What's that about? Do you know?'

'I don't, Mate. It could mean the vehicle's assigned to some bigwig within MOD. For reasons of his personal safety, no information regarding who's using it, nor which section of MOD he's serving in, can be disclosed. Alternatively, it could simply be one of their surveillance vehicles. For obvious reasons, MOD wouldn't want the target of their surveillance to run a DVLA check and be given confirmation that it's an MOD vehicle which is parked outside their house.'

'I see,' Dave frowned.

'Unfortunately, it also means MOD security will get an instant notification that I've run a check on the number. It'll run up a red flag. I did the check using my own warrant number, so MOD will know the enquiry came from Thames House.'

'Oh, I hadn't realised that would happen. I haven't got you in any trouble, have I?'

'No, Mate. But if the reason for you requesting the check was because someone at MOD has been a bit naughty, then they'll know the Security Service is looking at them. It could put them on their guard. Anyway, I'll make sure Adrian knows all this when he comes in on Monday.'

'Thanks, Harry. I'll call Adrian on Monday and discuss it with him.'

Carole overheard Dave's side of the conversation and saw he had become quiet and thoughtful for a moment.

'Is everything okay?' She asked.

'You said that retired detective, Walter Gerrard, knew you were ex-Security Service?'

'Yes. Why?'

'Well, the vehicle Tom clocked is registered to MOD, but it's also on the system in such a way that anyone running a check on it gets flagged up to MOD security. They'll now know MI5 are interested in that vehicle.'

'Is that bad?' Carole asked.

'It might not be good. You said Tom didn't see the men who arrived in the vehicle?'

'No, he didn't.'

'Well, let's hope the men didn't see him.'

Chapter 27

Carole and Dave decided to put the whole murder and Misbourne contamination issues out of their heads and spend the following week exploring more of the local area instead. Carole decided fresh air and a change of scene would be good for Dave now that he was more mobile. Packing the dogs and a picnic into the rear of Carole's car, they drove out along the Misbourne Valley. Their fun plan for the day was to track the course of the River Misbourne to its source. This proved to be an enjoyable exercise, since it took them through a series of beautiful villages, in one of which, they parked up and tried to gauge the speed of the river flow by dropping twigs over one side of the bridge and timing their progress until they reappeared from beneath the other side of the bridge.

'I haven't played pooh-sticks since I was a nipper,' Dave laughed.

'It's not pooh-sticks,' Carole corrected him. 'It's science.'

Ultimately, the map brought them to a farmer's field where a small spring which, according to their map, was the source of the Misbourne, welled up and trickled along a gulley until its volume increased and it became a stream. The grass was still damp from all the recent rains, so they sat in the car to eat their picnic.

'According to Mary Keswick,' Carole announced as she poured Dave a cup of coffee from a vacuum flask, 'there used to be twelve mills in this valley, all powered by the mighty Misbourne.'

'That's hard to imagine, since it was little more than a stream until the rains caused it to flood. What do you suppose made it shrink?' Dave asked.

'Water extraction, according to Rob Younger. Still, considering what's in the water these days, it's probably as well people are no longer trying to make a living from it.'

Just then, Dave's mobile rang. After a fairly brief conversation, Dave ended the call.

'That was Adrian,' he announced. 'He asked if we'd be at home tomorrow, as he'd like to call on us. He said it's very important.'

***

It was around three o'clock that Thursday afternoon when Adrian appeared at their new front door.

'Adrian, thank you so much for expediting our replacement doors. You've made us feel a lot more secure,' Carole tole him as she ushered him in. 'Tea, or coffee, or a beer perhaps?'

'A coffee would be lovely, thanks, Carole. What a lovely spot you've picked to retire to. And I love your cottage.'

Over coffee and cake, Adrian explained the reason for his visit.

'As you know, last week, Harry ran a check on that vehicle number you gave him and he found it had a marker on it.'

'Yes,' Dave nodded, 'and I hope I didn't get him into any trouble.'

'No, not at all. But there have been some interesting developments. I had a call from a chap in MOD security later the same day, demanding to know why someone in my section was checking out one of their vehicles. Fortunately, Harry had forewarned me and I'd already decided what I was going to tell them.'

'Did you mention the Misbourne business?' Carole asked.

'No. Naturally, I wanted to get information out of them, not give them information. I told the caller we'd found the vehicle number in the possession of someone we suspected had links to terrorism. I told him that, in order to ensure the safety of the person or unit to which the vehicle had been issued, I would need to know who they were.'

'And did he tell you?' Carole asked.

'Not immediately. He went away to consult with someone, then he called me back a while later. He explained the vehicle in question is in use by BRAN.'

'Who?' Carole looked baffled.

'It's MOD's Biological, Radiological and Nuclear Laboratory over at Porton Down.'

'Porton Down?' she frowned. 'Where all the chemical nasties are created?'

'Well, seemingly they have a much broader remit than that, these days. So, I spoke with a chap named Blunt, the Chief Executive Officer of BRAN's Special Projects Division, the SPD.'

'That's a lot of letters,' Dave remarked. 'Do you know what they do?'

'Well, as the CEO explained it, they're pursuing a lot of very positive projects. They've come up with a gadget which can very rapidly detect nerve agents the moment they're dispersed on a battlefield. The spinoff from that invention is that it can also be used in hospitals to detect such things as MRSA in the atmosphere. So, inventions developed primarily for defence also have useful applications for the rest of us, in public health and that sort of area.'

'That sounds very positive and laudable,' Dave said.

'Another invention of theirs, which was developed for use in war zones, to ensure retreating forces haven't poisoned water sources or food stores, is also proving useful for applying diagnostics in commercial food storage, to identify possible contaminants before those foodstuffs get onto supermarket shelves.'

'I imagine that would stop all those supermarket recalls,' Carole surmised. 'And did you ask him what his people were doing in the shed up at Gallows Hill? That place seems to be a repository for rusting drums which are leaking radioactive substances. Surely, they're not developing anything up there?'

'I didn't ask him specifically about Gallows Hill. I didn't want to alert him to the fact that someone in this neighbourhood had seen his unit's vehicle around here. If he or someone else at Porton Down should be behind the recent murder, it could put you two in danger.'

'Good thinking,' Dave agreed.

'Instead, I got him talking about modern germ warfare, then we got around to talking about the possibility of terrorists getting their hands on things like spent uranium and radioactive substances disposed of by hospitals. I asked him whether his MOD department also concerned itself with contaminated land, for instance old wartime sites.'

'And what did he say?' Carole asked.

'He assured me they did, and that they had carried out decontamination processes at all the UK's former wartime and cold war installations. The responsibility for redundant nuclear facilities and hospital waste comes under other agencies, he claimed. He did say that MOD continues to carry out routine annual checks at all their own wartime and experimental sites for air, soil and water contamination.'

'Well, if that's what his men were doing up at Gallows Hill last week, their tests mustn't be very good,' Carole surmised. 'Not sure how they could have missed the radium bromide which is leaking all over the place. And the shed is open to the elements. That's probably how the stuff's been leaking into the river.'

'I'm thinking I could persuade a different body to have a look at that place, maybe the Environment Agency,' Adrian suggested.

'Well, a friend of ours had a look around in there and he managed to get that stuff on his boots,' Carole said, carefully avoiding any mention of her own presence in the shed. 'He wrapped and sealed up the boots with a view to perhaps sending them to the government laboratory over near Abingdon – the lab that tested the river water for me.'

'It wouldn't be safe for him to send something toxic through the post, though,' Adrian warned. 'In fact, it'd be illegal. Supposing I take them over there in person? Where are the boots now?'

'They're in my friend Daisy Cooper's garage. When we've finished our coffee, I could take you over there to collect them.'

'Yes, let's do that. Before we do, though, I need you to tell me what was in the Misbourne file, the one that was taken from DI Hogget.'

'Okay,' Carole agreed. 'But you'll need to tread carefully, Adrian. Four people who knew what that file contained are dead – almost certainly murdered.'

Chapter 28

At Thames House the following Monday morning, Harry Edwards handed Adrian a printed list of the phone calls made from Walter Gerrard's landline over the past three months and the identities of the telephone subscribers linked to those numbers. As he sipped his coffee, Adrian perused the numbers. One was a mobile number the subscriber's details for which were withheld. Acting on a hunch, he flipped through a small collection of business cards in the top drawer of his desk until he came to the card he had been given by the CEO of MOD's Biological, Radiological and Neurological section. His hunch was correct. The unattributed mobile number was on the CEO's business card. He rang the number and was soon connected.

'Hello, again. It's Adrian Curtis from Thames House. We spoke last week. I would like to meet with you soonest, at your earliest convenience… No, I'm not yet able to tell you the name of the suspect I mentioned, but I'm hoping you'll be able to furnish me with some more information which will help our investigation into that suspect.'

The scientist confirmed he would be up in London for a meeting at the ministry on the Wednesday morning and so, rather than Adrian having to travel out to Porton Down, he offered to come to Thames House. When he had finished his call, Adrian scribbled the mobile number and a couple of dates on a post-it note. Slipping on his coat, he switched off his desk lamp and, exiting his office, headed for Harry's desk.

'Harry, this is a mobile number which was on the printout of Gerrard's phone records you gave me. It's an unlisted MOD number but I have his business card. Would you have a word with our techies and ask if they can track the phone's movements on the dates I've written here? It's be very helpful if I could have that information before Wednesday.'

'Will do, Boss. Where are you off to?'

'Abingdon. Going to deliver an important package to a scientist at the government laboratory down there.'

'Couldn't one of us take it down there for you?' Harry offered.

'Thanks, but I need to ask the scientist's advice. I need to talk to him about radium bromide, cobalt and polonium.'

On the Wednesday morning, the CEO of MOD's Special Projects Division arrived at Thames House promptly at eleven-thirty. The forty-one-year-old civil servant was escorted through security and upstairs to the Counter-espionage section. Soon, he and Adrian were drinking coffee together in Adrian's office. After Adrian had kicked off with some polite enquiries regarding his department's recent developments and their flourishing partnerships with big business conglomerates, he decided to grasp the contaminated nettle.

'May I ask you what business took you to Buckinghamshire on the ninth of April and the thirteenth of May?'

The scientist looked puzzled at first but then he swallowed. It was only a small gesture, but it was one which Adrian interpreted as significant.

'I would probably have been having lunch or dinner at the *Austen Arms* in Gaunt's Cross. It used to be my family's home, you see. But my grandfather sold it to a hotel chain. I'm friends with the owners of the hotel and I like to pop back occasionally and see the place.'

'And you also visited Briarfield on the ninth of April and Chalfont St George on the thirteenth of May?'

'Yes, I like to visit my grandfather's old stomping ground. It's a nice part of the world. But how did you …'

'Did you visit the MOD site at Gallows Hill?'

'No, I'm not sure I even knew we had a site there.'

'Well, you do have a site there. And I'd be surprised if you didn't know that, because, in fact, your grandfather used to own over two hundred acres of land around Gallows Hill, until he sold it to the MOD.'

'Okay, that's true,' the scientist conceded and he shifted uncomfortably in his chair. 'My department doesn't routinely declare which sites it owns. It's the kind of information that's kept on a need-to-know basis, for security reasons. But, since you already know about the Gallows Hill site, I can confirm we do own it. Until a few years ago, though, it was leased out to a commercial company, and it's been abandoned for quite a while now.'

'Since it's abandoned, I'm surprised you feel the need to deny ownership. Could that be because of the highly toxic chemicals stored there? Or perhaps because of the fact that the land has been dangerously contaminated ever since World War Two?'

The scientist looked extremely uncomfortable now. He appeared to be struggling to respond.

'I'm not sure we should be having this conversation,' he said, at last. 'I don't see what this has to do with your terrorism suspect.'

'I understand there are poisonous and radioactive substances stored up there. It would be unfortunate if a terrorist were to get his hands on those, wouldn't it? But what I want to know is why MOD haven't removed those contaminants. Why hasn't the land been cleaned up?'

'You clearly have no idea how incredibly expensive that would be,' the scientist protested. 'It would cost many millions to clear that land. It's contaminated all the way down to the river. Every inch of soil would have to be lifted and removed by a professional clean-up squad and then we'd have to find somewhere safe to dump it – down a mine, probably.'

'Well, that sounds achievable.'

'And the mine would have to be sealed up with a massive amount of concrete. Have you seen how much the price of concrete has soared since they started building HS2? And that's assuming you can find enough concrete for the job. Most of it's going into the HS2 rail tunnels. The taxpayers would have to foot an astronomical bill.'

'But your division's funding last year was almost six hundred million. Surely some of those millions could have been spent on the clear up?'

'No, you don't understand. We're in partnership with big business these days. Half of our funding comes from government, but the rest comes from those businesses, and they're mostly American-owned. We're answerable to them on spending, as well as to government.'

'So, what *are* you spending your massive budget on?' Adrian asked.

'In case you hadn't noticed, we've been fighting wars in Iraq and Afghanistan in recent decades. Most of our funding goes into research and development of defence measures. We have to ensure our military is well-equipped with the latest weaponry for World War Three when it comes. And it could come any time now. But I also told you the other day how useful our defence projects have been in terms of public health.'

'But what about the health of the public living below Gallows Hill?'

'There's no danger to them. I personally arrange for soil and water testing up there each year. The levels of toxins up there fall well within the acceptable ranges.'

'I don't know who does your testing, but I can tell you that is not the case,' Adrian argued. 'Twenty-five years ago, a scientist at that site, Doctor Emerald Isacson, tasked local GPs with testing the levels of toxins in the bloodstreams of local children. They were dangerously high then. I imagine they'll be just as high now, if not higher still.'

'Nonsense. The county's health authority would tell me if there was a problem.'

'And how would they know to even look for a problem? If they're unaware of the presence of toxins and radioactive substances leaching into the soil and the water in the area, they wouldn't have cause to test the local population. Nobody's monitoring the levels of cancer and other serious illnesses in the area, are they?'

'Well, that's not my responsibility. I'm not in public health. And, anyway, I wasn't working with MOD twenty-five years ago. I'm not responsible for what MOD did back then.'

'No, but your father was, wasn't he? Back in the nineteen seventies, your father, Michael, was the Chief Scientific Officer at what is now BRAN. The land at Gallows Hill had already been contaminated ever since the war, so no-one else would have bought it. And your family had owned that land. Your grandfather was lucky to have MOD as a buyer. And, of course, he had already moved his family down to Wiltshire, so they wouldn't be affected by the toxic environment. And it seems MOD, as well as subsequent outfits leasing the land, have continued to contaminate it.'

'I can assure you there aren't any toxins leaching into the environment, at least not in any substantial quantities. As I said, we take samples every year and test them. The levels are acceptable.'

'By whose standard? Who's doing the testing? I've seen the results of recent testing by an independent laboratory. The water in the river there is highly toxic, and it's radioactive. They stopped issuing fishing licences there years ago because the local anglers were dying from environmentally caused cancers.'

'But you really don't understand. Hardly surprising as you're not a scientist. *All* rivers have heavy metals and other toxins in them. Stuff like that comes down in acid rain, and it comes off the roads from vehicle wear and tear. People die all the time from toxins in their environment. I'm sure the number of deaths locally is within acceptable parameters.'

'Did you kill Emerald Isacson?' Adrian asked suddenly.

'What?' Adrian's visitor seemed deeply shocked. 'Of course not. She died twenty-five years ago, didn't she? I would have been sixteen. I was at school in Wiltshire. I didn't know the woman.'

'No. Emerald Isacson died on the ninth of April this year. It was her sister Euphemia who was murdered twenty-five years ago.'

Adrian scrutinised the scientist's countenance to try to gauge whether that revelation would come as a surprise to him. Clearly, however, it did not. The man's unchanging expression persuaded him Carole and Dave's theory about Euphemia Isacson having been killed by mistake was probably correct and that the man in front of him knew this. Adrian gained the distinct impression the MOD man had indeed known that the woman who lived as Euphemia was really Emerald.

'Rubbish,' the scientist persisted in his defiant denial. 'The papers said it was Emerald who was murdered all those years ago.'

'You took an interest in the case, then? Even though you were just a sixteen-year-old schoolboy when it happened?'

'Well, I mean, it was in all the papers, wasn't it? And it happened in the area where my father had spent his childhood. I remember my grandparents discussing the murder. Naturally, it interested me.'

The scientist stood up suddenly and looked at his watch. He had turned quite pale.

'I have to go now. I take it I am free to go?'

Adrian stood up, too.

'Yes. For now. I'll escort you downstairs.'

As they took the lift down to the ground floor, Adrian noticed his visitor was shaking slightly. He knew he was on the right track. He also knew, however, that this wasn't exactly an issue warranting Security Service involvement. He decided he would give DI Hogget a call right after lunch. Once back at his desk, however, he decided to call a number at the American Embassy. As the embassy's US National Security Agency head, Corey Hart was one of Adrian's most trusted contacts.

'Corey, it's Adrian. Fine, thanks. I just wanted to pick your brains on something. A couple of US companies seem to be bankrolling a branch of our own Ministry of Defence, and there's a whisper that some of their joint projects may be a little dubious. Oddly, one of the US companies is a major insurer with connections to the US military. Yes, I have their details. And may I also ask, has the US ever had problems with water pollution? I'm looking specifically at PFOs – *perfluoro-octane sulphonates*?'

Adrian began to scribble down notes of Hart's lengthy response.

'Newburgh? Where's that?' he continued writing.

'New York State? I see. And how many died? Good God! Do they know how the PFOs got into the drinking water? And it was from a military base, you say? That's extremely helpful, Corey. Many thanks.'

Chapter 29

A month had passed and so had the rains. Yet the floods had not yet abated and nor had the Misbourne returned to its former levels. The village of Chalfont St George was still not open for business, despite the continued pumping out efforts by Isis Water's tankers. Dave no longer had need of the neoprene ankle support, however, and he was relieved to be able to get out and about even more. He was pleased he could now drive himself into the village to select his own library books. Having promised Carole he wouldn't be climbing any more trees, he had booked a local gardening service to give their cottage garden a much-needed overhaul.

Once again, Carole was preparing to go to the village shopping for groceries and had put on her coat and boots when, on opening the front door, she saw DI Hogget and DS Caulfield walking up the path.

'Good morning, Carole,' Hogget smiled. 'New front door, I see?'

Carole was relieved to note Hogget's friendly tone. Hopefully, the matter of her having been in possession of the diaries and the birdwatching book was forgotten.

'Yes, Bernie. No more break-ins now, I hope. Do come in. Once again, I'm afraid, we're out of milk. I was just heading to the shops.'

'Well, we won't keep you long. Just wanted to update you and Dave on developments.'

Carole ushered the detectives in and removed her coat and boots.

'I understand the Misbourne file has gone for good,' Dave said when they were all seated in the living room.

'Yes, that's unfortunate,' Hogget agreed. 'But the test results on the samples Carole took seem to have done the trick. The Environment Agency has served a notice on the Ministry of Defence under the EPR – that's their Environmental Permitting Regulations. MOD have been ordered to clear up the Gallows Hill site and also Percival's Wood.'

'Percival's Wood?' Carole queried.

'Yes. They took samples of the land all the way from the old laboratory site right down through the wood and down to the river. It seems that, as well as the stuff they had stored in the barns at the old labs, they'd also been burying contaminated substances in the woods for years. Looks like they'd been taking mechanical diggers into the woods, digging out clearings and burying the stuff in there. They must've been doing it at night. No-one visits woods at night so their activities had never been spotted.'

'Presumably, though, Doctor Isacson found out,' Carole reasoned. 'She probably showed the journalist Charlie Herron signs of a dump site in one of the clearings, perhaps even in the very clearing where her sister was murdered. And that's almost the same spot where Herron died. I'm pretty certain he was murdered, too.'

'But the cause of death in Herron's case was given as suicide by hanging, wasn't it?' DS Caulfield said.

'Officially, yes, but according to his undertaker, his skull had been fractured,' Carole explained. 'The coroner thought it might have happened when his body was cut down, as he was quite a heavy man. But he could equally have been hit on the head before he was hanged.'

'How do you know this?' Hogget asked Carole.

'A local journalist found out. I've passed that information on to a former colleague of Dave's. Geoff Jackson is on your force's unsolved cases team. He's currently looking at the file on Emerald Isacson's murder and he now has Herron's autopsy report, too. You might find it useful to liaise with him, as you'll find there are similarities in the way the two sisters and Herron were killed.'

'How's the murder investigation going, by the way?' Dave asked.

'Slowly,' Hogget acknowledged. 'But we weren't able to prove your theory about Euphemia Isacson being Emerald Jackson. Unfortunately, the recently murdered sister wore dentures. She'd had all her teeth extracted years ago. Her current set of replacement dentures were fitted five years ago at the dental surgery in Briarfield. Miss Isacson registered with the surgery around that time, after her previous dentist passed away. We've not been able to locate her earlier dental records nor those of her sister. Seems a dental comparison won't be possible.'

'That's a shame,' Carole said. 'Still, it's good news on the environmental issue. Emerald would have been pleased, even if it has taken a quarter of a century to resolve. It'll be a shame if you can't solve her murder, though.'

'Well, it's going to cost MOD many millions to clear up hundreds of acres of ground. Blunt is hopping mad,' Hogget grinned.

'Who?' Dave asked.

'Robert Blunt. He's in charge of their Biological, Radiological and Nuclear unit. He's footing the bill. As well as the clean-up costs, MOD will also be hit with a massive multi-million pound fine for the contamination offences.'

'But, so far, you have no suspects in your murder case?'

'Well, unfortunately, we don't know what if any valuables Miss Isacson had in her flat. Couldn't find any other family members who might know, and she rarely had visitors. It looks like a robbery gone wrong, but we've no way of knowing if anything was stolen. We're looking at a few known local burglars.'

'And do you think there's any connection with her sister's murder?' Dave asked.

'After twenty-five years?' Hogget said. 'Seems most unlikely. I guess it's just a tragic coincidence.'

Dave frowned and Carole knew exactly what he was thinking. Her husband was not a man of strong beliefs but, as he so often said, one thing he most definitely did *not* believe in was coincidence.

'Anyway, we just wanted to let you know the good news,' Hogget said. 'You'll be seeing diggers operating up there for the next few months. And, once the topsoil's been cleared away and the buried substances removed, the Environment Agency will take over responsibility for regular testing of the river water. So, we're grateful to you for exposing the scandal, Carole. Now then, we won't hold you up any longer.'

The detectives departed, leaving Carole and Dave to consider their news.

'Well, Love, I think you should be proud of yourself,' Dave told her. 'It's all thanks to you that our rare chalk stream will soon be running clear again. Who knows, the trout might even return one day.'

'Yes, I'm relieved about that. But Hogget didn't sound too hopeful about solving his murder. I'm not too sure robbery was the motive.'

'Nor am I, Love. But we'll just have to let him get on with it.'

'I can't help thinking that solving the most recent Isacson murder would also help solve the previous one. They must be connected.'

'I agree, but it's not our job, Love. Leave it to the professionals.'

'Okay, well, at least I'll have some good news to give the *Third Agers* on Tuesday.'

***

All twenty-one members of the U3A's local history group turned up the following week. This time, however, the room was not so stuffy. The milder weather meant the community centre's heating boiler had been turned off and so things were a little more comfortable in the meeting room. When the last member of the group had taken their seat, Carole asked Mary's permission to make a small announcement about the river pollution scandal. She related the discovery which had been made – not mentioning MI5's involvement – of the buried contaminants, as well as the stored toxins found on Gallows Hill, and she told of the fines and clear up costs incurred by the Ministry of Defence.

'So, going through Charlie Herron's files wasn't a waste of time and effort after all,' she assured them. 'We got Emerald Isacson's revelations into Hogget's hands, even if only briefly. The water samples I took confirmed Emerald's findings and showed the contamination was still ongoing. Thanks to your help, Daisy, and Kitty, Betty, Tom and Mary, it'll soon be safe enough to go walking in the woods and along the river banks again,' she assured them.

'But what about the murders?' Kitty asked.

'Well, DI Hogget of the local CID is still investigating the murder of Miss Isacson in Briarfield, and the three historic deaths are being re-investigated by Thames Valley Police's unsolved murders team.'

'But there must be a connection between all four deaths, surely?' Tom Sharples protested. 'Don't these police units speak to each other?'

'Bernie Hogget doesn't think there's a connection,' Carole explained. 'He believes the most recent murder was a robbery gone wrong.'

'But *you* don't believe that, do you, Carole?' Daisy asked. 'I mean, the odds against two sisters being murdered in exactly the same way by two different individuals but for different reasons must be astronomical. Not to mention the similarity with Charlie Herron's death – and he knew Emerald and he knew about the contamination.'

'No, I don't believe it was a robbery. I think they must be connected. Proving it will be tricky, though.'

'It's one thing imposing fines on MOD,' Tom added, 'but surely, they should be bringing criminal charges? I mean, those toxins have been making folks ill for decades now. They've been killing people. Somebody should be jailed for that. Who's in charge at MOD?'

'Well, the current CEO of their department which is responsible for biological and radiological stuff is the man in trouble,' Carole confirmed. 'I don't know if any of you caught this morning's news? Only, it seems Sally Grey, our local member of Parliament called out

MOD over their contamination of our chalk stream. In fact, she used her parliamentary privilege to name and shame MOD's head of special projects.'

'So, will he be prosecuted?' Kitty asked.

'Unlikely,' Carole said. 'I expect he'll simply lose out on a gong in the New Year's honours list.'

'Anyway, People,' Mary raised her hand to get everyone's attention. 'May I suggest we turn to the topic of our history project? Who's got an update for us?'

There was much shuffling of papers and it was Elaine who announced her findings.

'I've found twenty-seven stars of stage and screen who've lived around here at one time or another. I think that's me done. Can't find any more.'

'And I've managed eighteen musicians so far,' Kitty added. 'Half of them are classical composers and performers and the rest are or were in pop bands. Found one music promoter and manager, too.'

'How are the infamous people shaping up, Tom?' Mary asked.

'Found around a dozen highwaymen,' Tom added proudly. 'Thing is, you see, what's nowadays the A40 was always the main route out of London to the wealthy wool estates of the West Country. There were rich pickings on the stage coaches back in the day. Chalfont Heath was swarming with highwaymen.'

'Have you got Hanging Judge Jeffreys in your list?' Kitty asked. 'Only he had quite a few of the highwaymen hanged on his personal gibbet down by *The Whippet*.'

'Oh yes, he's on the list. He was a most infamous and despised individual. I think there was some sympathy around here for the highwaymen, though,' Tom informed them. 'I'd always wondered why one of the local pubs, the Blue Angel, has a room named 'The Jack Shrimpton Bar'. Seems Shrimpton was one of the highwaymen who operated locally.'

'We'll have to have a drink in there,' Betty suggested. 'I'm doing the writers and I've found two local poets who used to frequent that bar.'

'I'm making progress on
 Malcolm's research into the war heroes,' Mo Durrani added. 'His widow, Dorothy tells me he'd taken some shots of the Blounts' photos which are on display in the bar at the *Austen Arms*. Unfortunately, that

was on the night he died, and they were on his phone, but he must have dropped it when he was injured.'

'The Blounts?' Mary asked. 'Who are they?'

'Ernest Blount VC and his son.'

'I think you mean Blunt, surely?' Mary queried. 'Malcolm was looking into the Blunt family who used to live at the *Austen Arms*.'

'Ah, according to his research notes, the family name is spelled Blount but is pronounced Blunt. Malcolm had phoned the VC holder's great grandson, Robert Blount – or Blunt, as he prefers to be called.'

'Robert Blunt?' Carole exclaimed. 'Robert Blunt, spelled Blount, is also the name of the MOD CEO – the man who's in charge of their special projects division.'

'Robert Blunt, spelled Blount?' Mo said. 'Yes, that's the same man, Anthony's civil servant grandson.'

'May I ask, what have you and Malcolm learned about this Blount or Blunt family so far?' Carole asked.

'Well, they lived in the area for several generations. Ernest and Anthony were naval men and war heroes, but Anthony's son Michael was a scientist. He joined the Civil Service in some science capacity. Robert is Michael's son, and he, too, is some kind of scientific civil servant. Robert's father, Michael grew up around here, but when Michael's father, Anthony, sold their house and moved out to Wiltshire, their former house became the *Austen Arms*. They do a nice steak in the restaurant there, Dorothy says. Sadly, that steak proved to be Malcolm's last supper.'

'So, the Blunts were the original owners of what's now a local hotel?' Carole queried.

'Yes. In fact, Malcolm spoke to Robert on the phone. Robert told Malcolm he occasionally has lunch or dinner at the *Austen Arms*, whenever business brings him back to the area.'

'I wonder what business he would have in this area?' Carole ruminated.

'I don't know. I mean, the family used to own a lot of land around here, but they sold it off a long time ago.'

'Do you know which lands they owned, Mo?' Carole asked, although she suspected she knew the answer.

'Well, I know they owned the Gallows Hill site – you know, where the laboratories used to be. But they sold it and moved to Wiltshire.'

'It was sold to the Ministry of Defence,' Tom added. 'That's the land that got contaminated. I imagine it was already contaminated when the Blunts sold it. This wants looking into. I'll have a look at land registry records.'

'And I'll do a bit of research into the Blunt family history,' Carole promised. 'If the Robert Blunt Malcolm was in contact with is the MOD CEO Robert Blount, he might be more culpable than the Environment Agency thinks.'

'I can help you with the family history research,' Daisy offered. 'Genealogy is my thing.'

Chapter 30

Carole was hard at work that afternoon, looking through the Blount family tree Daisy had sent her based on her research on various ancestral research websites. Carole was so engrossed in the task that she didn't notice Dave peering over her shoulder.

'Blount?' he queried. 'Is that one of the administrators you're supposed to be researching.'

'No, I've given up on the admins. Wasn't very interesting. This is actually a family of war heroes which Malcolm in our group was researching. Mo, another group member is researching them now.'

'If he's researching them, why are you looking at them, too?'

'Well, two of them are scientists. To be honest, though, I think one of them might be our murderer.'

'What? You're not serious?' Dave seemed alarmed.

'Well, it's just a hunch. I mean, we strongly suspect all these killings are connected to the MOD contamination scandal, don't we? So, it turns out the current CEO of their Special Projects Division is one Robert Blount, great grandson of a VC recipient who lived in what's now the *Austen Arms* in Gaunt's Cross. The surname's pronounced 'Blunt', apparently.'

'Right.'

'And his father, Michael Blount-call-me-Blunt, held a scientific grade post in the Civil Service. In fact, he was Chief Scientific Officer working for MOD's forerunner of the Biological, Radiological and Nuclear arm.'

'So? Many sons follow in their father's footsteps. My old man was a copper.'

'Yes, but Michael Blunt was in charge of all MOD's biological, radiological and nuclear projects back when Emerald Isacson – or the woman who was identified as Emerald – was killed. And we believe she was killed because she was about to uncover an MOD contamination scandal all those years ago.'

'Okay.'

'And Michael's son, Robert, is also with MOD and he is Chief Executive Officer of MOD's Special Projects Division when the contamination continues and when the other Miss Isacson is murdered.

And this murder occurs right after yours truly starts poking her nose into the contamination of the river.'

'So, what are you thinking?'

'I'm thinking maybe Robert Blunt is our killer.'

'But how old is he? I mean, how old would he have been twenty-five years ago when the first sister was killed?'

'He would have been ... um, sixteen.'

'Isn't it more likely that his father was the killer?'

'Yes, probably. But he couldn't have killed the second sister.'

'Why not?'

'Because Michael Blunt died three years ago. Maybe a more feasible conclusion would be that Michael killed the first sister and his son Robert killed the second.'

'Two murderers in one family?' Dave's expression reflected his scepticism. 'It's stretching the bounds of credibility a bit. What motive would each of them have?'

'The same one. Both wanted to stop the sisters revealing what the Blunts believed they knew about the contamination.'

'Well, it's a theory. Though it's as far-fetched a theory as my idea about Euphemia being Emerald and Emerald being Euphemia.'

'But we haven't yet disproved your theory, Dave.'

'No, but we haven't proved it either. Not sure how we could. And how would you go about proving your theory about the Blounts – or Blunts?'

'Not sure, Love. But I might have an idea about how we could prove yours.'

'I thought we were going to step away from the murders, Carole. We've seen how dangerous these people can be, and we promised Adrian we'd butt out.'

'Well, of course I wasn't suggesting we'd get involved ourselves. But Adrian said he'd spoken with MOD's Robert Blunt. Robert's the one who's arguing over the fines imposed by the Environment Agency. I thought we could just pursue a few enquiries about the Blunts via the internet and pass on anything we find out to Bernie Hogget and to Geoff Jackson.'

'So long as that's all we do. How do you propose to go about this?'

'Well, first I need to give Tom Sharples a call. He's been checking out land registry records, to confirm the Blunts' former ownership of the contaminated land, and I might have an idea for another check he can make.'

'What shall I do?'

'Make us a cup of tea, Love. That'll help the thought processes.'

Whilst Dave went to put the kettle on, Carole took out her mobile and called Tom.

'Hi Tom, it's Carole. Got a favour to ask you. Your neighbour who used to teach at Briarfield High School, I know it's been twenty-five years since he worked with Euphemia, but I wonder if you could ask him to give you a physical description of her. What colour were her hair and eyes, and if he remembers her having any distinctive physical characteristics, and that sort of thing. And maybe you could ask him if he'd be willing to go to the police mortuary to identify the body to see if he recognises her as Euphemia. If he is willing, I could arrange it with DI Hogget … You will ask him? Great. Now, any joy with the Land Registry?'

By the time Dave re-appeared with a pot of Earl Grey tea and a plate of Carole's favourite lemon madeleines, she had some more information on the Blounts.

'Tom just confirmed that Anthony Blunt, Robert's grandfather, sold the family home, *Ferndown House* in Gaunt's Cross, to the hotel chain in nineteen-forty. But he only sold the land at Gallows Hill to the MOD nine years later. Between nineteen-forty and nineteen forty-nine, MOD were leasing the land from him. You know what that means?'

'No. What does that mean?'

'It means he sold the land to the MOD because it was *already* contaminated with those PFO things, you know, the carcinogenic things that were in the RAF's fire-fighting foam. Back then, nobody knew PFOs were so harmful, not until half a century later, when Emerald tried to tell MOD this.'

'Poor Em,' Dave reflected, as he poured the tea. 'Or poor Effie, if it was Effie who was killed back then. Em, Effie, FE, and all over those PFOs. They do go in for a lot of acronyms and initialisms, these scientists. Oh, … hang on a minute. D'you remember those initials that were in Emerald's last diary entry?'

'Don't remember them, but I did write them down somewhere. Why?'

'Can you find where you wrote them? We might now be able to decipher them.'

Carole fetched the notebook in which she'd been recording her jottings about the murders. Flipping through the pages, she eventually found the note she had made regarding the diary entries.

'Yes, here it is: 'MB of SPD to compare test results this lunchtime AA.'

'We didn't know what SPD was when we read the diaries. Now we do know. That could be *'Michael Blunt of Special Projects Division to compare test results this lunchtime'* ... but what is AA?'

'Austen Arms? The hotel which used to be the Blunts' home. Of course. This suggests that, the day before she was murdered, Emerald was to meet MOD's Michael Blunt at the hotel to discuss the test results. She was probably intending to challenge him over the fact that MOD's test results were so very different from her own. There's your motive for murder.'

'Hmmh. She must have arranged to meet him again the following afternoon in the woods, to challenge him about soil contamination she'd found there, too,' Dave reasoned.

'She probably took Charlie Herron, the journalist, along with her. And maybe, when Michael Blunt got there, poor Euphemia was already in the woods, watching her beloved birds. He thought she was Emerald and he killed her to silence her. When, as his widow says, Charlie found the body, Emerald was probably with him.'

'Maybe Herron and Emerald between them came up with the idea of identifying the body as Emerald, in order to keep her safe.'

'That makes sense,' Carole agreed. 'Emerald would have been in shock. She might not have been thinking that clearly. Herron was a smart man. He had the good sense to write that a dog walker had found the body. That put a distance between him and the discovery of the body.'

'But since Michael Blunt is dead now, there's not much the unsolved cases team will be able to do to prove that's what happened.'

'Maybe not, but I think they owe it to the families of Charlie Herron and Andrew Maudsley to pursue that line of investigation,' Carole said. 'It's never too late to crack a cold case.'

'But even if they find enough evidence to conclude that the late Michael Blunt did murder the first Isacson sister, how will Hogget make a case against Robert Blunt?'

'Well, first things first, Love. Let's see what else Tom and his friend Callum come up with.'

Chapter 31

Carole met with Tom and his neighbour Callum Dennis at *The Whippet*. In his forties, Callum looked every inch like the high school teacher he was, even down to the leather patches on the elbows of his corduroy jacket. Once Tom had made the introductions, he went to the bar to order three coffees.

'So, Tom told you why we need your help to identify the woman who was murdered recently in Briarfield, did he?' Carole asked.

'Yes. He told me you think maybe she wasn't Euphemia Isacson. You think she might have been her sister, the one they thought died twenty-five years ago. Well, I have to say I'm intrigued. Why d'you think she was pretending to be her sister all these years?'

'Well, I think the killer back in 2000 intended to kill Emerald Isacson but killed her sister by mistake. Emerald may have realised she, herself, was the intended target and that, if the killer realised his mistake, he'd come back for her. So, posing as Euphemia, she identified her deceased sister as Emerald.'

'That would explain why she never came back to work after the murder,' Callum said. 'She submitted her resignation by post, too. In view of the tragic circumstances our headmaster didn't insist on her working out her notice. It was near enough to the Easter break, in any case, so he was able to get a supply teacher to replace her by the start of the next term.'

'Did you see Euphemia again after she left?'

'No. Nobody did. A few of our colleagues called at her house to offer their condolences, but they got no answer. They saw the house was up for sale. And she was invited to a member of staff's retirement party that June, but she didn't come. Didn't even RSVP. We assumed she was too distraught over her sister's death.'

'Callum, did it strike you as odd that she dropped out of teaching altogether?'

'At the time, we didn't know she had. The head told us she'd got a teaching post overseas. At least, that was the reason she'd given in her resignation letter. As far as I know, none of the staff ever saw her again.'

'Then, what made you think she'd taken on the tearooms instead?' Carole asked.

'She had a subscription to the Royal Society for the Protection of Birds,' Callum explained. 'She used to have their member magazines delivered to the school. She would read them in the staffroom then donate them to the school library, for pupils to read. Well, long after she'd left, the magazines kept turning up at the school. The secretary asked me what she should do with them.'

'And what did she do with them?' Carole asked.

'I suggested she take them to Briarfield post office and see if they could be re-directed to Euphemia's new home address. The post office people said they couldn't do that without permission from Miss Isacson herself, and that would incur an additional fee for her to pay. They did confirm, however, that she'd arranged a re-direct of mail from her former home address but they wouldn't disclose her forwarding address. They weren't entirely unhelpful, though. They suggested that, if the secretary took the magazines to the *Elsinore Tearooms* and handed them in there, they'd reach Euphemia.'

'And did she?' Carole asked.

'Yes. She gave them to the lady in the tearoom who told her Euphemia was the owner of the business and was actually living on the premises. The magazines stopped coming to the school after that, so we presumed Euphemia had informed the RSPB of her new address. But it struck me as very odd.'

'What did?' Tom asked.

'Well, the fact that, in all the years since then, not a single member of the teaching staff, or any one of our eight hundred pupils who were here in Euphemia's time, ever bumped into her around the town. The school is just a few blocks away from the tearooms and many of us would head to the shops at lunchtime, but we never saw her again. She must have been living like a hermit.'

'Or she wasn't living at all,' Carole said. 'So, can you describe Euphemia?'

'She was, I dunno, medium height for a woman, I suppose. Dark hair, fair complexion.'

'Any particular distinguishing marks, like moles or scars?'

'No, not that I recall. But she did have very pale blue eyes.'

'Blue eyes? You're sure about that?'

'Yes. I remember that because once, in the staffroom, somebody complimented her on her blue eyes, and Effie said she'd inherited her mother's Irish eyes. Another member of staff whispered under his breath that she had an Irish temper to match. Luckily for him, she didn't hear him. You see, she was a difficult woman to like. Morose. Short-tempered. Always complaining.'

'Complaining about what?' Carole asked.

'Oh everything. New homes being built in the valley, farmers killing birds of prey, that kind of thing. She didn't exactly have any friends on the staff. I was in my early twenties then and, as a newly qualified teacher, I found her a bit fierce and unapproachable.'

'Did she ever say anything about her relationship with her sister?'

'From conversations I overheard in the staffroom, I got the impression her sister was her only friend. I had the feeling she was envious of her sister, but it seemed Emerald was always there for her. I think she was fond of Emerald really, and they were close, but she was jealous of Emerald's career.'

'Now, that's interesting, Callum. Because I met the woman who was living as Euphemia Isacson in the flat above the *Elsinore Tearooms* in Briarfield. She seemed to have quite a sweet disposition, and, what's more, I'm pretty certain she had brown eyes.'

'Well, I never met Emerald, so I wouldn't know what she was like or what colour eyes she had, but I can say for certain that Euphemia who worked with me all those years ago definitely had blue eyes. No doubt about that.'

'Oh, but I've just remembered,' Carole said, 'I saw a graduation photo of Emerald on the police's cold case file. And I think in the photo she had blue eyes, so maybe I'm mistaken.'

'And who do you think would have given them that photo, Carole?' Tom asked.

'Her sister. Of course! She'd have given them Euphemia's graduation photo to maintain the pretence.'

'Would you be willing to speak to the police, Callum?' Tom asked. 'They might want you to have a look at the deceased and help with the identification. It might not be pleasant, though.'

'That's no problem. If it helps get justice for the poor woman – whoever she is.'

***

The following day saw Carole back at *The Whippet* and again enjoying a latte, but this time with Helen Chandler. Carole's earlier reticence about speaking to a journalist was eclipsed now by her excitement at the way the evidence was slowly coming together. She outlined the situation as succinctly as she could and Helen took notes.

'Wow!' Helen marvelled. 'That's some story. Three historic deaths, and also the woman who died more recently, all bashed on the back of the head, but you don't think it's the same killer?'

'Well, the first three probably were, but the man I believe killed them died three years ago now, so he couldn't have been responsible for the most recent Isacson murder. I think his son carried out the murder of the surviving sister.'

'Why would he do that?'

'Probably because they were both involved in the same dreadful long-term cover-up on behalf of MOD. I believe it's all to do with that MOD site up on Gallows Hill.'

'And, let me get this right, you suspect the first victim wasn't Emerald but her sister Euphemia, and that the sister killed most recently was really Emerald?'

'Yes, and I've persuaded the detective inspector in charge of the case to allow someone who worked with Euphemia Isacson to view the body of the most recent victim. Her former colleague may be able to say whether or not it's Euphemia lying in the mortuary.'

'Didn't the police get someone to identify the body before now?'

'They didn't think they needed to. She was found dead in her flat where she lived alone. I suppose I was responsible for telling the police she was Euphemia, because that's who I believed she was.'

'Is there any other way of establishing for certain who she was?'

'Yes. The detectives say that, if her former work colleague says that's not Euphemia in the mortuary, they'll check out both the sisters' passport and driving licence records. Any identity documents issued to the sisters prior to the first murder would have had photos of Emerald and Euphemia in them for comparison.'

'But what made you even suspect there'd been a switch of identities in the first place?' Helen asked.

'Well, it was my husband's theory really. Dave's brilliant at anagrams.'

'Anagrams?'

'Well, all kinds of puzzles, but that's not important,' Carole said, not wishing to go into the issue of the bird-watcher's book and its dedication. 'It was Dave who first suspected the earlier victim was Euphemia and that she was killed by mistake. When Emerald realised she herself was the intended victim, she must have deliberately misidentified her sister and assumed her sister's identity in order to protect herself.'

'This will make great copy, Carole. It'll be the biggest story I've ever written.'

'Well, it'll be an even bigger and better story when the current killer is caught.'

'So, this suspect of yours, Blount, was it? Are the police going to arrest him?'

'He pronounces it 'Blunt' by the way. Sounds a bit of an arse, if you ask me. Well, so far, there isn't enough evidence for an arrest.'

'Have they even questioned him yet?'

'No. I told you about Charlie Herron's papers that have been stolen, well DI Hogget had read them. From those papers, he's established a possible motive, but he's still looking to see whether Robert Blunt had the means and the opportunity. Inspector Hogget says Blunt's a person of interest, and they will bring him in for interview in due course, but their best hope of getting a conviction is if he confesses. And he's not likely to do that.'

'That's true. But, Carole, how did you find out about him? How did you even hear about the historic Isacson murder?'

'Oddly enough, it all emerged through my research for a project my U3A local history group are putting together. We're researching local people who were famous and infamous, and I was assigned to research the scientists and medics. But one of my fellow *Third Agers* remembered the case of a scientist who had been murdered. When he said it had never been solved, I was hooked. I've always loved research, you see.'

'Me, too. I think I heard some rumours about that MOD site. So, Carole, tell me everything you know about it. I think I need to do some digging into this myself.'

***

The following day, Carole drove Tom Sharples and Callum Dennis over to the mortuary at the local hospital. They sat patiently in the visitors' waiting area awaiting DI Hogget's arrival. Soon, he appeared and Carole introduced Tom and Callum. Callum explained his connection with the late Euphemia Isacson and Hogget asked if he would be okay with entering the body display area and looking at her remains. He confirmed he would be fine. They all rose to enter the facility, but Hogget raised a hand.

'Sorry, you can't all go in. Only Mr Dennis here will be needed. Carole, you already saw the body. No need to see it again.'

Reluctantly, Tom and Carole sat back down in the waiting room.

'Have you ever seen a dead body, Tom?' Carole asked, while they waited.

'Yes, I'm afraid so. I saw several during my time in the Fire Service. Not always in the best of conditions, either. How about you? Apart from the Isacson woman, obviously?'

Carole had indeed seen several bodies previously. Besides finding that of the Isacson sister, she had seen various deceased persons in a variety of circumstances during her career, not least the unfortunate defector and car bomb victim Vasilevsky, but, since she hadn't actually disclosed to her *Third Ager* friends any details of her former occupation, she thought she should be measured in what she said.

'Only my late parents, and an elderly aunt – in a funeral parlour setting,' she said.

Moments later, Hogget was back, with a pale-faced Callum Dennis. Callum glanced at Carole and Tom and he shook his head.

'That isn't Euphemia Isacson,' he said, firmly. 'Admittedly, it's twenty-five years since I saw her last, and her hair is no longer brown but white. But although the deceased woman in there looks a little bit like Euphemia, it's definitely not her.'

'You're absolutely sure?' Hogget asked.

'Absolutely. Euphemia had very distinctive pale blue eyes. The mortuary attendant let me see the eyes of the deceased. She has brown eyes, just as you thought, Carole. It's not Euphemia.'

'This does add weight to my Dave's theory – that Euphemia was killed back in two thousand and one, and Emerald took on her identity,' Carole said. 'And we're convinced the two murders are linked.'

'Yes,' Hogget agreed. 'It's looking as though you might be right. But we still don't have any firm suspects, only your man Blunt, and apart from motive, we don't have any evidence of his involvement.'

'I have an idea which might help you with that,' Carole told him. 'Let me explain.'

Chapter 32

It was little after eight in the evening when a black Citroen saloon pulled up outside the Chalfont St George home of journalist Helen Chandler. Robert Blount climbed out and, glancing up and down the high street, he locked his car, stepped smartly up to the front door and rang the bell. Helen Chandler came to the door.

'Mister Blount,' she smiled.

'It's pronounced Blunt,' he said with undisguised irritation.

'Sorry. Do come in, Mister Blunt. May I take your coat? It's good of you to come all this way to see me.'

'I was happy to come to you. Seems only fair as you're taking the trouble to write a feature on my illustrious forebears. I'm only sorry I couldn't make it during business hours. Got rather a lot of irksome stuff going on at the Ministry at the moment.'

Helen ushered him into her little study at the front of the house and offered him a seat.

'All on your own this evening?' he asked.

'Yes. I live alone. And don't worry about the hour. We freelancers work whatever hours are necessary. Can I get you a tea or coffee?'

'No thank you, Miss Chandler. I've brought you some photographs, by the way. It'll be fairly obvious which ones are of my grandfather in his World War Two naval uniform, and which are of my great grandfather, in his Edwardian naval uniform and with his Victoria Cross. This one is a shot of my father as a lad. As you can see, he's standing with his parents outside our family home. This was before my grandfather sold *Ferndown*.'

'Ah, that's the house which nowadays is the *Austen Arms*, isn't it?'

'That's right.'

'May I scan the photographs so I can use them with my article?' Helen asked.

'These are copies so you can keep them if you like. I have the originals.'

'So, *Ferndown* looks like a charming Edwardian house. And the gardens look delightful. Why did your grandfather sell it?'

'I imagine he wanted to move to somewhere even more rural. There was a lot of house building going on in the village of Gaunt's Cross back then. It was becoming less rural, and it's recently been given town status, hasn't it? I think he liked the idea of raising his children in the country.'

'So, your father, Michael Blount ... er Blunt ... he didn't follow his forebears into the navy?'

'No. He studied science and became a government scientist, and so did I.'

'Actually, a lady I know is researching prominent and famous scientists who were born or lived in this area. It's for a project being run by the U3A's local history group. I expect she'd be interested to know more about your father. Was he a high achiever, too?'

'Oh, yes, he was,' Blount sat back in his chair, relaxed now and eager to talk about his family's achievements. 'Michael Blunt. He rose to the post of Chief Scientific Officer at the Ministry of Defence. He set up the unit we now call BRAN.'

'BRAN?'

'The Biological, Radiological and Nuclear branch. It's now based in and around Porton Down. My father established the SPD, the Special Projects Division, and he helped develop the division into what it is today, the world's leading centre for research and development in defence science.'

'And I understand you followed in your father's footsteps. You joined MOD also.'

'That's right. He would have been proud of what the department has become today. And I like to think he'd be proud of me, too. I've steered MOD into collaboration with private industry and I'm now CEO of a hugely successful organisation, an amalgamation of defence personnel with funding from industry and commerce. The fusion of military know-how and commercial finance, especially from America, has been a major success.'

'But I understand the rise of BRAN wasn't without its problems and its detractors,' Helen said. 'Wasn't there some controversy over some kind of biological warfare experiments they were conducting from the nineteen forties and right up to the nineteen seventies?'

'Oh, well, the public and the press are always suspicious about chemical and biological defence development, and you only have to mention 'Porton Down' and the rumour mongers start to get twitchy.'

'But didn't it emerge that the MOD scientists had been deliberately releasing all kinds of harmful bacteria and chemicals on pockets of the population, just to see what effects they would have?'

'Absolutely not. That was the press's distortion of the truth. The scientists back then were simply *measuring* the effects of elements already present in the water and the soils in certain areas, to assess the effects these might have *if* a hostile state were to drop vast quantities of substances on an unsuspecting population.'

'But these 'elements' as you call them, were substances such as e-coli, anthrax, carcinogenic metals and radium.'

'But these are naturally occurring in nature anyway.'

'But isn't it true that certain villages and communities were used as guinea pigs and, without their knowledge or consent, had these toxins dumped on them as part of a long-term experiment? And some of those toxins are still being leached out onto communities today, even here in this locality.'

'That's nonsense,' Blount frowned. 'We don't do that sort of experiment. We only measure what's already in the environment and we gauge its effects.'

'But a number of concerned individuals discovered that your father was heavily involved in dubious experiments back then, didn't they?'

'No, that's not accurate,' Blount snapped, looking less comfortable now.

'They actually uncovered evidence that MOD were storing and releasing chemicals from the Gallows Hill site here in this very village onto an unsuspecting community. They challenged your father, and they ended up dead – murdered. Your father killed Miss Isacson in an attempt to cover it up, didn't he?'

'So, this is the real reason you wanted to interview me,' Blount sneered. 'Well, you can't prove any of that.'

'Charlie Herron and Andrew Maudsley were also murdered by him, weren't they? He was a smart man, your father, but not smart enough to have killed the right sister. He killed Euphemia Isacson by mistake, didn't he? How stupid was that?'

'Yes, he had no choice but to kill them,' Blount said, rising to his feet. 'But you can't prove that either.'

'Yes, I can,' Helen stood up also and, picking up a manila folder from her desk, she edged towards the open door which led to the hallway. 'I have Doctor Isacson's original notes and test results here, and I'll be taking them to the police.'

Blount suddenly sprang at the reporter and pinned her against the wall by her shoulders.

'You really haven't a clue, have you?' he spat. 'They were interfering in something so important it was beyond their comprehension. The Russians and other hostile states were, and still are developing all manner of nerve agents and biological weapons. We have to understand how they affect human biology in order to develop the means to counteract them, to offset their effects.'

'But the terrible effects those experiments had,' Helen gasped as she writhed beneath his grip. 'Premature deaths, terrible illnesses, children born handicapped. You people had no right to do that. And you're still doing it. You've still got all that stuff stored up on Gallows Hill.'

'You don't understand. It's for the greater good. Experimentation was and is necessary in order to save millions of lives. Look, in wartime, men like my father and my grandfather risked their lives for their country. The few sacrificed their lives for the good of the many. That's how it should be in peacetime, too. A few people may get sick or die because of it, but that's a small price to pay for the survival of the nation. Yes, my father killed that interfering cow Isacson and the others. But it was necessary.'

'And when you realised your father had stupidly killed the wrong woman, you murdered her sister, didn't you? You tracked her down to her flat over the teashop. You killed Emerald Isacson.'

'My father realised he'd killed the wrong sister as he was leaving the woods that day and he saw Emerald arrive with that journalist. He couldn't attack her there and then, not while she had that big burly Herron chap with her. Dad would have made another attempt to kill her but she disappeared for a while. Then one day, he spotted her. She was still living in Briarfield and using her sister's name. Dad had a tame detective who lived nearby keep an eye on her over the years. So long as she said nothing of what she might know or suspect, we left her alone.'

'So, why ...' Helen began but Blount gripped her throat, choking off her question.

'But then others came, interfering. So, yes, I killed her. And they kept coming. That ex-MI5 woman who visited Emerald, and that man who was asking questions in the bar at the *Austen Arms*. They weren't going to leave it alone. I had no choice. And you've interfered now, too, so you'll understand why I now have to kill you. And there won't be any proof of that either. I'll take that file, now.'

Blount snatched the manila folder from her and tighten his grip still further on her throat. She could no longer speak and her peripheral vision began to darken. Suddenly, however, Blount's arm was gripped by another stronger one and was yanked away from the reporter's throat and twisted up his back. The two uniformed police officers who had appeared fairly smartly from the hallway now wrestled him to the ground and slipped handcuffs on him before pulling him back to his feet. DI Hogget and his sergeant, DS Anna Caulfield, now also appeared.

'You cut that a bit fine, Inspector,' the journalist gasped, as she rubbed her reddened throat.

'Sorry, Helen, but you did a grand job. Are you okay? Do you need a medic?'

'No, I'm all right,' she replied and, bending down, she retrieved the folder from the floor where Blount had let it fall. She placed it back on her desk. She would not reveal to Blount that the folder was empty.

Hogget then formally arrested Blount for the murders of Emerald Isacson and Malcolm Rawlinson and for the attempted murder of Helen Chandler and he cautioned him. He warned him that other charges might follow. The detective walked across to the journalist's desk and moved aside a small stack of books. Taking the mini recording device from behind the books, he checked it and switched it off.

'Looks like you got all of that, Helen,' he grinned. 'Well done. Take him out, Officers.'

Slipping the recording device into his pocket, he shook Helen's hand.

'Thank you so much. I'll get this confession transcribed. It wasn't made under caution, of course, but I'll come back tomorrow and get a full supporting statement from you. That should be enough to enter the recording into evidence. We'll give him a full interview tonight down at the station. He can't get out of the attempted murder charge and, if he's wise, he'll plead guilty to the murder charges, too, even if he tries to argue in mitigation that it was for the benefit of mankind.'

'Oh, and you might want to contact Geoff Jackson over at your unsolved cases unit.'

'Why?'

'Because Carole Murray's been liaising with him about Walter Gerrard. Gerrard was the lead detective on the original Isacson murder. He still lives locally. Carole's convinced he failed to pursue suspects back then. She thinks he may have been paid off.'

'Has she any proof of that?'

'It seems that, not long after his investigation was shelved, he bought a substantial property in Spain. Jackson's looking into the source of the money he used for the purchase. Carole says Gerrard turned a blind eye to that case. She says he also misdirected the coroner in two more deaths, those of Charlie Herron and Andrew Maudsley.'

'Oh, Carole says that, does she?' Hogget said, with more than a hint of sarcasm. 'Well, where would we be without Carole Murray?'

Hogget bid the reporter good night and stepped out into the street to watch the officers marching Blount to their car. As he turned to walk towards his own vehicle, he spotted a car parked on the opposite side of the street, a car with five adults and two greyhounds all squeezed inside. With an ironic grin, he raised his hand and gave the driver the thumbs-up sign to signal that she needn't worry. He had everything in hand.

Seated in the driver's seat, Carole slapped both hands on the steering wheel and gave a whoop of joy, echoed immediately by her front seat passenger Tom, and by Kitty, Daisy and Betty who were squeezed into the rear. From the very back of the hatchback, two more little heads popped up. Ronnie and Reggie looked baffled by the humans' sudden hysteria.

'Fantastic,' Kitty declared. 'Well done, Carole, the plan worked. And well done to Helen.'

'Well done all of us,' Carole grinned. 'We've done the right thing now by Emerald. Her killer's been arrested at last. Can't wait to tell Mary. She'll be sorry she missed the arrest.'

'Oh, no! Look!' Tom warned.

They all looked out to see a struggling Blount suddenly headbutt the constable who was attempting to put him into the back of the police car. Breaking free, and despite the fact that his hands were firmly cuffed behind his back, Blount took off down the high street. The stunned constable took off after him, to be followed by his colleague who had climbed into the driver's seat of the police car but now jumped out again. The two detectives also bounded across the street and gave chase.

'Come on!' Carole shouted and she leapt out of the car, too, leaving the car door ajar. The others quickly followed.

The fleeing Blount careered down the high street, past the darkened shops, assisted in his escape by the downward momentum of the hill, but with the two uniforms, two detectives, five *Third Agers* and two greyhounds all in hot pursuit. As he came to the bridge, Blount made a sharp right-hand turn and sprinted along the towpath by the side of the river. Soon, he was enveloped by the darkness as he disappeared beneath the willow trees which lined the unlit path along the river bank. The police continued to give chase, as did the *Third Agers*. The greyhounds, Ronnie and Reggie, easily overtook the human pursuers and also disappeared into the darkness ahead of them.

'Watch that hip, Kitty!' Tom called out, as he led the friends' charge along the towpath.

All of a sudden, there was a loud and anguished yell and a couple of loud barks, followed by an even louder splash. Tom slowed to a halt and held up his hand.

'I don't think they're going to need any further help from us, Ladies,' he said. 'I think we should withdraw. Anyway, they're still serving at *The Whippet*. What do you say? I'm buying the first round.'

Carole called the dogs back and the friends retreated back along the path and crossed over the bridge, heading towards the riverside pub, leaving it to the police to fish their suspect out of the Misbourne. Whilst Tom went to the bar to order the drinks, Carole took the packet of antiseptic wipes from the pocket of her jacket and proceeded to give the dogs' feet a good clean. She then fished around in another pocket for some doggy treats. She told herself Ronnie and Reggie had definitely earned them. She then called Helen Chandler and invited her to join them at the pub.

It was around eleven o'clock that night when Carole and the dogs arrived home. Dave was waiting up for her. He made them both some hot cocoa and they sat together on the sofa.

'I got your text, Love,' he said. 'You said the plan worked well. So, I suppose you lot have been out celebrating?'

'We have. And, yes, Robert Blount-call-me-Blunt confessed and Helen got it all on tape. Whether it'll stand up in court remains to be seen, but Hogget is hopeful of a conviction. And Helen Chandler's got the scoop of a lifetime. But she deserves it. He only tried to choke the life out of her.'

'Well, I hope this turns out to be your last case, Love. I don't think I want military police kicking our door down again, or Ronnie and Reggie being doped. And I don't think we can rely on Adrian and our old firm to bail us out of trouble again. Maybe the quiet village life is what we need after all.'

'Oh, I don't know, Love. I quite enjoyed it all really. I mean, I've had all the satisfaction of the investigation, plus the thrill of the chase, but zero paperwork to complete. Anyway, you did say you were finding retirement a bit dull, didn't you? You must have found it just a *little* bit exciting.'

'Well, there's exciting and there's downright scary,' Dave conceded. 'At least we can sleep well tonight knowing the killer's in Briarfield nick now.'

'Well, unfortunately, he did a runner right after they arrested him. He isn't actually in the nick.'

'He isn't?'

'No. He tripped over the dogs and fell into the Misbourne. You know, it's really hard to keep your head above water with your hands cuffed behind your back.'

'So, where is he? Did he get away?'

'No. He's in hospital tonight under police guard – having his stomach pumped out.'

'Well, that's ironic,' Dave laughed.

'Like I told you, Dave, there's a lot of dodgy stuff in that river. And there's a lot of dodgy goings-on in these supposedly quiet Misbourne villages.'

ALSO BY THIS AUTHOR

Look out for more cozy crime novels coming soon in the Misbourne Murder Mysteries series.

Books in the series *The Thames House Files*, a series of standalone international espionage novels include:

The Hunt for WOTAK
When the Grey Wolf Sings
A Long Road to Revenge
Shearwater Point
The Kohat Connection
The Nevsky Prospekt Affair

True crime:
Odd Man Out: A Motiveless Murder?
The Wronged Man: A Miscarriage of Justice
The Forgotten Forty-Four: Victims & Survivors of America's First Serial Sex Killer*
*Awarded a 'Highly Commended' in the True Crime Awards 2024 'Book of the Year' award

ABOUT THE AUTHOR

Denise Beddows is an award-winning author of best-selling crime/espionage fiction and true crime. With a background in research, investigation and intelligence analysis, and having lived, worked and played in various countries across three continents during a career in government service, she speaks six languages. Based in Buckinghamshire, she is a member of the Society of Authors and the Crime Writers Association. She actively supports the Chalfont St Giles & Jordans Literary Festival, and founded 'Chiltern Kills' Crime Writing Festival, based in Gerrards Cross. Writing also as DJ Kelly, she has published the following local histories:

The Chalfonts and Gerrards Cross at War
Buckinghamshire Spies and Subversives
The Famous and Infamous of The Chalfonts and District
Chalfont St Peter Old Burials and Curious Deaths

www.ingramcontent.com/pod-product-compliance
Ingram Content Group UK Ltd.
Pitfield, Milton Keynes, MK11 3LW, UK
UKHW040435180325
456385UK00003B/41